AMAZING GRACE IN ABUNDANCE

Michael Nwaduba

Grosvenor House
Publishing Limited

The right of Michael Nwaduba to be identified as the author of this
work has been asserted in accordance with Section 78
of the Copyright, Designs and Patents Act 1988

The book cover picture is copyright to Michael Nwaduba

This book is published by
Grosvenor House Publishing Ltd
Link House
140 The Broadway, Tolworth, Surrey, KT6 7HT.
www.grosvenorhousepublishing.co.uk

NOTE:
This book is a work of fiction and most of the characters are fictitious
as well as some of the places mentioned. If any fictitious character resembles
anyone living, it's simply a coincidence, and the author is truly sorry for that.

The information and views expressed in this book by the author should
not be used as a substitute for professional medical advice or treatment,
always consult your doctor. Any use of the information in this book is
entirely at the reader's discretion and risk. The author or publisher cannot
be held liable for any loss, claim, or damages arising out of the use or
misuse of the suggestions made in this book.

Due to the dynamic nature of the internet, website addresses or links used
in this book may have changed since publication and may no longer be valid.
Hence, the author and publisher hereby disclaim any responsibility for them.

A CIP record for this book
is available from the British Library

Paperback ISBN 978-1-78623-413-1
Hardback ISBN 978-1-78623-397-4
eBook ISBN 978-1-80381-277-9

PASTOR LEKE SANUSI

FOREWORD

This is one book you will not drop once you start reading it. It is set in a storyline, which though fictional, points directly at practical and real issues of life. Every reader will identify with the realities of the pictures being painted by the author.

Life is war and is full of many challenges, trials and battles. The flood and afflictions of life oftentimes do not give you notice. The enemy indeed comes in like a flood! Also, trials come irrespective of all your trying. Afflictions come to the affluence and riotous rain storm do fall upon the righteous. *"Many are the afflictions of the righteous..." Psalm 34:19.*

The good news is that this book: AMAZING GRACE IN ABUNDANCE offers you the panacea to the turbulence of life, from a purely and truly biblical point of view, for that is the RIGHT VIEW, THE RIGHT WAY, THE RIGHT TRUTH: *"...but the Lord delivereth him out of them all."*

There is a supernatural facility called the GRACE OF GOD. You will see that divine spirit at work in this book. You will discover that no matter what you may be going through or what may be coming your way, if you take the right approach which this book counsels, advocates, teaches and encourages, you will become a beneficiary of the Amazing Grace of God in abundance.

The grace of God is the currency of heaven. It is what makes the race of life easy to run. It is said that where the grace of God is busy, the race of life will be easy. Jesus Christ enjoyed it, for the grace of God was upon Him. Paul the Apostle benefited and overcame by it, for His Grace was sufficient for him. Peter knew the wonders of it, for he called Him the God of all Grace.

This book is very easy to read, interesting to enjoy, comforting to the soul, healing balm to the sick, encouragement to the discouraged, lifting to those struggling with their faith and belief in God and it is ready to launch you to a higher level in your walk with God.

I recommend this great book to you and to all your loved ones. You will be thankful you owned and read a copy.

God bless you richly.

Pastor Leke Sanusi
Special Assistant to The General Overseer (SATGO)
RCCG Europe Continent Overseer

CONTENTS

ABOUT THE BOOK AMAZING GRACE IN ABUNDANCE

I published my first book entitled *"A Simple Guide for Bible Study"* in 2008. This book was followed by my second book, *"Questions and Answers on Tithes: Covenant of Prosperity,"* which was published in 2009. After the publication of this book, I tried and tried to write another book but I couldn't. Every time inspiration to write came, it always ended up in an article. It never translated into a book. So I ended up writing many articles through the inspiration of the Holy Spirit. I wrote over three hundred articles between 2009 and 2017.

On the 2nd of July, 2017 at exactly 9 pm, the inspiration came, and I commenced writing *"Amazing Grace in Abundance."* When the inspiration to write came, I immediately thought this was another article and I said, *"Oh, another article to write. Let me write it,"* but I was wrong. After I had written for about an hour and half it suddenly dawned on me that it was a book I was writing and not an article, after nearly a decade since my last book was published. I screamed out joyfully, *"It's a book! It's a book! Oh my God! Thank you, Jesus!"* This was how this book was born.

Prior to writing this book, I was emotionally distraught and in pain, but I noticed that day that after writing for about two hours that I was feeling better and getting healed emotionally. To me, this is God demonstrating with me, the author, what He will do for readers of this book. That was an outright confirmation to me that this book is a healing book. The Bible says in *2 Timothy 2:6*, *"The husband man that laboureth must be the first partaker of the fruits."* As the author of this book, God allowed me to be the first person to partake of the fruits – Healing! As you read this book, open your heart and be ready to receive your healing by faith in Jesus' name. Amen!

After writing for about four hours, the heavens opened up and God spoke to me loud and clear saying, *"This book will be used for a movie."* I immediately jumped up for joy and this scripture was fired up in my spirit - *1 Samuel 10:7, "And let it be, when these signs are come unto thee, that thou do as occasion serve thee; for God is with thee."* I said, *"I must take part in the movie."* So my first reaction was to create a role for myself in this book that I will play in the movie – Reverend Dr. Lawrence Nduka Chukwuemeka. I had the pen so I had to write what I want as the author. I did as occasion served me because I knew God was with me and He is still with me.

From that point, I wrote *"Amazing Grace in Abundance"* doing two things - writing the book and also imagining it as a movie. The inspiration to write was awesome! God did not tell me when the film will be released, but I reckon it will happen soon. He is true and faithful to His word. The fact that *"Amazing Grace in Abundance"* has effectively turned out to be a book as God said, contrary to my initial thought that it was an article, is evidence that the movie will definitely manifest as well. How and when this will happen is entirely up to God because He spoke the words to me, and I believe and trust His word.

This book comes as a story wrapped with teachings based on biblical principles embedded in it to make it come alive, and also embellish it.

I continued to write the book and God manifested again for the third time instructing me to include chapter 8 about the honeymoon in the book. This chapter later turned out to be a book. This is another beautiful aspect of this book which lies in the fact that it has an offshoot titled – *"Mr and Mrs Evans' Honeymoon on the Island of Majorca, Spain."* This book is a sequel to Chapter 8 of Amazing Grace in Abundance. Chapter 8 is just a foretaste of the honeymoon. For full details of this exciting honeymoon get the book.

Finally, the Holy Spirit further inspired me to write the second Honeymoon book titled, *"Mr and Mrs McGregor's Honeymoon on the Island of Santorini, Greece."* This is a sequel to *"Amazing Grace in Abundance,"* and it is a deeper dimension of a marriage honeymoon featuring a mature Christian couple. Extraordinary honeymoon in paradise. You can't afford to miss this. Get your copy now. God bless you.

MICHAEL NWADUBA

CHAPTER ONE

THE TRIALS OF MARY JENKINS

All day she's in pain. Mary Jenkins keeps wondering how and when she will be completely healed and eventually be free indeed from the terrible afflictions she's going through. No serious relationship with a man at the moment to lead to marriage. This is a serious concern for her considering she is now in her mid-thirties. Her parents are also concerned about this.

The last time they met for the Easter holiday, they said to her, "We are looking forward to meeting your fiancé someday." And those words have not stopped ringing bells in her ears since then. Her friend Jane Foster in Sydney, Australia is happily married with two children and Priscilla Jenkins, her cousin, is getting ready to tie the knot this winter. Friends and family are keen to see her married, and this is mounting pressure on her. She worked for Elohim Car Company in London as a Senior Marketing Officer for nearly a decade before she was made redundant a month ago. She is now aggressively searching for a replacement job.

Mary has a first class Bachelor of Science (BSc) degree in Marketing and a Master's degree in Business Administration (MBA) from Oxford University. And most things about her are indeed first class. Good moral upbringing. She regularly works out in a gym, and she strictly watches her food in order to maintain a good physique as a single lady; her favourite food is salad. She stands at 5 feet 8 inches tall, with a moderate stature to easily fit into a size 14 dress. White-skinned with a pointed nose, dark brown eyes, and slim lips enclosing her white set of teeth, all fitted into a round face with long blonde hair falling right down to her shoulders and beyond. She is indeed of Anglo-Saxon descent. A born-again Christian, she worships at Shekinah Pentecostal

Church. The daughter of a Police Superintendent and her mother is a Professor in Mathematics at Manchester City University.

"Oh my God, what the hell is going on here?" Mary screamed out.

She has just read a letter from Dr Joseph Moore confirming the results of the two recent tests she had. She had been previously hinted. The lump in her left breast is confirmed to be breast cancer, and the other test confirms a fibroid that needs to be removed immediately through surgery. With trembling hands, speechless, a rising temperature and sweat coming out on her forehead and neck, she dropped the letter on the table and screamed out loud.

"Satan, you are a liar. My body is the temple of the Holy Spirit. Therefore, no sickness is permitted in my body. I will not die but live to declare the works of God on earth. I shall surely fulfil my days on earth. Nothing will cut my life short. With long life you will satisfy me Lord, and also show me your salvation in Jesus' name. Amen!"

She immediately felt relieved. Composing herself, and not allowing fear but faith to rule her, she reached for her mobile phone and rang her mother in the city of Manchester.

"Hello Mummy," she greeted, as she got through to her mum.

"Hello Mary," replied her mum. "I hope you are alright Mary because your voice sounds a bit shaky."

"Mummeeee! You and this discerning of spirits!" replied Mary.

And Brenda said, "Tell me, what's the matter my dear?"

"I got a terrible letter from my doctor a while ago saying my enemy has breast cancer and fibroids," replied Mary.

"What! I reject it for you. It will never be your portion in Jesus' name. Have you told your daddy?"

"No Mummy."

"You better hang up now and let him know too, you know your Daddy is a prayer warrior, and he loves you dearly."

"I will call him now."

"Before you go darling, please always remember who you are in Christ. He has said He will never leave you nor forsake you. Therefore, you are not alone in this raging storm. Christ is with you. He says, 'Lo, I am with you till the end of the world.' He says again, 'Be still and know that I am God.' Therefore, remain calm, and don't panic, avoiding all fears and worries. Bye love."

"Thanks Mummy, bye."

As she put down the phone, a feeling of confidence ran through her spirit and she felt strengthened.

"Shame on you devil," she declared as she scrolled down the phone address book searching for Daddy's number. "Hello Daddy, it's me Mary."

"Ah! My darling Mary, how are you doing? I'm so excited to hear your voice now."

"Daddy, there is a bit of a problem here, but God is absolutely in control."

"What's the matter, dear?"

"The devil is lying again. He says my enemy has got breast cancer and fibroids. That's the doctor's report in a letter I received today. But I have rejected that report in Jesus' name. I choose to believe the report of God that I am made whole by the stripes of Jesus."

The phone went silent for a moment as Police Superintendent Paul Jenkins tried to process the information he was receiving about his only lovely daughter. "I will commence serious fasting and prayers for you regarding this matter. Please do not allow any fears or worries at all. Effectively slam the door against the devil. Remain confident in the Lord, and put your trust in Him. You are in God's hands. The enemy has already been defeated on the Cross of Calvary. Your body is the temple of the Holy Ghost. Therefore, sickness will never be your portion in Jesus' name. Amen! I hope your mummy knows about this?"

"Yes, Daddy."

"Alright, I will talk to you later my dear. Bye for now".

"Bye, Daddy."

She lives in the exclusive and quiet area of East Dulwich in South East London. Not far from the Dulwich home of former British Prime Minister, Margaret Thatcher after she left office in 1990. The house is a Victorian-style detached building with three bedrooms. Sitting down, her eyes started moving round from one end of the beautifully decorated living room to the other and the artworks displayed on the wall caught her attention. She drew near to one of the beautiful scriptural inscriptions in a frame given to her as a first-degree graduation gift by her cousin Priscilla, who's getting ready for a wedding this winter in December. The verse says, *"No weapon that is formed against thee shall prosper:..." – Isaiah 54:17*. She began to absorb those holy words and as she pondered on them she muttered, "No weapon of breast cancer, fibroids, and unemployment formed against me shall ever prosper in Jesus' name. Amen!" As she meditated on these words, she began to be filled with more confidence and trust in the Lord through the power of the Holy Ghost that all is indeed well.

Her mobile phone started ringing and she spoke these words into it, "Hello, good afternoon, who's on the line?"

With a trembling voice, the caller spoke and said, "This is Shirley Brown, Alan Brown's sister. Sorry, it's sad news. There was a suspected terrorist attack on the American Airlines flight NY3351 from New York City heading to London according to the Mayday call received from the pilot. A device was said to have exploded and all one hundred and fifty people on board, including the pilot and crew members, crashed into the Atlantic Ocean and they have all been confirmed dead after a rescue search team dispatched immediately to the scene saw the debris of the plane with most of the passengers floating in the waters. Sadly, Alan was on board the American Airlines flight."

"Really? This is unbelievable. I am stunned and devastated with this sad news," said Mary, and yelling and crying followed.

"Sorry, I've got to go now," said Shirley, and Mary replied, "Bye, Shirley."

Mary met Alan Brown just three months ago, but it felt like they had known each other for years because of the care and love they both shared. They met at an International Marketing Trade Fair organised in Chicago, in the United States of America and it turned out to be that he also lives in London and even worshiped in the same Pentecostal Church as Mary; Shekinah Pentecostal Church in central London. A Senior Manager in a multinational car company called Posh Cars Limited. Alan was in his early forties, a devoted Christian, with very promising career prospects, handsome, and jovial.

"How can I cope with this tragedy?" Mary asked as she cried aloud with tears running down her cheeks like a tap gushing out water. Her handkerchief was now drenched with tears, and within seconds she was looking pale and emotionally distraught. "Why me Lord?" She asked.

And the devil whispered into her ears saying, "How come you are not quoting scriptures now?"

"Get thee behind me Satan," she retorted.

This is the anguish the young lady, Mary Jenkins, is facing. The pain is overwhelming. Heartbroken! Alan Brown, her best friend is no more. No job. Then, the sad news of breast cancer and fibroids is there. How can she possibly pull through all these? Has the world turned upside down for her to perish?

Mary Jenkins is known for her resilience in life. She is a tough fighter. She has fought wars in the past, so to say, and won victories, but this seems to be an insurmountable mountain. The pains and sorrows are placing enormous pressure on Mary. One of her favourite scriptures is *Psalm 119:71* in which the Psalmist declared, *"It is good for me that I have been afflicted: that I might learn thy statutes."* But not this time! The affliction is too much, and she wished the scripture reads, "It is *bad* for me that I have been afflicted...." That's a true expression of how deep the emotional wounds and pain are. Excruciating! However, she cheered up a bit as she remembered what Jesus said in *John 16:33*, *"These things I have spoken unto you, that in me ye might have peace. In the world ye shall have tribulation: but be of good cheer; I have overcome the world."*

The fear of cancer kills more than actual cancer. However, as she dwelt on the scripture that says, *"God has not given us the spirit of fear but of power, and of love, and of sound mind,"* she felt reassured and calm. The Word of God comforts and heals. She needs to defy and conquer fear by staying connected to the Word of God. She goes onto the internet to have more awareness of fibroid and breast cancer, to investigate the sicknesses further and find out measures she could take to help herself regarding achieving a permanent cure. She found loads of information regarding what to eat and what not to eat, the kinds of medicines to take, and the kind of treatments to undergo. As good as this information appears to be, she concluded she would still have to see her doctor and get professional advice, and get answers to the questions she may have. This certainly makes a lot more sense to her.

It's been a bright, sunny, summer day, and the sun is gradually winding down. She now decides to get into the bath to have a shower again to refresh herself and go down to Classic Food Stores to pick up some groceries. They specialise in selling high-quality freshly made food, fruits, vegetables, and other foodstuffs. This classy food store is situated close to other food stores, including Tesco, Sainsbury's, and Marks & Spencer in East Dulwich. As she gets into the bathroom she gazes at the beautiful white wall tiles with flowers, and the Jacuzzi bath. She reached for the white robes and girded herself. And then she stood up to feel the lump on the left breast and her mental imagination is that it has grown much bigger since she received the doctor's letter.

"Whao! I hope this is not a malignant cancer!" She exclaimed. "Lord Jesus, help me overcome these afflictions."

And as she said that the Holy Spirit quickened her to remember the scripture, *Psalm 34:19, "Many are the afflictions of the righteous: but the LORD delivereth him out of them all."*

She declared, "Yeah! Father, I thank you because you are already delivering me from all these afflictions in Jesus' name. You are not a man that you should lie. Whatever you say in your Word, you are committed to do because you are a faithful God." She got into the bath, and had a quick wash, dressed up, and sprayed on her favourite perfume, Fahrenheit.

As she was about to step out, three Church members who had heard the news about the plane crash and the death of Alan Brown came in unannounced. These are Angela, Deborah, and Felicia, all from the choir department of Shekinah Pentecostal Church.

"So sorry to hear the sad news," they all said almost simultaneously.

Mary started sobbing and crying, laying her head on Deborah's shoulders, while she gave her a pat on the back pulling out a handkerchief to wipe the tears. "This has left me gutted and in pain since Shirley gave me the news this afternoon," she declared.

"Something has to be done about terrorism by the nations of the world," said Deborah. She is stoutly built with muscles gained from lifting weights at the London 2012 Olympic Games where she won a gold medal for Britain.

Stepping back into the living room, they all sat down and made themselves comfortable on the soft sofa.

"My brother James sends his condolences," says Deborah.

And Mary answered and said, "Thanks. What can I offer you ladies?"

They all answered and said, "Nothing! We are fine."

Mary got the television remote control and tuned to the British Broadcasting Corporation (BBC) News channel, the 6 o'clock news was on and the headline gave an update about the crash of flight NY3351, showing pictures of the devastating scene with the debris of the plane and human remains floating on the waters of the Atlantic Ocean. Horror! Tears started gushing from her eyes again as she beheld the television pictures. The Newscaster read on saying, "The President of The United States of America, Barack Obama, has vowed to get down to the root of this cowardly monstrous act, to catch the people responsible and bring them to justice. The Central Intelligence Agency (CIA) has already commenced investigations into the matter. The Hitman terrorist group has indicated involvement in the planting of the explosive device in the airplane claiming the lives of seventy-seven Americans out of the one hundred and fifty people on board."

Felicia cleared her throat and gave a few words to comfort her. She said, "I would like you to be strong and of good courage in this painful, difficult time. Alan has translated to be with the Lord, and there is absolutely nothing anyone can do about this. But we all have to take solace in the fact that when our Lord Jesus appears again, we shall all get to meet again. Please remain strong in the Lord as always, feeding yourself with the Word of God. Don't allow the enemy to bombard your mind with lies of any kind. Remember you are not alone. He has said, 'He will never leave you nor forsake you.' The Lord will continue to comfort you and fill you with peace in Jesus' name."

They all said, "Amen!"

"Let's pray," says Deborah and continued, "Angela, please lead us with a song and pray." Angela began to sing the song, '*It is well with my soul,*' based on 2 Kings 4:26 while others joined.

"Heavenly Father, we thank you because it is indeed well with our soul. Thank you for this day that you have kept us alive to see. We are grateful that we are healthy and well. Thank you for your provisions. Thank you for your protection over our lives and those of our family and friends. We commit our dear sister Mary into your hands, as we ask that you comfort and console her during this trying time. Thank you, Lord because our brother Alan Brown is resting in perfect peace in your bosom. And regarding terrorism, Lord, we ask for your peace to reign across the nations of the world. Let there be an immediate stop to terrorism through your mercy. And we ask that those who have committed this atrocity of the plane crash will give themselves up willingly to the Police to be prosecuted. There shall be no peace for the wicked, says your Word. Deny the terrorists peace in Jesus' name. Amen!"

"We are going now," says Felicia. "Please take very good care of yourself."

"Alright ladies. Thanks for coming to cheer me up. Much appreciated."

After they left, the whole apartment looked like a graveyard. The serene atmosphere gradually started turning scary. "I hope Alan doesn't appear here as a ghost," she thought. She now decides to cancel going to Classic Food Stores to buy groceries.

While she is seated there on the sofa, her mind started wandering about from one thing to another regarding the various challenges she is facing. The devil is busy now highlighting all the trials. Alan's death is a gruelling one that has left her dazed and heartbroken. But thank God for the scripture in **Psalm 147:3** that says, *"He healeth the broken in heart, and bindeth up their wounds."*

"Lord, thank you because I know you are healing my shattered heart in Jesus' name. Amen!" She said.

These positive confessions seem not to bring forth an immediate solution to restore her much needed peace. As she lay on the sofa trying to relax and have a nap with her eyes closed, she started having a dream, seeing herself in the dream with her left breast swelling beyond normal proportions. And she suddenly woke up, grabbed her left breast as she walked towards the bathroom to see the mirror and compare the pair. The lump is there quite alright, but the size has slightly increased beyond normal. This is not a fake mental imagination. "I've got to see Dr Joseph Moore again, and also see Bishop John Barnes for prayers, and anointing oil to rub on this," she declares.

Thank God for the well-organised National Health Service (NHS) and social welfare system. She is likely to get a lot of support towards her medical treatment now that she's not working. So, the medical bill is not something to start worrying too much about and putting herself through unnecessary burden. Driving down to see Dr Joseph Moore without booking an appointment might not be easy on a busy day, but she definitely needs to see him. She got into her luxurious *Lexus* car to drive down to Shalom University Teaching Hospital (SUTH), and this is not far from King's College Hospital in Camberwell. The car has comfortable leather seats, and is fitted with modern gadgets. Music is the food of life. It refreshes the soul. She reached for her worship CD player and started playing one of them while the air conditioner was turned on to cool down the car, because of the high sun temperature. The hospital is not a good place to visit especially if you have to go to the wards to see people going through pain. She imagined herself being in one of those beds, and detests it saying, "Lord have mercy, and help me."

After registration, she stayed in the waiting area for her turn. About twenty minutes later, the Receptionist calls out her name, "Mary Jenkins, please go to Room 6 and see Dr Joseph Moore."

Mary says, "Thank you," and starts walking down briskly. She knocked on the door and walked in without waiting for a response. "Good morning Dr Joseph."

"Good morning Mary, please take a seat. We have conducted our tests, and I sent you a letter regarding the results. Sorry for the outcome of the results. However, it's a good thing we are aware of what's happening at a very early stage. I'm confident we will deal with it effectively. Have you been sleeping well, eating well, and are there pains around the breasts, or abdomen?"

"The lump and swelling on my left breast is giving me concern and I would like treatment to commence immediately."

"That's exactly what I will line you up for. You have already been for a mammogram. That means I will put you on a special medication and see how you respond to treatment. I assure you, it will not get to the stage of carrying out a mastectomy, because it's pretty much at an early stage, therefore controllable. And regarding the fibroid, you will be having a surgical operation in three weeks' time to have it removed. I will write to you again to give you details of what you need to do to get ready for the surgery."

After checking her blood pressure to find out her systolic and diastolic reading, he said, "Please lie down on this bed for a brief check-up before you go."

He pulled out his stethoscope and placed it just below the left side of her breast, and requested her to breathe in and out which she did thrice. He also placed it on the right side and held her left hand wrist for a few seconds to check her pulse rate. He laid hands on her stomach pushing it gently and asked, "Do you feel any pain as I do this to your stomach?"

She answered, "No Doctor."

And he said, "That's fine. Please get up."

She got up from the bed she lay on for the check-up feeling relieved it was not one that she had to undress for, showing her nudity. A few years ago, she had to change her General Practitioner (GP) because he would ask her to take off her clothing for a check-up, even for sicknesses she considered minor. She was just not happy about that idea and she became suspicious of the young doctor, and eventually changed him. Since then, she had even wished her doctor was a female. She remembered in a flash one of the ugly encounters she had with Dr Anthony Griffiths before she changed him and grimaced her face in anger, hissed, and muttered, "Nonsense! Does he think he could have had his hands all over me and still expect me to come back to him? No way! My body is the temple of the Holy Spirit and not for every Tom, Dick, and Harry to rough handle."

"If it was Dr Anthony Griffiths that checked me today, he would have taken advantage of the breast cancer as an opportunity to start fondling my breast. This is professional misconduct and patient abuse. Well, I'm glad I have given him the boot," she said in a low tone as she navigates the final bend in the road close to a traffic light not far from her home.

In spite of the assurance she got from Dr Joseph Moore, she is still having growing fears about her general health condition, and emotional pain from the loss of Alan Brown. The pain keeps her awake almost all the time at night as she is filled with negative thoughts. To alleviate the pain, she plays Christian praise and worship songs which she believes will penetrate her and restore her soul and confidence, and bring forth healing supernaturally. She has tried to pray in tongues and understanding, but the weight of the affliction is just too much, and perhaps she needs a higher vessel to jump start her, or a prayer partner to join her because two indeed are better than one, for they shall have a good reward for their labour. Besides, whatsoever two of you shall agree together and ask my Father in heaven, He will do it. As she pondered on things, her phone rang.

Her daddy spoke saying, "Hello Mary."

She answered and said, "I'm fine Daddy, how are you?"

He answered, "I'm fine. Your mummy is alright too. She's already sleeping. I just thought I should give you a call now to encourage you and also pray with you."

"Fantastic! I need that now because I've been up having silly thoughts."

"Silly thoughts? Have you seen Dr Joseph Moore?"

"Yes Daddy. He's prescribed medication for me, and I'm due for surgery regarding fibroids in three weeks' time."

"How are you feeling generally? Confident?"

"Not quite."

The Bible says in *1 Corinthians 10:13*, "*There hath no temptation taken you but such as is common to man: but God is faithful, who will not suffer you to be tempted above that ye are able: but will with the temptation also make a way to escape, that ye may be able to bear it."*

"My dear Mary, the trials you are going through today, as tough as they are, they are common to men. God is indeed faithful and will not allow you to be tempted more than you can bear and He has already made a way of escape regarding these trials. There is a way out honey."

Isaiah 43:2 says, *"When thou passest through the waters, I will be with thee: and through the rivers, they shall not overflow thee: when thou walkest through the fire, thou shalt not be burned: neither shall the flame kindle upon thee."*

"You are not alone in these trials. The Most High God is with you. He says, 'He will not leave you nor forsake you.' So you will come out unhurt from these crises just like Shedrach, Meshach, and Abednego came out of the fire. Jesus was with them in the fire of the fiery furnace, and protected them under the Old Testament. He is much more with you now to save you in the New Testament. No shaking! Be at peace. 'Heavenly Father, I commit your daughter into your hands, and I ask for your protection over her. I declare you are made whole by the stripes of Jesus. Thank you, Lord, because the surgery she is going for is a success. Thank you because Doctor Jesus, the Doctor of all Doctors, is the one performing the surgery. Thank you, Lord, for perfecting all that concerns your daughter in Jesus' name. Amen!' Please remain confident and focused on the Lord. I am praying for you darling. Take care."

"Amen! Thanks Daddy for the prayer and word of encouragement and greetings to Mummy. Bye Daddy."

CHAPTER TWO

MUSICAL PERFORMANCE OF THE LIFE OF KING DAVID AT THE EL SHADDAI THEATRE, LONDON

He is a Computer Engineer, of medium build, in his late thirties, with a full beard. He has a visible scar on the left side of his face below his eye, with a scorpion tattoo on the left side of his neck and other tattoos on his left hand. He is 6 feet 4 inches tall with a broad chest and robust biceps like a weightlifter. He has been to prison twice. The first time he went in was for rape, and the second time for assaulting a Police Officer. He has also had several warnings for different offences. That's how bad his record is. The man has been described as extremely dangerous by the Manchester City Police. They have advised the general public to steer clear of him. Anyone with information about him should report him to the nearest Police Station or dial the emergency number 999 immediately. His name is Theophilus Anderson alias, 'Commotion.'

This time, Commotion has gone into a more sophisticated crime. He has successfully hacked into the financial computer system of Apex Bank limited, and five hundred million pounds sterling (£500m) was stolen. In addition to that, a malicious virus was released which has led to the crash of the bank's computer system. The Police have been alerted, and a team from the Manchester City Police, Fraud Investigation Department is handling the matter. Commotion has caused commotion for the Apex Bank. Business is severely disrupted, and the man is on the run.

The phone rings, "Hello, this is Sergeant Linda Thompson, and you are through to Manchester City Police Station. What is your name, and address, and how can I help you?"

"Sorry, I choose to remain anonymous. I've just spotted the bloke, Theophilus Anderson, alias, 'Commotion' whom you are looking for. He just went into a tower block at Piccadilly Circus, on Beverly Street. He disguised himself by wearing a long brown robe, a black top with a hood and black eyeglasses. That's it. Bye."

As soon as Superintendent Paul Jenkins received the message from Sergeant Linda Thompson, he declared, "Right! Gentlemen, we don't have a second to waste. I need six armed Police officers to be on their way to Beverly Street straightaway in two cars and keep in touch on your radios. I am also dispatching a helicopter to the scene to start combing the area, taking pictures, and monitoring Commotion. We must nab him."

He immediately informs Scotland Yard in London of the latest developments.

Commotion had already changed to jeans, and he moved swiftly right to the top of the building, the 50th floor, the highest floor of the building carrying a bag and a gun. The police sighted him and gave him a hot chase, exchanging bullets with him in a movie-style manner while on the 45th floor.

"Stop there and put your gun down," shouted one of the Bobbies, but he kept on running. As soon as he got to the top, he got out a parachute and went for a fast landing right on the top of a ten story building next to Howard Williams block, and within seconds, he was out of police sight. The area is cordoned off, and the investigation and search continues. This is the sort of situation Superintendent Paul Jenkins deals with. Tough! That's why as a Christian, he is on his knees most times asking for God's guidance and protection.

Crime is taking a new dimension in cities across the country. London, Manchester, Birmingham, Leeds, Newcastle, Liverpool, Cardiff, and Glasgow have all recently experienced shocking new crime waves. And the Police are working tirelessly to ensure law and order is maintained. The police are continually busting gangsters, and suspected terrorists' attacks are regularly foiled. Sadly, a seventeen-year-old teenager, Johnson Smith, one of the 'chimpanzee gang' on the Bradley Taylor estate in Manchester was stabbed to death following a squabble on how to share their loot from a recent theft operation.

His mum, Elizabeth Smith, a lone parent, is crying and mourning but it's too late to cry after death has struck. The police have arrested the suspect and he will be charged soon. That's a precious soul lost. Why should a teenager abandon being meaningfully engaged in his studies to have a decent education and life to join a bandit's gang? Perhaps parents are to be blamed for not doing enough to train up children to follow a godly path in life. The Bible says in **Proverbs 22:6,** *"Train up a child in the way he should go: and when he is old, he will not depart from it."*

Children need a solid foundation to put them on the right path in life. If the foundation be destroyed, what can the righteous do? Children should start reading their Bible from an early age. God is our Creator, and He has provided us with the Bible to serve us as a manual to fix our lives. The Bible says in **2 Timothy 3:15,** *"And that from a child thou hast known the holy scriptures, which are able to make thee wise unto salvation through faith which is in Christ Jesus."* Timothy read his Bible and knew the holy scriptures as a child, and that made him wise. Children should follow this godly example.

Mary lay on the bed with Alan's picture laid on her chest, and her mind filled with his thoughts. She goes down memory lane in her thoughts, dwelling on the good times they both shared. The one that she found so exciting was her first outing with him. Alan had called her earlier on the phone to ask her out.

"Where are you taking me out to this weekend Alan?"

"It's a surprise. I've got loads of exciting things lined up for us this Saturday. All I need is for you to get dressed and be ready by 5 pm."

She replies and says, "That's fine."

It's just three days to Saturday, but it seems like forever. She sleeps and wakes up with great expectation that she's going to have a real good time with him. And she thought within herself, "Is it right for me to accept having a date with Alan without first letting Bishop John Barnes know about it as a Christian? Oh well, I see him as a gentleman, and a good Christian."

Looking through her wardrobe, it's like there are no suitable clothes for the Saturday date, and she decided she will be at Magnificent Superstores shopping complex for a dress and a hair do first thing Saturday morning. Magnificent Superstores is a great shopping centre at Oxford Circus in Central London, and it is a fantastic place to be on a Saturday to shop. This complex is situated close to Selfridges, and Marks & Spencer. There are loads of beautiful items on display for sale at Magnificent Superstores, and they are irresistible.

"Oh, that's a beautiful Italian black dress designed by *Giorgio Armani*." She quipped.

Immediately, she is flanked by a sales lady who said, "Hi, that's a nice Italian dress. We have it in all sizes, an elegantly made long sleeve dress by *Giorgio Armani* with a blend of cotton, very comfortable fabric, and embroidered suitable for an evening outing. We also have nice designer *Dolce & Gabbana* handbags and shoes here to go with it. The prices are reasonable as well and we are currently offering a 20% sales discount on all our products."

"I love it. Can I try them on?"

"Please try them on."

She tries a size 14 dress along with the shoes and bag, and it was a perfect match. "I will go for it."

"That's fine."

She pays for the items.

"Thanks for shopping at Magnificent Superstores. We look forward to seeing you again. Bye."

Off she goes to the Salon for a manicure and pedicure, and to get her hair done in another section of the same Magnificent Superstores complex. A good colour combination is very important for her as she needs her nails to match the rest of her outfit. And as for her hair, she needs a style that will make her look young and highlight her beauty more. Fortunately, there wasn't a queue at that time, so she quickly had it done and left. And as she drove back home, she kept imagining how the outing will go. "It's going to be fun," she thought. She has not had a date with any man for a long time before today so she's pretty much excited.

She quickly starts making up with her *Estee Lauder* products, and then puts on her clothes while ensuring she will be ready before the 5 pm date with Alan. She's determined not to give a bad impression on her first date with him or be late. And 5 pm on the dot, there he comes in his white Range Rover car. He got out of the car with a bunch of beautiful flowers from the florist in his hand. The landscape in front of the house is beautifully made. He went straight for the doorbell and Mary opened the door with a broad smile on her face exposing her beautiful white set of teeth. While Alan drew near her with a broad smile as well, he reached for her and held her gently close to him. Mary smells the *Hugo Boss* Cologne and the fresh breath oozing out from his macho physique as he warmly wraps her in his arms for a peck.

"These flowers are for you. How are you? You look absolutely gorgeous in that black dress."

"Thanks Alan for the flowers and the compliments. You are looking good as well in your brown suit. And your cologne smells nice."

He replies, "Thanks darling."

Alan is 6 feet 3 inches tall. A strong man with a fine physique developed over the years from working out in the gym. He holds a Bachelor of Science degree in Economics and a Master's degree in Marketing from Harvard University. He is in his early forties, and he is a Marketing Manager at Posh Cars Limited with international responsibility. He is a Christian from a good family, and his parents are originally from Canada.

"Right! Let's be on our way," says Alan as he reaches out for her hand and they head for the front door ready to leave. "We are heading first to Oriental 5-star hotel in Hyde Park, close to the Dorchester 5 star hotel, Park Lane, in central London for our dinner, and then to El Shaddai Theatre, in London for a live performance. I hope that's fine with you?"

"That's fine."

They exit the house, and slowly walked down to the car while holding hands. He reaches for the car door and opens for her to get in. And he goes to his own side and he drives off. She already has a note in her mobile phone diary that she will be with Alan this time. She also left a note on the kitchen table that she is with Alan at this time, as she didn't tell anyone. This is their very first date, though they attend the same Church.

Alan spoke and asked her in a gentle tone, "What are the things you find very exciting in life as a woman?"

She replied and said, "That's a very interesting question. I find my relationship with God and my family exciting. Travelling to different nations of the world on holiday and lodging in a 5-star hotel is exciting to me. I find romantic and musical movies exciting. I also love sports, and sports cars." She giggled. "I hope you got an exciting answer here?"

"That's an exciting answer. But I think there is something that needs to be added to that answer."

"What needs to be added?"

"For me, I would like to add that I find it exciting to have you, a very beautiful lady by my side, going out on a date with me. I also find it exciting to have a romantic, caring, and loving partner."

"That's a good one Alan. I concur."

As they approach the Hotel, he carefully slows down and drives in to park the car and they get out and head straight for the restaurant area.

"Have you been here before Alan?"

"Yes I have, and the food and service are excellent."

"Good evening sir and madam. Please come this way to the special table reserved for both of you." That's the greeting from a waiter as he hands over the menu and wine list to them. It's a long list of assorted food and drinks.

"I like the interior and exterior decorations of this hotel. It's very appealing to the eye," says Mary.

"Yes, it's lovely. Please feel free to order whatever you like darling."

They make their order for food and drinks.

While they wait for their order to arrive, Alan continues the conversation by asking her, "What's the most exciting book you've ever read?"

Mary answered, "The Bible is by far the most exciting book I have ever read and I still read. I call it the book of life."

He asked again, "What makes it the most exciting book?"

AMAZING GRACE IN ABUNDANCE

"It's the most exciting book because that's God communicating with me as I read. Jesus says in *John 6:63*, '...*The words that I speak unto you, they are spirit, and they are life.*' The holy book is full of anointing to empower, strengthen, and heal. *Hebrews 4:12* also says, '*The Word of God is quick, and powerful, and sharper than any twoedged sword...*' The Bible is full of words of wisdom that refreshes the soul."

"Great! Who's your favourite character in the Bible apart from Jesus?" inquired Alan.

The waiter turns up with the food and drinks.

"Let's pray," says Alan. "Thank you, Lord, for the wonderful opportunity you've given us to be together today. Thank you for the food and drink, we are grateful. I bless and sanctify this meal. Let it nourish our bodies as we eat in Jesus' name." And they both say, "Amen!"

Now it's time to get down to action and enjoy the meal. As she helps herself to a few bits of the salads and seafood, she says, "Whao! The food is delicious."

"Yeah, I agree."

She continues, "My favourite character in the Bible is King David, God's beloved. I love him so much because he is a Psalmist and a true worshipper. He single-handedly wrote about three quarters of the entire book of Psalms. And God described him in the book of Acts as a man after His own heart because of his lifestyle of praise. He is also a warrior. He killed Goliath the Philistine that defied the army of Israel with just a sling and a stone. He lived a life of royalty. His story in the Bible has greatly influenced my life. The same goes for other areas of my life as I apply the words the Spirit of God inspired him to write in my life. Sorry, I am only dwelling on the positive side of King David. I'm not looking at the adultery he committed with Bathsheba, Uriah's wife, or the many people he killed in different wars that he fought that made God say to him, 'You can't build me a Temple because you have shed much blood.'

"Well done my dear. That's a great answer."

"Please pass me that toothpick," Alan requested as they begin to round up. He continued, "I enjoyed the meal. This is *Espora Fitness Tinto Cabernet Sauvignon* non-alcoholic red wine.

It's very nice. You can fill your glass. Let's have a toast to our health and prosperity."

They raised their glasses and said, "Cheers!" and continued to listen to the mid-tempo instrumental Jazz music.

"Thanks Alan for the meal."

"Oh, please don't mention it. It's my pleasure to do it," he replies, and calls out saying, "Waiter, please come over so that I can settle the bill with my debit card."

The waiter turns up and he pays, and says, "This ten quid is a tip for you. Thanks for the food and lovely service. Much appreciated. See you next time."

The Waiter replies, "Thank you very much sir."

They get going and she is walking on Alan's left hand side as they hold hands laughing and chatting as they make their way down to the car to head for the El Shaddai Theatre to see the powerful musical live performance about the story of King David in the Bible, directed by the internationally acclaimed award winner John Walker. Alan didn't know King David was Mary's favourite character in the Bible when he booked the tickets for them to see the performance about King David.

"Here you are. What a coincidence! This is your chance to see your favourite character in the Bible, a King David theatre performance. Hopefully, you will get to love him more."

Mary replies, "I'm excited about the theatre performance."

Alan pulled up the car at the National Car Park (NCP) and obtained a parking ticket for the evening before they made their way to the El Shaddai Theatre, which is just a stone's throw away. This is not far from Trocadero Entertainment Centre, in Piccadilly Circus, London.

THE EL SHADDAI THEATRE, LONDON

They got to the entrance and found that the queue stretched right down the street, but thankfully they went to the front of the queue because they had special front row tickets. As they are seated waiting for the performance to commence, they got busy fiddling with their mobile phones. The El Shaddai Theatre is a very big theatre with a seating capacity for 5,000 people, and it is always packed full because of the life-changing King David musical performance. People from all walks of life including Christians and non-Christians, bourgeoisie, tycoons, top celebrities, top government officials, and tourists from across the nations of the world are always in attendance. And security is always tight in there. The interior is well-decorated with biblical Hebrew traditional and cultural musical artworks of ancient times. The seating layout is such that people can have a good view of the stage wherever they are seated, with screens mounted at strategic places. The performance is mostly presented in opera style. Every King David musical performance lasts for a maximum of two and a half hours, but you will wish it would continue when it ends, because the performance on stage will surely grab your attention fully. Excellent!

On the stage lie the musical instruments used by the *orchestra*, with seating arrangements in a uniform way according to instruments. All manner of *string* instruments including the violins, violas, cellos, banjos, guitars, and harps are here. A complete set of *woodwind* instruments including flutes, piccolos, clarinets, and saxophones are present. *Brass* instruments including cornets, trumpets, baritones, trombones, horns, and tuba are here. They also have *percussion* instruments on display, which include timpani, piano, drums, cymbals, xylophones, gongs, and bells.[1-2]

The instruments on display clearly show a reflection of similar musical instruments mentioned by the Psalmist in *Psalm 150: 3-5* saying:

> [3] *Praise him with the sound of the trumpet: praise him with the psaltery and harp.*

> [4] *Praise him with the timbrel and dance: praise him with stringed instruments and organs.*

> [5] *Praise him upon the loud cymbals: praise him upon the high sounding cymbals.*

The Bible says we should praise the Most High God with all kinds of musical instruments. That's exactly what happens in this Theatre. For Christians who have read 1st and 2nd Samuel, and the

Book of Psalms in the Bible before coming to see this King David live performance, and are connected to the performance, the feeling they get is more like being in a Church rather than a Theatre. Awesome!

The characters of the musical are dressed in costumes as described in the Bible. The clothing, armour, shields, and weapons, all reflect the Hebrew culture. It's indeed fascinating! The story of King David in the Bible becomes more real when you see this life-changing performance.

ANNOUNCER: Ladies and gentlemen, it's time to start the live musical performance about the life of King David. Please sit back, relax, and enjoy it.

ORCHESTRA: Everyone in the orchestra takes their rightful place in a uniform manner according to their instruments, with the Conductor, John Walker in front on the podium with his music book.

THE CHARACTERS: All the major characters appear on stage for their introductions in turn including; King David, Jesse and the sons, Prophet Samuel, King Saul, Goliath, the armies of Israel, the Philistine army, the women of Israel, Jonathan and his brothers, Michal, Abner, Joab, the sons of David – Absalom, Adonijah, Solomon and the rest, Bathsheba, Uriah, and Prophet Nathan.

ORCHESTRA: Commences by playing a beautifully composed song based on Psalm 23 written by King David as the characters are ushered onto the stage. The tempo of the music begins to steadily rise up and down, captivating the audience to join in and stay connected. Meanwhile, the presence of God is already filling up the whole atmosphere.

PSALM 23 – THE LORD IS MY SHEPHERD

¹ The LORD is my shepherd; I shall not want.

² He maketh me to lie down in green pastures: he leadeth me beside the still waters.

³ He restoreth my soul: he leadeth me in the paths of righteousness for his name's sake.

⁴ Yea, though I walk through the valley of the shadow of death, I will fear no evil: for thou art with me; thy rod and thy staff they comfort me.

⁵ Thou preparest a table before me in the presence of mine enemies: thou anointest my head with oil; my cup runneth over.

⁶ Surely goodness and mercy shall follow me all the days of my life: and I will dwell in the house of the LORD for ever.

PSALM 100 – A PSALM OF PRAISE AND THANKSGIVING

¹Make a joyful noise unto the LORD, all ye lands.

² Serve the LORD with gladness: come before his presence with singing.

³ Know ye that the LORD he is God: it is he that hath made us, and not we ourselves; we are his people, and the sheep of his pasture.

⁴ Enter into his gates with thanksgiving, and into his courts with praise: be thankful unto him, and bless his name.

⁵ For the LORD is good; his mercy is everlasting; and his truth endureth to all generations.

AUDIENCE: There is a roar of excitement in the air, as they sing along to Psalm 23 and Psalm 100 with joy, radiating the Shekinah glory of God. People are already getting emotional as they are being moved by the beautiful songs. This is just a little part of the show because much more is on the way. Mary and Alan joined in the singing. Exciting!

PROPHET SAMUEL: The story begins from 1ˢᵗ Samuel 16, as he appears in the house of Jesse as instructed by the Lord to go and anoint one of his sons. The seven sons are paraded before the

Prophet. They were all rejected by the Lord, and they had to go to the field where David was looking after his father's flock to fetch him, and he was finally anointed to be a replacement for King Saul who had disobeyed the Lord by not wiping out the Amalekites completely as instructed.

KING SAUL: He is attacked by evil spirits from the Lord. And the servants suggested he should get a minstrel to be performing for him, and David was brought to the palace to play for King Saul.

ORCHESTRA: The Bible says in *1 Samuel 16:23, "And it came to pass, when the evil spirit from God was upon Saul, that David took an harp, and played with his hand: so Saul was refreshed, and was well, and the evil spirit departed from him."* The orchestra plays another beautiful song based on this scripture.

AUDIENCE: The audience goes absolutely ecstatic emotionally as this scripture is actually being fulfilled in the lives of people in the audience whilst the orchestra played the stringed instruments, and performed. The atmosphere in the auditorium changed and you could feel the strong presence of God for real and as a confirmation, evil spirits started crying out, and different forms of manifestations among the audience started happening and deliverances and healings began to take place. Praise God! Hallelujah!

My prayer as you read this book and stay connected is that the power of God will be abundantly made available to you and touch you as you behold wondrous things from the pages of this book to bring forth deliverances and healings to you in Jesus' name. The power of God is present and available to you now, and all you've got to do is open your heart by faith and you shall be healed indeed in Jesus' name. There is this twelve-year-old boy in a wheelchair that has seen this live performance six times before and he is there in the audience for the seventh time. He felt the power of God so much that he walked after the doctors had said he will never walk again due to a severe injury to his spinal cord, sustained in a motor accident a year ago. The boy and a few other people shared their testimonies after the live performance. There is amazing grace in abundance to heal.

ORCHESTRA: They played again the following songs taken from the Psalms, reproduced and directed by John Walker, the Musical Director.

PSALM 47:1-9

¹ O clap your hands, all ye people; shout unto God with the voice of triumph.

² For the LORD most high is terrible; he is a great King over all the earth.

³ He shall subdue the people under us, and the nations under our feet.

⁴ He shall choose our inheritance for us, the excellency of Jacob whom he loved. Selah.

⁵ God is gone up with a shout, the LORD with the sound of a trumpet.

⁶ Sing praises to God, sing praises: sing praises unto our King, sing praises.

⁷ For God is the King of all the earth: sing ye praises with understanding.

⁸ God reigneth over the heathen: God sitteth upon the throne of his holiness.

⁹ The princes of the people are gathered together, even the people of the God of Abraham: for the shields of the earth belong unto God: he is greatly exalted.

PSALM 8:1 & 9

O LORD, our Lord, how excellent is thy name in all the earth! who hast set thy glory above the heavens.

PSALM 48:1

Great is the LORD, and greatly to be praised in the city of our God, in the mountain of his holiness.

PSALM 108:5

Be thou exalted, O God, above the heavens: and thy glory above all the earth;

AUDIENCE: People became so emotional expressing joy with deep sighs of relief. The entire audience got up on their feet as they joined in singing along to the lyrics of the songs in a jubilant and vibrant manner. It's indeed exciting! Mary and Alan are marvelled at what they see. It is more like a Church service than a live theatre show. They joined the audience in the singing, clapping, and dancing, participating fully. They are having a good time. Exciting!

DAVID VERSUS GOLIATH'S FIGHT: The storyline takes us further to the great fight between David and Goliath featured in 1st Samuel chapter 17. Goliath's costume, especially the armour depicts so much of the description in the Bible, and that is fascinating. You certainly cannot talk about David without talking about this fight. And thank God David killed Goliath the uncircumcised Philistine who defied the armies of Israel. David was able to kill Goliath through the power of Almighty God. There are a few important lessons to learn from this fight between David and Goliath which the Announcer gave as follows: *Firstly,* David was not afraid of Goliath. *Secondly,* he made enquiries from the soldiers in the camp about the man he has set his eyes on to fight in order to know his strengths and weaknesses. *Thirdly,* he found out that the reward to kill Goliath is freedom from paying tax, as well as marrying the king's daughter. That was a motivation for him. Everyone in the army camp saw Goliath as a big challenge, but David saw him as an instrument for his promotion, freedom, and fame. *Fourthly,* David remembered how God delivered him and gave him victory over the lion and the bear that attacked his father's lamb and him, and concluded the same

26

God will help him kill Goliath. **Fifthly,** he did not use Saul's armour because he was not used to it, neither did he use weapons he was not used to. He got himself a sling and five smooth stones. **Sixthly,** when Goliath engaged him in a war of words, he did not close his mouth. He promptly responded because a closed mouth is a closed destiny. He did not cower. He declared in **1 Samuel 17:47**, *"...The battle is the LORD's..."*

The story continues in chapter 18 telling us how much Jonathan loved David. He loved him as his own soul and they made a covenant.

1 Samuel 18:1-4 says:

> *¹ And it came to pass, when he had made an end of speaking unto Saul, that the soul of Jonathan was knit with the soul of David, and Jonathan loved him as his own soul.*
>
> *² And Saul took him that day, and would let him go no more home to his father's house.*
>
> *³ Then Jonathan and David made a covenant, because he loved him as his own soul.*
>
> *⁴ And Jonathan stripped himself of the robe that was upon him, and gave it to David, and his garments, even to his sword, and to his bow, and to his girdle.*

Jonathan has just demonstrated one main undeniable quality of love which is giving. When you truly love somebody you have to also give gifts to the person to express it.

ORCHESTRA: Plays a song of victory for King David based on the scripture below, and sung by the women of Israel. The women infuriated King Saul as they sang the song ascribing more glory to David. The Bible says in **1 Samuel 18:6-7**:

> *⁶ And it came to pass as they came, when David was returned from the slaughter of the Philistine, that the women came out of all cities of Israel, singing and dancing, to meet king Saul, with tabrets, with joy, and with instruments of musick.*

⁷ And the women answered one another as they played, and said, Saul hath slain his thousands, and David his ten thousands.

KING SAUL PURSUES DAVID EVERYWHERE TO KILL HIM. The story continues as we see King Saul getting very jealous of David to the extent that he even set out to kill him by twice throwing a javelin at him to pin him to the wall. Jealousy and envy!

1 Samuel 18:10 - 11 says:

¹⁰ And it came to pass on the morrow, that the evil spirit from God came upon Saul, and he prophesied in the midst of the house: and David played with his hand, as at other times: and there was a javelin in Saul's hand.

¹¹ And Saul cast the javelin; for he said, I will smite David even to the wall with it. And David avoided out of his presence twice.

The Bible says that in all this, David behaved himself wisely and God was with him. **1 Samuel 18:14** says, *"And David behaved himself wisely in all his ways; and the* LORD *was with him."*

The story continued telling us that King Saul's daughter Michal loved David, and King Saul was pleased to hear that because he would use that as opportunity to plot against David, for him to die through a set-up in a fight with the Philistines and for him to be his son-in-law and marry his daughter.

1 Samuel 18:25-27 says:

²⁵ And Saul said, 'Thus shall ye say to David, the king desireth not any dowry, but an hundred foreskins of the Philistines, to be avenged of the king's enemies'. But Saul thought to make David fall by the hand of the Philistines.

²⁶ And when his servants told David these words, it pleased David well to be the king's son-in-law: and the days were not expired.

²⁷ Wherefore David arose and went, he and his men, and slew of the Philistines two hundred men; and David brought their foreskins, and they gave them in full tale to the king, that he might be the king's son-in-law. And Saul gave him Michal his daughter to wife.

The plan to kill David continued in chapter 19 to the extent that King Saul sent messengers to David's house to monitor him and kill him, but God was with him and used his wife to save him. The Bible says in *1 Samuel 19:11-18:*

¹¹ Saul also sent messengers unto David's house, to watch him, and to slay him in the morning: and Michal David's wife told him, saying, if thou save not thy life to night, tomorrow thou shalt be slain.

¹² So Michal let David down through a window: and he went, and fled, and escaped.

¹³ And Michal took an image, and laid it in the bed, and put a pillow of goats hair for his bolster, and covered it with a cloth.

¹⁴ And when Saul sent messengers to take David, she said, He is sick.

¹⁵ And Saul sent the messengers again to see David, saying, bring him up to me in the bed, that I may slay him.

¹⁶ And when the messengers were come in, behold, there was an image in the bed, with a pillow of goats hair for his bolster.

¹⁷ And Saul said unto Michal, Why hast thou deceived me so, and sent away mine enemy, that he is escaped? And Michal answered Saul, He said unto me, Let me go; why should I kill thee?

¹⁸ So David fled, and escaped, and came to Samuel to Ramah, and told him all that Saul had done to him. And he and Samuel went and dwelt in Naioth.

When David escaped and fled, he was now on the run as King Saul pursued him everywhere determined to kill him. David fled from

Ramah where he saw Prophet Samuel in *1 Samuel 20:1;* From there he came to Nob where he saw Ahimelech in *1 Samuel 21:1;* And from there he fled to Gath in *1 Samuel 21:10* where he met with King Achish and pretended to be mad, and he further fled to the cave of Adullam in *1 Samuel 22:1.* David further ran to Kellah in *1 Samuel 23:1;* and from there to the wilderness of Ziph in *1 Samuel 23:14.* From here David moved to Hachilah hill in *1 Samuel 23:19.* From here he fled again to Moan wilderness in *1 Samuel 23:24.* From here David ran again to Engedi wilderness in *1 Samuel 24:1.* He further fled to Paran wilderness in *1 Samuel 25:1,* and back to Ziph wilderness in *1 Samuel 26:1-2;* and to Gath of the Philistines in *1 Samuel 27:1 & 3.* From there he further fled to Ziklag in *1 Samuel 27:6.* These are places David had to run to in order to escape the wrath of King Saul.

Surprisingly, David caught up with King Saul, but refused to kill him saying in **1 Samuel 24:6,** "*And he said unto his men, The LORD forbid that I should do this thing unto my master, the LORD's anointed, to stretch forth mine hand against him, seeing he is the anointed of the LORD.*"

All David did was to cut off part of King Saul's skirt as evidence that the King should have been captured and killed, but he spared his life. **1 Samuel 24:11** says, "*Moreover, my father, see, yea, see the skirt of thy robe in my hand: for in that I cut off the skirt of thy robe, and killed thee not, know thou and see that there is neither evil nor transgression in mine hand, and I have not sinned against thee; yet thou huntest my soul to take it.*" And **1 Samuel 24:17** says, "*And he said to David, thou art more righteous than I: for thou hast rewarded me good, whereas I have rewarded thee evil.*" What an evil thing for a king to be envious of his subordinate! David had another opportunity to kill King Saul but he refused to lay hands on him claiming King Saul is God's anointed. The Bible declares in **1 Samuel 26:7-11:**

> [7] *So David and Abishai came to the people by night: and, behold, Saul lay sleeping within the trench, and his spear stuck in the ground at his bolster: but Abner and the people lay round about him.*

8 Then said Abishai to David, God hath delivered thine enemy into thine hand this day: now therefore let me smite him, I pray thee, with the spear even to the earth at once, and I will not smite him the second time.

9 And David said to Abishai, destroy him not: for who can stretch forth his hand against the LORD's anointed, and be guiltless?

10 David said furthermore, As the LORD liveth, the LORD shall smite him; or his day shall come to die; or he shall descend into battle, and perish.

11 The LORD forbid that I should stretch forth mine hand against the LORD's anointed: but, I pray thee, take thou now the spear that is at his bolster, and the cruse of water, and let us go.

The story continues and tells us that David married Abigail after Nabal misbehaved and the Lord smote him and he died. *1 Samuel 25:39* says:

"And when David heard that Nabal was dead, he said, blessed be the LORD, that hath pleaded the cause of my reproach from the hand of Nabal, and hath kept his servant from evil: for the LORD hath returned the wickedness of Nabal upon his own head. And David sent and communed with Abigail, to take her to him to wife."

King Saul and his three children died in a fight against the Philistines. The Bible says in *1 Samuel 31:4-6:*

4 Then said Saul unto his armour bearer, draw thy sword, and thrust me through therewith; lest these uncircumcised come and thrust me through, and abuse me. But his armour bearer would not; for he was sore afraid. Therefore Saul took a sword, and fell upon it.

5 And when his armourbearer saw that Saul was dead, he fell likewise upon his sword, and died with him.

6 So Saul died, and his three sons, and his armour bearer, and all his men, that same day together.

The Bible tells us that David lamented the death of King Saul and Jonathan in *2 Samuel 1:17:*

> *"And David lamented with this lamentation over Saul and over Jonathan his son:"*

ORCHESTRA: The Orchestra played their instruments softly while the story is told. They now play more songs based on the following Psalms.

PSALM 18:3

> *I will call upon the LORD, who is worthy to be praised: so shall I be saved from mine enemies.*

PSALM 25:1-2

> *¹ Unto thee, O LORD, do I lift up my soul.*
>
> *² O my God, I trust in thee: let me not be ashamed, let not mine enemies triumph over me.*

PSALM 30:11

> *Thou hast turned for me my mourning into dancing: thou hast put off my sackcloth, and girded me with gladness;*

PSALM 32: 7

> *Thou art my hiding place; thou shalt preserve me from trouble; thou shalt compass me about with songs of deliverance. Selah.*

AUDIENCE: Meanwhile, the audience is still very much connected with the story and the Orchestra's music performance and they are participating fully by singing along, clapping, and dancing. It's really soul-refreshing. Mary and Alan are not left out. They are also participating fully.

DAVID IS ANOINTED KING OVER JUDAH AND ISRAEL. After the death of King Saul, David was anointed officially again by the house of Judah in **2 Samuel 2:4** that says, *"And the men of Judah came, and there they anointed David King over the house of Judah. And they told David, saying, That the men of Jabeshgilead were they that buried Saul."*

All the elders of Israel also anointed him in Hebron to be king over Israel. **2 Samuel 5:3-5** says:

> ³ *So all the elders of Israel came to the King to Hebron; and King David made a league with them in Hebron before the* LORD: *and they anointed David King over Israel.*

> ⁴ *David was thirty years old when he began to reign, and he reigned forty years.*

> ⁵ *In Hebron he reigned over Judah seven years and six months: and in Jerusalem he reigned thirty and three years over all Israel and Judah.*

Before David was anointed king of Israel, the Bible says that as a result of the long war between the house of Saul and the house of David, the house of Saul waxed weaker and weaker and the house of David waxed stronger and stronger. David went ahead and had six children from six wives in Hebron. **2 Samuel 3:1-5** says:

> ¹ *Now there was a long war between the house of Saul and the house of David: but David waxed stronger and stronger, and the house of Saul waxed weaker and weaker.*

> ² *And unto David were sons born in Hebron: and his firstborn was Amnon, of Ahinoam the Jezreelitess;*

> ³ *And his second, Chileab, of Abigail the wife of Nabal the Carmelite; and the third, Absalom the son of Maacah the daughter of Talmai, King of Geshur;*

> ⁴ *And the fourth, Adonijah the son of Haggith; and the fifth, Shephatiah the son of Abital;*

> ⁵ *And the sixth, Ithream, by Eglah David's wife. These were born to David in Hebron.*

The Bible tells us that King David took more wives and concubines and had eleven more children in Jerusalem including King Solomon who succeeded him. *2 Samuel 5:13-16* says:

> [13] *And David took him more concubines and wives out of Jerusalem, after he was come from Hebron: and there were yet sons and daughters born to David.*

> [14] *And these be the names of those that were born unto him in Jerusalem; Shammuah, and Shobab, and Nathan, and Solomon,*

> [15] *Ibhar also, and Elishua, and Nepheg, and Japhia,*

> [16] *And Elishama, and Eliada, and Eliphalet.*

The Bible further tells us in 2 Samuel 6:12 that when king David heard the Lord has blessed the house of Obededom because of the ark of the Lord, he went and brought the ark of the Lord from the house of Obededom to the city of David with gladness.

ORCHESTRA: They played a powerful song based on the scripture below when music was played and King David danced with all his might as the ark of the Lord was brought while Michal his wife despised him. *2 Samuel 6:14-15* says:

> [14] *And David danced before the LORD with all his might; and David was girded with a linen ephod.*

> [15] *So David and all the house of Israel brought up the ark of the LORD with shouting, and with the sound of the trumpet.*

AUDIENCE: The audience went wild here as it seemed they all got into a dancing competition and they all danced like David danced, with all their might. They are still very much connected with the story and the Orchestra's music performance and they are participating fully by singing along, clapping, and dancing. This time around, people were already sweating, and it felt as if the air conditioner was not on, when in fact it was on full blast. It's really fun. This time offered the opportunity for Mary and Alan to dance and shake their bodies down to the ground. It was indeed fun as the pair danced feeling free with one another while they also sang.

GOD TELLS KING DAVID HE IS NOT TO BUILD HIM A TEMPLE

The Bible tells us in *2 Samuel 7:1-2:*

> *¹And it came to pass, when the king sat in his house, and the LORD had given him rest round about from all his enemies;*
>
> *² That the king said unto Nathan the prophet, See now, I dwell in an house of cedar, but the ark of God dwelleth within curtains.*

But the Lord told King David that he will not be the one to build him the Temple but his son Solomon because King David has shed much blood fighting in many wars. *1 Chronicles 22:8-11* declares:

> *⁸ But the word of the LORD came to me, saying, Thou hast shed blood abundantly, and hast made great wars: thou shalt not build an house unto my name, because thou hast shed much blood upon the earth in my sight.*
>
> *⁹ Behold, a son shall be born to thee, who shall be a man of rest; and I will give him rest from all his enemies round about: for his name shall be Solomon, and I will give peace and quietness unto Israel in his days.*
>
> *¹⁰ He shall build an house for my name; and he shall be my son, and I will be his father; and I will establish the throne of his kingdom over Israel for ever.*
>
> *¹¹ Now, my son, the LORD be with thee; and prosper thou, and build the house of the LORD thy God, as he hath said of thee.*

KING DAVID SETS UP URIAH TO DIE IN THE BATTLE AND MARRIES HIS WIFE BATHSHEBA.

> The Bible says in *2 Samuel 11:2, "And it came to pass in an evening tide, that David arose from off his bed, and walked upon the roof of the king's house: and from the roof he saw a woman washing herself; and the woman was very beautiful to look upon."*

The Bible says again in *2 Samuel 11:14-15:*

> *14 And it came to pass in the morning, that David wrote a letter to Joab, and sent it by the hand of Uriah.*

> *15 And he wrote in the letter, saying, Set ye Uriah in the forefront of the hottest battle, and retire ye from him, that he may be smitten, and die.*

And finally, the Bible says in *2 Samuel 11:26-27:*

> *26 And when the wife of Uriah heard that Uriah her husband was dead, she mourned for her husband.*

> *27 And when the mourning was past, David sent and fetched her to his house, and she became his wife, and bare him a son. But the thing that David had done displeased the* LORD.

The Lord was not happy with the adultery King David committed with Bathsheba and also set up the husband to die in the battlefield. Therefore, the Lord sent Prophet Nathan to warn him of the consequences, and King David acknowledged that he had sinned against the Lord. *2 Samuel 12:11-14* declares:

> *11 Thus saith the* LORD, *Behold, I will raise up evil against thee out of thine own house, and I will take thy wives before thine eyes, and give them unto thy neighbour, and he shall lie with thy wives in the sight of this sun.*

> *12 For thou didst it secretly: but I will do this thing before all Israel, and before the sun.*

> *13 And David said unto Nathan, I have sinned against the* LORD. *And Nathan said unto David, The* LORD *also hath put away thy sin; thou shalt not die.*

> *14 Howbeit, because by this deed thou hast given great occasion to the enemies of the* LORD *to blaspheme, the child also that is born unto thee shall surely die.*

ORCHESTRA: They stepped in and played a very moving song of confession, forgiveness, and repentance of sin written by King David after he committed adultery with Bathsheba. They played:

PSALM 51 – CONFESSION AND FORGIVENESS OF SIN

[1] *Have mercy upon me, O God, according to thy loving kindness: according unto the multitude of thy tender mercies blot out my transgressions.*

[2] *Wash me thoroughly from mine iniquity, and cleanse me from my sin.*

[3] *For I acknowledge my transgressions: and my sin is ever before me.*

[4] *Against thee, thee only, have I sinned, and done this evil in thy sight: that thou mightest be justified when thou speakest, and be clear when thou judgest.*

[5] *Behold, I was shapen in iniquity; and in sin did my mother conceive me.*

[6] *Behold, thou desirest truth in the inward parts: and in the hidden part thou shalt make me to know wisdom.*

[7] *Purge me with hyssop, and I shall be clean: wash me, and I shall be whiter than snow.*

[8] *Make me to hear joy and gladness; that the bones which thou hast broken may rejoice.*

[9] *Hide thy face from my sins, and blot out all mine iniquities.*

[10] *Create in me a clean heart, O God; and renew a right spirit within me.*

[11] *Cast me not away from thy presence; and take not thy holy spirit from me.*

[12] *Restore unto me the joy of thy salvation; and uphold me with thy free spirit.*

[13] *Then will I teach transgressors thy ways; and sinners shall be converted unto thee.*

[14] *Deliver me from blood guiltiness, O God, thou God of my salvation: and my tongue shall sing aloud of thy righteousness.*

¹⁵ O Lord, open thou my lips; and my mouth shall shew forth thy praise.

¹⁶ For thou desirest not sacrifice; else would I give it: thou delightest not in burnt offering.

¹⁷ The sacrifices of God are a broken spirit: a broken and a contrite heart, O God, thou wilt not despise.

¹⁸ Do good in thy good pleasure unto Zion: build thou the walls of Jerusalem.

¹⁹ Then shalt thou be pleased with the sacrifices of righteousness, with burnt offering and whole burnt offering: then shall they offer bullocks upon thine altar.

AUDIENCE: The audience continued to be connected to the story and songs. As Psalm 51 was played, most people were moved to tears, and the atmosphere was solemn, but still entertaining. People got their handkerchiefs out and wiped their tears, and shook hands and embraced their neighbours out of an expression of deep emotion. They could see genuine confession in the lyrics of Psalm 51 originally written by King David and now played. Meanwhile, Mary Jenkins wished King David didn't commit adultery with Bathsheba. As her favourite character and mentor in the Bible, she wished he didn't do anything bad to spoil his record.

INCEST IN KING DAVID'S HOUSE

The Bible says in **2 Samuel 13:1,** *"And it came to pass after this, that Absalom the son of David had a fair sister, whose name was Tamar; and Amnon the son of David loved her."* Amnon burned with infatuation and went ahead and raped his step-sister. Tamar tried to resist him, but **2 Samuel 13:14** says, *"Howbeit he would not hearken unto her voice: but, being stronger than she, forced her, and lay with her."* This heinous act angered Absalom and after two years he plotted with his servants, and Amnon was slain. And he fled in exile to Geshur for three years, while King David mourned the death of Amnon.

ABSALOM REBELS AGAINST KING DAVID AND HE FLED

It came to pass that Absalom set his eyes on the throne and set out to topple the father, King David. The Bible says in *2 Samuel 15:10-14:*

> *10 But Absalom sent spies throughout all the tribes of Israel, saying, As soon as ye hear the sound of the trumpet, then ye shall say, Absalom reigneth in Hebron.*

> *11 And with Absalom went two hundred men out of Jerusalem, that were called; and they went in their simplicity, and they knew not anything.*

> *12 And Absalom sent for Ahithophel the Gilonite, David's counsellor, from his city, even from Giloh, while he offered sacrifices. And the conspiracy was strong; for the people increased continually with Absalom.*

> *13 And there came a messenger to David, saying, The hearts of the men of Israel are after Absalom.*

> *14 And David said unto all his servants that were with him at Jerusalem, Arise, and let us flee; for we shall not else escape from Absalom: make speed to depart, lest he overtake us suddenly, and bring evil upon us, and smite the city with the edge of the sword.*

It came to pass that in a battle between the men of Absalom and the servants of David, that Joab, King David's captain of host smote him to death. *2 Samuel 18:9* says, *"And Absalom met the servants of David. And Absalom rode upon a mule, and the mule went under the thick boughs of a great oak, and his head caught hold of the oak, and he was taken up between the heaven and the earth; and the mule that was under him went away."* The Bible also says in *2 Samuel 18:14, "Then said Joab, I may not tarry thus with thee. And he took three darts in his hand, and thrust them through the heart of Absalom, while he was yet alive in the midst of the oak."*

When Absalom died, King David wept bitterly, and this is confirmed in *2 Samuel 18:33* that says, *"And the king was much* moved, *and went up to the chamber over the gate, and wept: and as he went, thus he said, O my son Absalom, my son, my son Absalom! would God I had died for thee, O Absalom, my son, my son!"*

After the death of Absalom, King David went back to assume his throne.

ORCHESTRA: The Orchestra starts performing more Psalms of victory and thanksgiving taken from 2 Samuel 22. They performed using the following scriptures.

2 SAMUEL 22:2

[2] And he said, The LORD *is my rock, and my fortress, and my deliverer;*

2 SAMUEL 22:4

[4] I will call on the LORD, *who is worthy to be praised: so shall I be saved from mine enemies.*

2 SAMUEL 22:7

[7] In my distress I called upon the LORD, *and cried to my God: and he did hear my voice out of his temple, and my cry did enter into his ears.*

2 SAMUEL 22:18

[18] He delivered me from my strong enemy, and from them that hated me: for they were too strong for me.

2 SAMUEL 22:20

[20] He brought me forth also into a large place: he delivered me, because he delighted in me.

KING DAVID IS DESCRIBED AS THE SWEET PSALMIST OF ISRAEL

The Bible described King David as the sweet Psalmist of Israel in **2 Samuel 23:1** saying, *"Now these be the last words of David.*

David the son of Jesse said, and the man who was raised up on high, the anointed of the God of Jacob, and the sweet psalmist of Israel, said,"

KING DAVID ORDERS A CENSUS OF JUDAH AND ISRAEL THAT LED TO A PLAGUE

The Bible says that king David ordered a census of Judah and Israel which he later admitted was wrong in **2 Samuel 24:10**, *"And David's heart smote him after that he had numbered the people. And David said unto the LORD, I have sinned greatly in that I have done: and now, I beseech thee, O LORD, take away the iniquity of thy servant; for I have done very foolishly."* This led to a plague on Israel in **2 Samuel 24:15** that says, *"So the LORD sent a pestilence upon Israel from the morning even to the time appointed: and there died of the people from Dan even to Beersheba seventy thousand men."* David had to give a quality offering unto the Lord that cost him for the plague to stop in **2 Samuel 24:24-25**:

> *24 And the king said unto Araunah, Nay; but I will surely buy it of thee at a price: neither will I offer burnt offerings unto the LORD my God of that which doth cost me nothing. So David bought the threshing floor and the oxen for fifty shekels of silver.*
>
> *25 And David built there an altar unto the LORD, and offered burnt offerings and peace offerings. So the LORD was intreated for the land, and the plague was stayed from Israel.*

SOLOMON IS ANOINTED KING OF ISRAEL

After one of the sons of King David, called Adonijah, attempted and failed to seize power forcefully and become the King, the Bible says Solomon the son of King David was anointed to be King of Israel in **1 Kings 1:33-34**:

> *33 The king also said unto them, Take with you the servants of your lord, and cause Solomon my son to ride upon mine own mule, and bring him down to Gihon:*

³⁴ *And let Zadok the priest and Nathan the prophet anoint him there king over Israel: and blow ye with the trumpet, and say, God save king Solomon.*

THE DEATH OF KING DAVID

King David finally dies as stated in *1 Kings 2:10-12*:

¹⁰ *So David slept with his fathers, and was buried in the city of David.*

¹¹ *And the days that David reigned over Israel were forty years: seven years reigned he in Hebron, and thirty and three years reigned he in Jerusalem.*

¹² *Then sat Solomon upon the throne of David his father; and his kingdom was established greatly.*

ORCHESTRA: Plays more music based on the scriptural Psalms below and the music rose to a crescendo. Marvellous!

PSALM 103:1

Bless the LORD, O my soul: and all that is within me, bless his holy name.

PSALM 89:1

I will sing of the mercies of the LORD for ever: with my mouth will I make known thy faithfulness to all generations.

PSALM 107:15

Oh that men would praise the LORD for his goodness, and for his wonderful works to the children of men!

AUDIENCE: The audience really got into a state of ecstasy as they continue to sing, clap, dance, and heading for a closure of the performance. Awesome!

TESTIMONY

After the live performance, they usually give time for testimonies. This is the moment John Palmer, the twelve-year-old boy who was healed of his spinal cord injury has been waiting for. This is the seventh time John has seen the King David live performance, and he has always come full of expectations that he will be healed. And behold, this day that the Lord has made is his day to rejoice and be glad as he received his healing. He went straight for the microphone and began.

"I thank the Most High God for His mercy and for healing me today. I had a car accident a year ago, and it affected my spinal cord. Doctors did all they could do for me to be healed but to no avail and I was now paralysed and could not walk and ended up in a wheelchair. The consultant told me I can never walk again. But I still had strong faith in God, who created me, that I will definitely walk again. I believed His word that by His stripes I am healed. I held on to that word. And while in the wheelchair, I glued my eyes to healing scriptures from my Bible, and also prayed regularly for God to heal me. I kept coming to see the King David live performance because I believed so much in the musical ministrations, and today the power of God touched me and I rose up from my wheelchair unaided for the first time in a year. Praise God! Hallelujah!"

As he gave the testimony, he sobbed and tears of joy flowed down his tender cheeks on his handsome face. There was absolute tranquillity and everyone rejoiced with him. Mary and Alan immediately went to him, shook hands with him and embraced him. News of John's miraculous healing spread all over the City of London and beyond through different social media, and that boosted the live performances' attendance. Our God is awesome. This performance is a life-changing event for Mary Jenkins who is seeing it for the first time.

ANNOUNCER: Ladies and gentlemen, after an exciting two-and-half-hour live musical performance about the life of King David,

I want to announce that we have now come to *the* end of this show. Thank you for attending and God bless you all in Jesus' name.

AUDIENCE: Amen!

As they made their way back to the National Car Park (NCP) to pick up the car, Mary said, "What a glorious outing! You made my day Alan. I loved every bit of today's outing."

"I'm glad you did."

They got into the car and he drove off. And in half an hour they were already at Mary's home in East Dulwich, South East of London. They got out of the car and went to the living room. They both went straight for the sofa seat, and sat down next to each other and she rested her head on his shoulder, while he gently held her a bit closer and said, "I will see you in Church tomorrow, Sunday, by God's grace. And I would like us to work out together after service at the New Look Gym at Waterloo, close to the River Thames. So get ready your workout gear for tomorrow. I hope that's alright?"

"That's fine."

"Right! I will be on my way back home now. Thanks for agreeing to go out with me. I enjoyed your company." As he said this, he held her close to him so she could feel his warmth. And they looked at each other eyeball to eyeball and she lowered her eyes with a gentle smile and deep breath while resting her head on him. They are both aware of the rules of the game as Christians, knowing the boundaries and ensuring no one crosses it by going deeper than required.

The Bible says in *1 Corinthians 6:18-19:*

> *18 Flee fornication. Every sin that a man doeth is without the body; but he that committeth fornication sinneth against his own body.*

> *19 What? know ye not that your body is the temple of the Holy Ghost which is in you, which ye have of God, and ye are not your own?*

It says again in *1 Corinthians 6:9-10:*

⁹ Know ye not that the unrighteous shall not inherit the kingdom of God? Be not deceived: neither fornicators, nor idolaters, nor adulterers, nor effeminate, nor abusers of themselves with mankind,

¹⁰ Nor thieves, nor covetous, nor drunkards, nor revillers, nor extortioners, shall inherit the kingdom of God.

The consequences of adultery and fornication are clearly spelt out. So the best thing to do as a wise Christian is to flee fornication. In *Genesis 39:7-14,* Potiphar's wife cast her eyes on Joseph asking him to lie with her. He refused because he had the fear of God saying in verse 9: *"...how then can I do this great wickedness, and sin against God?"* Verse 13 says he fled from Potiphar's wife. They are expected to have the fear of God to be obedient to the Word of God. Christian dating should be without sex until after marriage. That's what the Bible says.

Alan reached for the door, and she said, "Good night Alan. Please call me as soon as you get home."

"Alright darling," replies Alan.

He got out to his car and drove off straight to Golders Green where he lives. He lives in a three-bedroom house with a beautiful front view landscape, and a well-maintained horticulture garden with grass, plants, and flowers. He also has a garden shed which he uses as storage for junk. He arrived home safely, and went into his well-decorated living room. He went upstairs and undressed himself ready to have a shower before retiring to bed. He went into the bathroom and took a quick shower, and he put on his pyjamas. He got on the phone to Mary, "Hello Mary, this is Alan. I'm at home."

"Oh! That's great."

"Let's have a short prayer before we retire to bed. 'Heavenly Father, we thank you and give you all the praise for our lovely outing today. You have begun a good thing in our lives and this relationship, and we ask that you perfect all that concerns us in

Jesus' name. As we go to bed, we ask for your protection all night, and by your special grace enable us to see tomorrow in Jesus' name. Amen!' Good night."

"Amen! Thanks Alan. See you tomorrow in Church. Good night."

CHAPTER THREE

SHEKINAH PENTECOSTAL CHURCH SERVICE AND NEW LOOK GYM

The Church service is due to officially start 10 am at the Shekinah Pentecostal Church (SPC) but by 9.30 am, Alan and Mary have already arrived in Church as workers to help with the necessary preparations in their various departments. Alan is in the Outreach/ Evangelism department while Mary is in the Choir department. Shekinah Pentecostal is an international Church in Hyde Park, central London, with forty thousand members, and thirty thousand seats in the auditorium, conducting two services on Sundays for the adults, youth, and children simultaneously. People come in from different cities and towns within Britain on Sundays and other service days to receive the Word of God, prayers, encouragement, counselling, blessings, and miracles. The Church has been in existence for twenty years, growing steadily in membership, and without any form of scandal.

It's a massive auditorium with three wings stretching out over a huge land area. This magnificent monumental edifice was designed by British Architect, Lord Jonathan Greenfield, and it reveals nothing but excellence for a modern building used as the Temple of God. The interior is lavishly decorated with furnishings of gold on the altar. The pulpit is made of mahogany wood with a smooth finish. And the chairs, both on the altar and in the main auditorium are made of fine wood, and upholstery finish, everything is perfectly arranged. Several large screens are displayed so that the congregation can have a good view from any part of the auditorium. The same goes for the camera coverage within the Church as well as online coverage. The speakers are properly positioned so that you can hear the music or preaching in any part of the auditorium with ease. The choir and technical department have all kinds of modern musical instruments and equipment for the efficient running of their departments. The auditorium is fully air-conditioned and has artistic wall decorations, assorted uniform beautiful chandelier ceiling lights, flower and plant displays at different meaningful locations. The congregation surely receives real comfort as they sit in there to hear the Word of God. No stress! The same goes for the youth and children's Church, offices, and the vicar's apartment. Everything displays excellence!

The health, safety, and security of members of the Church are of paramount importance to the Church management considering the horrible acts of violence going on in the world, and that department is headed by Retired Brigadier Samson Rogers, a no-nonsense retired soldier. Powerful security cameras are fitted all over the auditorium, and on other parts of the premises, along with powerful weapon detector equipment that can X-ray everyone entering or exiting the buildings. To the glory of God there has never been any incident of violence at Shekinah Pentecostal Church. The Bible says that He that keeps Israel (SPC) neither sleeps nor slumbers. What would have been an attack on one occasion was foiled by God. About three years ago, the Lord revealed to the Man of God, Bishop John Barnes in a vision that two men of Arab descent will be coming to the church dressed in blue jeans, and black jackets with hidden guns and knives on a Sunday morning about 9.30 am to attack people, and that he should be on the lookout and step up security. He told Retired Brigadier Samson Rogers who immediately swung into action and stepped up security. And as the two Arab men who fitted the description given by the Man of God approached the main entrance of the church at exactly 9.30 am on a Sunday, they were stopped, questioned, searched, and two pistols and four knives were found on them and they were effectively detained and handed over to the Police. Since then, there has never been any incident of violence or attempted violence. Never! That goes to show how much the Lord loves Bishop John Barnes, and the entire congregation. There has been absolute peace.

"Hello Madam, please sit on the fourth seat on the second row," says an usher politely and cheerfully.

"I don't like that position. I want to sit right here on this side," the woman replied rather impudently, and her facial expression looked confrontational. For peace to reign, the usher simply allowed her to have her way. This is one of the challenges ushers face on a typical service day. The church is a holy place of worship, filled with the presence of God. It's great to set out to church from home full of joy and expecting positive fellowship with other believers, and also connecting to the power of God through His Word peacefully. The church or any other venue should not be a place for a Christian to have strife with anybody, and certainly not regarding where to sit. Petty! Ushers are in a position of authority and they deserve full respect from Christians.

THE ORDER OF SERVICE IS AS FOLLOWS:

Opening prayer - Pastor Moses Elijah	10am – 10.15am (15 minutes)
Bible Study – Pastor Timothy Philips	10.15am – 10.45am (30 minutes)
Testimonies – Pastor Richard Berkley	10.45am – 10.55am (10 minutes)
Praise and Worship – Pastor Susan Edwards	10.55am – 11.25am (30 minutes)
The Word and Ministration – Bishop John Barnes	11.25am – 12.25pm (1 hour)
Tithes and offering – Pastor William Chapman	12.25pm – 12.35pm (10 minutes)
Screen Announcements – Media Team	12.35pm – 12.40pm (5 minutes)
Benediction & closing prayer – Bishop John Barnes	12.40pm – 12.45pm (5 minutes)
Total time	(2 hours 45 minutes)

OPENING PRAYER

It's 10 am and Pastor Moses Elijah is behind the pulpit to lead the congregation in a fifteen-minute opening prayer. Pastor Moses Elijah is Bishop John Barnes' deputy. He had very turbulent early years involving juvenile delinquency, and as a result of this, he struggled to finish his secondary school education, and was not able to attend university. However, the Holy Spirit arrested him at the age of twenty, and he became a born-again Christian and dedicated himself to intensive Bible study and general personal development, which has eventually transformed him. He is so knowledgeable and wise that if you were told he doesn't have a university education, you would be shocked and doubt it. He is very sound in knowledge, knowing very much about ministerial ethics, and he is very loyal to Bishop John Barnes. He has written five bestselling Christian books earning him substantial royalties. He is married to Pastor Derby Elijah, with two young children. He is popularly known as, 'The Fire Pastor.' When he ministers, fire actually falls down from heaven through the moves of the Holy Ghost, so intense to consume all evil and deliver and heal the people of God. He has a strong desire to see people receive salvation. He is in charge of evangelism.

PASTOR MOSES ELIJAH: Good morning Church. Please let's stand up on our feet for prayers.

CONGREGATION: Good morning Pastor Elijah, as they all rise up on their feet.

PASTOR MOSES ELIJAH: It's a beautiful Sunday morning, and I can see handsome and beautiful children of God gorgeously dressed in His presence. Please welcome your neighbour to the right and left and tell them, "Today is a special day of miracles for you in Jesus' name."

CONGREGATION: Greetings to neighbours saying, "Today is a special day of miracles for you in Jesus' name."

PASTOR MOSES ELIJAH: Please turn in your Bible to the book of *1Timothy 2:1-2* as I read:

¹ I exhort therefore, that, first of all, supplications, prayers, intercessions, and giving of thanks, be made for all men;

² For kings, and for all that are in authority; that we may lead a quiet and peaceable life in all godliness and honesty.

Let's pray for Her Majesty Queen Elizabeth and the entire royal family at Buckingham Palace, that the Lord will fill them with more wisdom and continually protect them from all evil in Jesus' name. Prayer!

CONGREGATION: Begins to pray.

PASTOR MOSES ELIJAH: In Jesus' name. We will pray now for the land of Britain that no kind of natural disaster or terrorist attack shall happen here, and that the peace of God shall continually reign in this land in Jesus' name. Prayer!

CONGREGATION: Begins to pray.

PASTOR MOSES ELIJAH: In Jesus' name! Let us pray for the Prime Minister David Cameron, all the cabinet ministers, and MPs that the Lord will grant them more wisdom to lead this nation well and that no unrighteous decree shall be made in the House of Commons in Jesus' name. Prayer!

CONGREGATION: Begins to pray.

PASTOR MOSES ELIJAH: In Jesus' name! Let us pray for Bishop John Barnes, the Pope, and all the Bishops, Pastors, Prophets, Evangelists, and the entire body of Christ, for God's protection, and that the gates of hell will never prevail against the Church of God in Jesus' name.

CONGREGATION: Begins to pray.

PASTOR MOSES ELIJAH: In Jesus' name! Please open your Bible and turn to **Psalm 107:20** as I read, *"He sent his word, and healed them, and delivered them from their destructions."*
  Let's pray that there shall be deliverances, healings, and miracles in this service and always in Jesus' name. Prayer!

CONGREGATION: Begins to pray.

PASTOR MOSES ELIJAH: In Jesus' name! Declare it powerfully saying, "Today is my day of deliverance, healing, and miracles in Jesus' name."

CONGREGATION: "Today is my day of healing, deliverance, and miracles in Jesus' name."

PASTOR MOSES ELIJAH: The service has started, and the Spirit of God is very much here. Please open your heart to receive the Word of God because the entrance of the word giveth light. It giveth understanding unto the simple. The Bible says again in **Proverbs 23:18,** *"For surely there is an end; and thine expectation shall not be cut off."*

The Lord shall exceed your expectations in this service by granting you all your heart's desires in line with the will of God for you in Jesus' name. Your coming here today shall not be in vain in Jesus' name. All you've got to do is be fully focused and connected to the Word of God as it comes forth. Don't let anything distract you. Make sure you are here in spirit, soul, and body. Don't let your mind wonder about, and as you stay focused you shall surely be blessed in Jesus' name.

Somebody shout "Amen!" as we sit on our seats. Pastor Moses Elijah exits the podium.

CONGREGATION: Ameeeeeeeeeeeen!

BRIEF NOTE ON PRAYER

Prayer is essentially a two-way communication between us and the Most High God. As you talk to God, you listen to Him also for answers. *Isaiah 65:24* says, *"And it shall come to pass, that before they call, I will answer; and while they are yet speaking, I will hear."*

For prayers to be effective, we must use the Word of God to pray, and also use the name of Jesus, which is the name above all names. We have to also pray both with understanding and in tongues. – See 1 Corinthians 14.

Prayer is a very useful tool for any Christian who wants to remain in faith and stay connected to the supernatural power of God. A Christian who does not pray cannot develop a strong faith. Hence, the Bible says in **Luke 18:1**, *"And he spake a parable unto them to this end, that men ought always to pray, and not to faint;"*

The Bible says again in *1 Thessalonians 5:17*, *"Pray without ceasing."* We ought always to pray, and prayer without ceasing is talking about having the consciousness of God at all times as well as praying always as a Christian. Always know and remember who you are in Christ Jesus. *Ephesians 5:19* says, *"Speaking to yourselves in psalms and hymns and spiritual songs, singing and making melody in your heart to the Lord;"*

From the above scripture, if we are to sing Psalms, and make melody in our hearts, then we can also pray in our hearts unto the Lord whenever and wherever including at work, school, in the car, bus, train, and home. Pray without ceasing.

In order not to have our prayers hindered, it's important for us to be quick at forgiving those who hurt us. The Bible says in, *Mark 11:25-26:*

> [25]*And when ye stand praying, forgive, if ye have ought against any: that your Father also which is in heaven may forgive you your trespasses.*

> [26]*But if ye do not forgive, neither will your Father which is in heaven forgive your trespasses.*

We must also avoid meddling with sin. The Bible says in *Isaiah 59:1-3:*

> [1]*Behold, the* LORD'*s hand is not shortened, that it cannot save; neither his ear heavy, that it cannot hear:*

> [2]*But your iniquities have separated between you and your God, and your sins have hid his face from you, that he will not hear.*

³For your hands are defiled with blood, and your fingers with iniquity; your lips have spoken lies, your tongue hath muttered perverseness.

May the Lord grant us all the grace to resist sin, and answer all our prayer requests in line with His will for us in Jesus' name. Amen!

BIBLE STUDY

It's now 10.15 am and for the next half hour, Pastor Timothy Philips who is already behind the Pulpit will deliver the Bible Study to the whole congregation numbering about thirty thousand, and that's why it's not going to be interactive as it should have been if it were to be done within a small group. The congregation is too large to be split for this exercise. However, there are many prayer and Bible study groups within the Shekinah Pentecostal Ministry in the City of London, and across other cities in Britain. And members can have further discussions of Bible study topics, asking questions, and making contributions within the cell group.

Pastor Timothy Philips is a great Man of God whose life depends solely on the Word of God. His whole life regarding his thoughts, meditations, words, and actions all revolve around the Word of God. He has read the Bible fifty-two times so far, and he is still reading it. He feeds his spirit with the Word of God regularly. He has a blessed memory to retain scriptures. When you come near him, and he opens his mouth to speak, you will obviously hear gracious words of wisdom that proceed from his mouth and the aura radiating from and around him confirming he is a mature Christian. He is of average height and stature, and graduated as a Theologian with first class honours degree from Cambridge University. He is popularly known as the 'Faith Pastor' having demonstrated great signs, wonders, and miracles, including raising the dead. He truly believes he can move mountains by faith. That's how strong his faith in God is. He is married to Pastor Janet Philips, who is also an MP in the House of Parliament, and a political juggernaut who always fights for the promotion of Christian values in the society.

PASTOR TIMOTHY PHILIPS: Good morning Church. You are all welcome to another special Bible Study session.

CONGREGATION: Good morning Pastor Timothy.

PASTOR TIMOTHY PHILIPS: Please open your Bible to the book of *Luke 24:45* as I read, *"Then opened he their understanding, that they might understand the scriptures."* I would like us all to lay both our hands on our head and make this powerful declaration. "Father, thank you because my understanding is open to understand scriptures in Jesus' name. Amen!"

CONGREGATION: "Father, thank you because my understanding is open to understand scriptures in Jesus' name. Amen!"

PASTOR TIMOTHY PHILIPS: Today's Bible Study topic is: *WHY DO WE HAVE TO STUDY THE BIBLE?* This topic is very important because when we know why we have to do something which essentially are the benefits; it does serve as a motivation for us to do it. We have to study the Bible as Christians for the following reasons:

1. *TO BOOST OUR FAITH:* The Bible says in *Romans 10:17*, *"So then faith cometh by hearing, and hearing by the word of God."* Continuous Bible study, whereby we spend quality time both *studying* and *meditating* on the Word of God will certainly boost our faith as Christians.

2. *TO RENEW OUR MIND:* Every Christian continually needs to renew their mind with the Word of God. The scriptures have the ability to renew polluted minds, and enable us continually to have the mind of Christ as we continue studying the Word of God. The Bible says in *Romans 12:2*, *"And be not conformed to this world: but be ye transformed by the renewing of your mind, that ye may prove what is that good, and acceptable, and perfect, will of God."*

3. *THE WORD OF GOD IS A PRAYER TOOL:* The only way you can effectively pray with understanding and not pray amiss is to pray using the Word of God, except you decide to pray in tongues. Praying without the Word of God is simply

more of blabbing, and such prayers are impotent lacking the power of God to produce desired results. The Bible says in **Hosea 14:2,** *"Take with you words, and turn to the LORD."* From where will you take words? – The Bible.

4. ***THE BIBLE CARRIES THE POWER OF GOD:*** The Bible as letters or Logos may be seen as powerless, but when you study and meditate on it and speak it out, it turns out to be a powerful Rhema word. **Hebrew 4:12** says, *"For the word of God is quick, and powerful, and sharper than any twoedged sword, piercing to even the dividing asunder of soul and spirit, and of the joints and marrow, and is a discerner of the thoughts and intents of the heart."*

5. ***THE WORD OF GOD BRINGS FORTH HEALING AND GOOD HEALTH: Psalm 107:20*** says, *"He sent his word, and healed them, and delivered them from their destructions."* The way you receive the Word of God determines the extent it will bless you. If you exalt the Word of God to the maximum in your life, and see it as medicinal, it will obviously heal you, and also deliver you from bondage when you receive it. On the other hand, if anyone despises the Word of God, it will not profit them anything. The Word of God is very powerful. It carries healing anointing in it. The Bible says in **Matthew 8:16** that, *"When the even was come, they brought unto him many that were possessed with devils: and he cast out the spirits with his word, and healed all that were sick."* How did Jesus cast out the evil spirits, and heal all that were sick? – With His word. There was no anointing oil, or laying of hands. **Proverbs 4: 20-22** also says:

²⁰*My son, attend to my words; incline thine ear unto my sayings.*

²¹*Let them not depart from thine eyes; keep them in the midst of thine heart.*

²²*For they are life unto those that find them, and health to all their flesh.*

King Solomon clearly stated in the above scriptures that as we study the Word of God, and hold them in the midst of our heart, it will bring forth divine health unto all our flesh. This again proves that the Word of God heals.

6. ***STUDYING THE BIBLE WILL MAKE GOD APPROVE US.*** The Bible says in ***2 Timothy 2:15,*** *"Study to shew thyself approved unto God, a workman that needeth not to be ashamed, rightly dividing the word of truth."* A thorough knowledge of the Bible causes us to be approved vessels of honour unto the Lord. God is pleased with people who are thoroughly furnished with His Word, having developed skills to interpret scriptures, as well as its application. The ability to compare scripture with scripture comes forth from studying. As we study the Bible, we also gain understanding and this helps us to rightly divide the word of truth. When we are able to do this, we are paving the way for God to use us as approved vessels.

7. ***TO AVOID CAPTIVITY AND DESTRUCTION: Proverbs 10:14*** says, *"Wise men lay up knowledge."* Knowledge is a source of strength. King Solomon says again in ***Proverbs 24:5,*** *"A wise man is strong: Yea, a man of knowledge increaseth strength."* The facts you have about a subject can save you from terrible situations. Lack of knowledge of a matter is synonymous to being in darkness. But light shines forth when adequate knowledge is in place. The knowledge to be acquired should not be limited to Bible knowledge only. Knowledge about other things in life is also essential as it also helps us make important decisions in life.

Prophet ***Isaiah*** likens lack of knowledge to being in captivity when he said in ***chapter 5:13*** of his book, *"Therefore my people are gone into captivity, because they have no knowledge: and their honourable men are famished, and their multitude dried up with thirst."* That is how terrible things can be for anyone who does not hunger to have general knowledge of things, and in particular, knowledge of the Word of God. King Solomon writes in ***Proverbs 19:2,*** *"Also, that the soul be without knowledge, it is not good."*

Hosea **4:6** says, *"My people are destroyed for lack of knowledge: because thou hast rejected knowledge, I will also reject thee, that thou shalt be no priest to me: seeing thou hast forgotten the law of thy God, I will also forget thy children."* The Word of God makes it clear here that lack of knowledge will lead to destruction. The only way to avoid this happening is to reach out for your Bible, and start searching it to know what God is saying about your situation, and apply the scriptures to your life.

8. ***TO AVOID MAKING MISTAKES:*** Jesus said to the Sadducees, in ***Matthew 22:29,*** *"Ye do err, not knowing the scriptures, nor the power of God."* Jesus is simply saying here that those who do not study their Bible make mistakes, and they do not know the power of God either. It is a shame for anyone to choose to live their life making errors. That will only retard the person. Studying the Bible will help us know the power of God, and also make fewer mistakes in life. Let us look at what Jesus said to the Pharisees when they made silly comments about His disciples in Matthew chapter 12 as they plucked and ate ears of corn because they were hungry. Jesus said to the Pharisees in ***Matthew 12:3 & 5,*** *"Have you not read in the law...?"* Meaning, you people ought to have read or studied your Bible before now to know what the right answer should be regarding this matter. But they did not, so they ended up challenging Jesus' disciples.

9. ***THE WORD OF GOD IS PROFITABLE FOR TEACHING AND CORRECTION:*** *2 Timothy 3:16–17* says:

[16] All scripture is given by inspiration of God, and is profitable for doctrine, for reproof, for correction, for instruction in righteousness.

[17] That the man of God may be perfect, thoroughly furnished unto all good works."

The Bible is authentic. It is also a book of authority. You cannot fault it the way other books are faulted because it has been tried like silver in a furnace of the earth, purified seven times and found to be pure, and therefore, a valuable tool for teaching and correction. The above scripture confirms that the Bible was written by men inspired by God.

10. *JESUS OUR ROLE MODEL STUDIED THE BIBLE:* As Christians, Jesus remains our number one role model. Hence, we have to continually follow His example. There is evidence in the Bible that Jesus read His Bible. Now, if Jesus our role model read His Bible, then we have to emulate Him and read ours.

In *Matthew 4:4, 7, & 10,* Jesus wrecked the devil big time by quoting the scriptures to the devil three times saying, *"It is written."* For Jesus to quote the scriptures shows He has read them because you can only quote what you have studied.

The Bible also says in Luke 4:16–17 that Jesus went to Nazareth where He was brought up and went into the synagogue and read the Bible as His custom was. This means that it was Jesus' practice to always go to the synagogue to read the Bible.

We will have to bring to a close today's Bible Study with the ten points given. We will continue next Sunday and I will give more points on this topic. However, you can find out more points on your own as you do your own personal Bible study. You can also discuss it further in your respective Bible study and prayer groups. Let's bow down our heads for a brief prayer. Heavenly Father, we thank you for ministering to us today through the power of the Holy Spirit. Thank you because the enemy will never steal these words from us, and we receive your grace to enable us practice what we have learnt today in our life, and as we do so let it bear good fruits in Jesus' name. He exits the podium.

CONGREGATION: Ameeeeeeeeeeeeeeen!

THE WORD OF GOD

We've got to keep hearing the Word of God in order to remain in faith. Unfortunately, present-day Christians don't spend quality time on the Word of God as they should. A lot of Christians don't even have a Bible. They come to Church without Bibles, and hardly care to even open the one on their mobile phone or tablet during Church services. They only depend on the one displayed on the Church screen. My friend, that's spiritual malnourishment. It can only lead to stunted growth or spiritual death. Read what the scripture says below.

Matthew 4:4 says, *"But he answered and said, it is written, Man shall not live by bread alone, but by every word that proceedeth out of the mouth of God."*

Job 23:12 says, "Neither have I gone back from the commandment of his lips; I have esteemed the words of his mouth more than my necessary food."

Jeremiah 15:16 says, "Thy words were found, and I did eat them; and thy word was unto me the joy and rejoicing of mine heart: for I am called by thy name, O LORD God of hosts."

Psalm 119:127 says, *"Therefore I love thy commandments above gold; yea, above fine gold."*

From the above scriptures, we can see that the Word of God is more precious than food and gold. Mary Jenkins and Alan Brown have standard, study leather-bound Bibles with legible print, centre column reference, words of Jesus in red, concordance, maps, and other features. They also have notebooks to jot things down during Bible study and sermons. This does not make them old-fashioned. A lot of Christians bring in their tablets and mobile phones to Church in order to use it to search for scriptures and take notes. However, they end up causing distractions both to themselves and others as they engage in internet searches and social media. Some even sleep during the sermon. Wake up!

TESTIMONIES

It's now 10.45 am and Pastor Richard Berkley just got up behind the pulpit to take the testimonies session for ten minutes. Pastor Richard Berkley has experienced many miracles in his life beyond human comprehension. He was born prematurely at almost six months at a time when medical science had not advanced so much, and he was meant to be thrown away because consultants wrote him off and said that he would die within hours, but his loving mother held on to him and he eventually miraculously pulled through and defied all medical assertions by so-called experts that he would grow up to be a vegetable. He fell from a five-storey building at the age of two and miraculously survived, despite being unconscious for one week in the hospital. He went to primary school, secondary school, and university with scholarships, graduating with distinction at all levels. He obtained his PhD in Mathematics from Imperial College London, where he also lectures as a Professor in the Mathematics department, at the age of thirty-six years. He was involved in a plane crash a few years ago, and all other persons on board perished and only he got out to safety with a parachute and he landed in a lion's den in the African jungle of Kenya and the lions didn't eat him up. He walked away unhurt and made phone calls with his mobile phone and he was located and rescued. What a miracle! He is popularly known as, 'The Miracle Pastor.' He has experienced a lot more miracles than the ones shared here. Heavily bearded, and wearing eyeglasses to help his hyperopia sight, he looked smart in his suit as he cleared his throat and began.

PASTOR RICHARD BERKLEY: Good morning Church. It's testimony time.

CONGREGATION: Good morning Pastor Richard.

PASTOR RICHARD BERKLEY: Please open your Bible to *Hebrews 2:12* as I read:

> [12]*Saying, I will declare thy name unto my brethren, in the midst of the Church will I sing praise unto thee.*

The Lord has done great things in the life of the following three brethren. Please come out to the altar and share your testimony as I call your names – Martin Finchly, Simon Howard, and Elizabeth Cameron. Please note that you only have two minutes to share your testimony. Straight to the point as you summarise.

MARTIN FINCHLY: Praaaaaaaaaaaise God! I thank the Most High God for saving my life in a motorbike accident. It's just a miracle that I'm alive. I was riding my motorbike dressed in my full leather gear and helmet on Chelsea Road three days ago, doing just thirty miles per hour, and suddenly I was swept off the road from behind by a lorry driver and I was flung up into the air to about fifty feet high according to eyewitnesses, and at that moment I felt like my spirit had left me because it happened unexpectedly. And when I came down, my motorbike was about thirty metres away from the accident scene, and people came to my rescue thinking I was dead, but amazingly, I stood up on my feet unhurt in any way. I have been to see my doctor, and he confirmed that I am one hundred percent alright. I thank God for the miracle.

SIMON HOWARD: The doctors confirmed that I had a brain tumour and it was growing bigger and bigger, and they quickly arranged for me to have surgery to remove it. Surprisingly, after the surgery, the tumour came back again growing at a much faster rate than before the surgery, to the extent that my head was now swollen to almost double the normal size in no time. Doctors were confused. I thought I was going to die. I hated to look into the mirror. I was looking horrible and scary. And then my case was mentioned to Bishop John Barnes through Pastor Moses Elijah. The Bishop prayed on a handkerchief and blessed anointing oil which Pastor Moses Elijah brought to me at the hospital. As soon as my head was anointed and the handkerchief was laid on my head, my head shrank to normal size in just an hour. Doctors couldn't understand what happened. I told them it's the power of God at work. Doctor Jesus healed me. I thank God for healing me. I want to also thank Bishop John Barnes, Pastor Moses Elijah and everyone who supported me in prayers during this trying time. Shame to the devil! Glory be to God!

ELIZABETH CAMERON: I was coming back from work last Thursday about 8 pm, and as soon as I got onto Robertson Lane, a man wearing a balaclava appeared in front of me from nowhere and pulled out a gun and started raining bullets on me both at my face and body, but surprisingly none of the five or more bullets he fired got into my body. He was afraid and dropped his gun and ran off. The police have got the gun and they are investigating the incident. I have seen my doctor who has confirmed that I am perfectly okay. I thank God for saving my life and for being my invisible whole armour that day to shield me from the devil's bullets. All bullets back to sender in Jesus' name. Praise God!

PASTOR RICHARD BERKLEY: Our God is awesome, and he is doing great things in the lives of our brethren in this Church. I declare that all testimonies received are permanent in Jesus' name. For those of us who did not testify today, be encouraged and know that the Lord is working behind the scene to perfect all that concerns you, and you shall surely testify in Jesus' name. Praise God! He steps off the podium.

WHY DO WE HAVE TO GIVE TESTIMONY?

God is continually performing miracles and great things in our life, and it's a good thing to openly appreciate Him in the congregation. The Bible says in *Psalm 35:18*, *"I will give thee thanks in the great congregation: I will praise thee among much people."*

It's good for us to give testimony for the following reasons. *Firstly,* when we openly acknowledge and testify of what God has done for us, He is likely to do more. *Secondly,* as we testify, somebody else in the congregation passing through a similar trial will be encouraged to know that our God who does not discriminate will also give them victory. *Thirdly,* our testimony can help convince unbelievers that there is God, and they will receive salvation.

PRAISE AND WORSHIP

It's now 10.55 am and Pastor Susan Edwards is already on stage with the choir to lead the ministrations for the next half hour. Mary Jenkins is already with her choir colleagues, Deborah, Angela, Felicia, and the rest of them. This is a big choir of about two hundred members. Pastor Susan Edwards is a highly anointed worship minister, and has been leading the choir since the inception of the ministry. She has released ten praise and worship albums, and she is also the author of two Christian books on praise and worship. She has composed many Holy Spirit-inspired songs. She is just forty years old, beautiful and slim, able to neatly fit into a size twelve dress. She lives a life of constant fasting, prayers, and Bible study. A lot of people are drawn to Shekinah Pentecostal Church because of the miracles they receive during her ministrations as a result of the powerful move of the Holy Spirit and her continued dedication. Her whole life is indeed a life of praise. She is supported by a powerful team of instrumentalists as follows: Pastor Jacob O'Brien on keyboard, Pastor Amanda Taylor on guitar, Brother Sylvester Smith on saxophones, and Pastor Stephen Thompson on drums, just to mention a few. As she steps forward on stage, the spirit-filled vibrant congregation is already earnestly full of expectation, expressing it through their jubilation and shouts of joy. People are already excited, clapping their hands, tapping their feet on the floor, humming, whistling, and moving their bodies. That's how exhilarating her ministration can be for the congregation.

PASTOR SUSAN EDWARDS: Somebody in the house praaaaaaaaaaise the Lord! Give Him shouts of praise as you clap your hands.

CONGREGATION: Hallelujaaaaaaaaaaaaaah! And they begin to clap their hands and make joyful noise unto the Lord.

PASTOR SUSAN EDWARDS: It's praise and worship time. Come on, let's go as you clap those blessed hands the more unto the Lord, and shake your body. Please refer to your bulletin or the screen for lyrics of the hymns and songs. She started her ministration by singing this great hymn by *Carl Gustav Boberg, written 1885:*

HOW GREAT THOU ART

Verse 1

O Lord my God
When I in awesome wonder
Consider all the works
Thy hands have made,
I see the stars,
I hear the rolling thunder,
Thy pow'r throughout
The universe displayed!

Chorus

Then sings my soul,
My Savior God, to Thee;
How great Thou art,
How great Thou art!
Then sings my soul,
My Savior God, to Thee;
How great Thou art,
How great Thou art!

Verse 2

When thru the woods
And forest glades I wander
And hear the birds
Sing sweetly in the trees,
When I look down
From lofty mountain grandeur
And hear the brook
And feel the gentle breeze,

Repeat Chorus

Verse 3
And when I think
That God, His Son not sparing,
Sent Him to die,
I scarce can take it in –
That on the cross,
My burden gladly bearing,
He bled and died
To take away my sin!

Repeat Chorus

Verse 4
When Christ shall come
With shout of acclamation
And take me home,
What joy shall fill my heart!
Then I shall bow
In humble adoration
And there proclaim,
My God, how great Thou art!

Repeat Chorus

The next hymn is:

TO GOD BE THE GLORY – *By Fanny Crosby,*
published 1875

Stanza 1
To God be the glory, great things He hath done;
So loved He the world that He gave us His Son,
Who yielded His life an atonement for sin,
And opened the life gate that all may go in.

Refrain
Praise the Lord, praise the Lord,
Let the earth hear His voice!
Praise the Lord, praise the Lord,
Let the people rejoice!
O come to the Father, through Jesus the Son,
And give Him the glory, great things He hath done.

Stanza 2
O perfect redemption, the purchase of blood,
To every believer the promise of God;
The vilest offender who truly believes,
That moment from Jesus a pardon receives.

(Refrain)

Stanza 3
Great things He hath taught us, great things He hath done,
And great our rejoicing through Jesus the Son;
But purer, and higher, and greater will be
Our wonder, our rapture, when Jesus we see.

(Refrain)

The next hymn is:

GREAT IS THY FAITHFULNESS – By Thomas Chisholm, 1866–1960

    1.   *Great is Thy faithfulness, O God my Father;*
          There is no shadow of turning with Thee;
          Thou changest not, Thy compassions, they fail not;
          As Thou hast been Thou forever wilt be.

Refrain
Great is Thy faithfulness!
Great is Thy faithfulness!
Morning by morning new mercies I see:
All I have needed Thy hand hath provided—
Great is Thy faithfulness, Lord, unto me!

2. *Summer and winter and springtime and harvest,*
   Sun, moon, and stars in their courses above
   Join with all nature in manifold witness
   To Thy great faithfulness, mercy, and love.

   (Refrain)

3. *Pardon for sin and a peace that endureth,*
   Thine own dear presence to cheer and to guide,
   Strength for today and bright hope for tomorrow—
   Blessings all mine, with ten thousand beside!

   (Refrain)

She now sings the song, **"My Redeemer lives,"** by Hillsong Worship, based on Job 19:25. Finally, she sang **"Alpha & Omega"** by Israel & New breed.

CONGREGATION: The whole congregation fully participates in the praise and worship session clapping, singing, and dancing unto the Lord. There are real shouts of joy in the house, and people are sweating as if the air conditioner isn't working, when in fact it's on full blast. You can hear evil spirits crying out of people, and others falling down as they are slain under the anointing, and the ushers are busy going round assisting screaming people, and those on the floor. After every service, many come out to share their testimony of healing and deliverance. It does truly feel as if one is already in heaven rejoicing with the angels, and saints.

PASTOR SUSAN EDWARDS: May the Lord grant all your good heart's desires, and be with you all in Jesus' name. And she steps out of the podium.

BENEFITS OF PRAISE, WORSHIP, AND THANKSGIVING

Praise, worship, and thanksgiving are very powerful Christian breakthrough tools, and you've got to use them regularly. King David writes in *Psalm 34:1,* *"I will bless the* LORD *at all times: his praise shall continually be in my mouth."*

No wonder God described him as a man after His own heart because of his lifestyle of praise. *Psalm 92:1* says, *"It is a good thing to give thanks unto the* LORD, *and to sing praises unto thy name, O Most High."* There are many benefits of praising God, but I would like us to look at the following:

1. As we praise the Lord, He will make our enemies destroy one another. See 2 Chronicles 20:22–23.
2. Praising God with instruments and shouts of joy unto the Lord will cause barriers and obstacles to collapse just like the wall of Jericho for us to possess our possessions. See Joshua 6:1–6.
3. Thanksgiving and praises unto the Lord will bring forth multiplications. *Jeremiah 30:19* says, *"And out of them shall proceed thanksgiving and the voice of them that make merry: and I will multiply them, and they shall not be few; I will also glorify them, and they shall not be small."*
4. Praises bring forth deliverance from chains and bondage. Praises brought Paul and Silas out of prison. *Acts 16:25-26* says:

    25 And at midnight Paul and Silas prayed, and sang praises unto God: and the prisoners heard them.

    26 And suddenly there was a great earthquake, so that the foundations of the prison were shaken: and immediately all the doors were opened, and everyone's bands were loosed.

5. Praises can lead to prophetic utterances to be made. As the minstrel played in 2 Kings 3:14–18, Prophet Elisha prophesied.

6. Note that we can also give thanks and praise unto the Lord with our substance and gain victory. In Genesis 4:4–5, Abel gave a quality offering that was acceptable unto the Lord. King Solomon also did the same in 1 Kings 3:3–5.

AVOID FALSE PRAISE AND WORSHIP

It's also important to avoid false worship. The Bible says in *John 4:24*:

> *24 God is a Spirit: and they that worship him must worship him in spirit and in truth.*

We need to worship God in spirit and in truth for our worship to be acceptable unto the Lord. The Bible says in *Amos 5:21-23*:

> *21I hate, I despise your feast days, and I will not smell in your solemn assemblies.*

> *22Though ye offer me burnt offerings and your meat offerings, I will not accept them: neither will I regard the peace offerings of your fat beasts.*

> *23Take thou away from me the noise of thy songs; for I will not hear the melody of thy viols.*

You can see from the above scriptures that people can be engaged in false worship in offerings, songs, and melodies and it's not acceptable to the Lord.

THE WORD AND MINISTRATION

It's exactly 11.25 am and Bishop John Barnes appears on the podium for the Word and Ministration. Bishop John Barnes is a lawyer by profession. He obtained his LLB Honours first class degree from Oxford University. After graduating, he went straight into the international Oil and Gas business which he did for nearly a decade and became a millionaire, before God called him into full-time ministry work. His company, Global Oil and Gas Company Limited, is still in operation and being managed by others. Initially, he was reluctant to answer the call, and resisted like Prophet Jonah, but God prevailed. He was forced to answer the call when, before his very own eyes, his business empire began to collapse, and he was fast losing all the wealth he acquired in the business. He immediately gave up the management of his business and entrusted it into the hands of others. Since he resigned from his business to start full-time ministry, his business is booming again and making a lot more profits than before. He immediately started doing personal Bible study, voraciously devouring the Word of God, reading over fifty chapters of the Bible daily, and also enrolled to study for a degree in Theology at Oxford University and graduated with a first class.

Bishop John Barnes is a man with very high business acumen. And his experience and success in business has helped him so much to build and run the Shekinah Pentecostal Ministry, which God has committed into his hands. He has a massive vision for the church to grow to greater heights in every ramification. He believes in accountability, and he is a very frugal person. A typical Yorkshire man except that his Yorkshire accent is no longer noticeable as a result of his excellent education, and by living in London for so many years. He is a conservative of culture and tradition. Hence, he has successfully preserved some heirlooms passed down to him by his parents.

Bishop John Barnes is stupendously wealthy. He is so immensely financially blessed to the extent that everything he has and uses speaks of excellence and royalty. The ministry God has committed into his hands, Shekinah Pentecostal Church is very prosperous. The Church is by far the biggest Church in membership in Britain, and also in turnover and assets. He has his own Private Jet *Gulfstream G650* airplane which he uses to do the work of God with ease, as he shuttles across the nations of the world evangelising. He has a luxury *Rolls-Royce* car, a customised *Mercedes-Benz* car, and lives in a beautiful seven-bedroom mansion with many amenities including a swimming pool, and massive garden with great horticultural work done to the plants and flowers. The Bishop already had most of these things as a millionaire from his oil and gas business before God called him into the ministry. Hence, those who know his background will never accuse him of going into the ministry to enrich himself financially with church collections. Bishop John Barnes has written thirty bestselling Christian books that have sold millions of copies worldwide, and are still selling, earning him millions of pounds in royalties. Since the inception of the ministry, he has always been the highest giver in tithes, offerings, and donations. The Bishop is blessed with his beautiful wife Pastor Martha Barnes, and two teenage children. Evelyn Barnes is a medical student at Oxford University, and Fredrick Barnes, an astronomy student in the same university.

A man of medium build, in his early fifties, white skin, pointed nose, light grey-blue eyes, always clean-shaven, with dark brown hair, and 6 feet 7 inches tall. He stands out wherever he finds himself because of his height, and his impeccable formal dressing. He loves his bespoke suits and designer ties which match his suit scarf. He also goes for designer shoes, wristwatches, handkerchiefs, and perfumes. He is a kind-hearted, humble man, and loves helping people by being involved in several charity works. He is a bookworm; he reads a lot. He always says, "Readers are leaders." If you are a member of Shekinah Pentecostal Church, you will certainly develop the habit of reading your Bible, and other Christian books. That's where Mary Jenkins developed her Bible study habits fully.

Bishop John Barnes is a highly anointed Man of God. He is given to constant prayers, fasting, and Bible Study. His presence alone makes demons cry out and flee from human beings. God has used him to wrought several miracles both in and outside the Church. God has used him to heal the sick, deliver those in bondage, and make the cripples walk, open blind eyes, heal the deaf and dumb, and raise the dead. And many come from all over Britain to hear the gracious words of wisdom that proceed from his mouth when he speaks. Prime Ministers, and Presidents of nations, plus other world leaders consult him for prayers and godly counsel. He is a highly respected bishop not just in the United Kingdom, but all over the world.

As soon as the Man of God, Bishop John Barnes appeared behind the pulpit, even without saying a word, evil spirits started crying out. He has been on three days dry fasting. He is a flexible Man of God who will always co-operate and yield to the leading of the Holy Spirit whenever he is ministering from the Podium. He will abandon whatever message he has prepared and allow the free flow of the Spirit of God, and this is part of the reason why he gets great results.

BISHOP JOHN BARNES: Good morning Church. I see very happy and glorious people of God. The blessings of the Lord will continually rest upon you all in Jesus' name. The Most High God has sent me to somebody in the house with a special message entitled: *WEEP NO MORE.*

> The Lord says, weep no more.
> For I have seen your cries.
> For I have seen your tears.
> For I have seen your sorrows.
> For I have seen your challenges.
> For I have seen your pain.
> And your time has come to be made whole in Jesus' name.

CONGREGATION: Ameeeeeeeeeeeeeeeen!

BISHOP JOHN BARNES: Please open your Bibles to *Psalm 42:3* as I read:

"My tears have been my meat day and night, while they continually say unto me, where is thy God?" The Psalmist says in the scripture I just read that he wept so much to the extent that his tears became food for him all day. And people now ask, *"Where is your God?"*

Perhaps you are currently going through storms, afflictions, weeping, and tears. Once again, the Most High God has sent me to you saying, weep no more. God has seen your tears. And He is working behind the scenes to perfect all that concerns you in Jesus' name. Shout Amen!

CONGREGATION: Ameeeeeeeeeeeeeeeen!

BISHOP JOHN BARNES: Please open your Bibles to *Luke 7:11-16* as I read:

> [11]*And it came to pass the day after, that he went into a city called Nain; and many of his disciples went with him, and much people.*

¹²Now when he came nigh to the gate of the city, behold, there was a dead man carried out, the only son of his mother, and she was a widow: and much people of the city was with her.

¹³And when the Lord saw her, he had compassion on her, and said unto her, **Weep not.**

¹⁴And he came and touched the bier: and they that bare him stood still. And he said, Young man, I say unto thee, Arise.

¹⁵And he that was dead sat up, and began to speak. And he delivered him to his mother.

¹⁶And there came a fear on all: and they glorified God, saying, that a great prophet is risen up among us; and, That God hath visited his people. (Emphasis mine)

What can be more devastating than for a widow (somebody who has already lost her husband) to also lose her only son? Ah! Satan is cruel, but I thank God for my Lord Jesus. He appeared on the scene and the dead man came back to life. As God's Anointed, and by the backing of God Almighty, and in the powerful name of Jesus, and through the tremendous power of the Holy Ghost, I declare as follows:

No more weeping.
No more crying.
No more sorrow.
No more storms.
No more afflictions.
No more shame.
No more disappointments.
Shout Amen!

CONGREGATION: Ameeeeeeeeeeeeeeeeeeen!

BISHOP JOHN BARNES: Please open your Bibles to **Psalm 30:5** as I read, *"For his anger endureth but a moment; in his favour is life: weeping may endure for a night, but joy cometh in the morning."*

I have come to announce to somebody that your weeping days are over in Jesus' name. Receive your permanent joy in Jesus' name.

CONGREGATION: Ameeeeeeeeeeeeeeeeeeeeeen!

BISHOP JOHN BARNES: Please open your Bibles to *Psalm 71:21* as I read, *"Thou shalt increase my greatness, and comfort me on every side."*

I prophesy to you today that in the name of Jesus Christ of Nazareth, all your weeping shall effectively be turned into greatness, and the God of all comfort shall comfort you indeed in Jesus' name. Shout Amen!

CONGREGATION: Ameeeeeeeeeeeeeeeeeeeeeen!

BISHOP JOHN BARNES: Henceforth, every arrow, curse, sickness, affliction of the enemy to cause pain and weeping, I say back to the sender in Jesus' name. You are free and free indeed forever in Jesus' name.

CONGREGATION: Ameeeeeeeeeeeeeeeeeeeeeen!

BISHOP JOHN BARNES: Please hold hands with your neighbour and begin to speak in tongues (the language of the Holy Ghost.)

CONGREGATION: The congregation began to speak in tongues. As they did this, the congregation became charged up even more, and the Spirit of God filled the atmosphere so much that evil spirits started crying out, and people were slain under the anointing, while deliverances and healings began to take place, and those in chains were set loose and freed.

BISHOP JOHN BARNES: Jesus is the only one that has the power to effectively end weeping in a man's life. If you have not given your life to Him to end all weeping, please signify by raising your hand wherever you are so that I can pray for you to receive salvation. Excellent! I can see loads of hands up. This is certainly a great decision you have made now and you will live never to weep again in Jesus' name. I will read **Romans 10:9-10:**

> *⁹That if thou shalt confess with thy mouth the Lord Jesus, and shalt believe in thine heart that God hath raised him from the dead, thou shalt be saved.*

> *¹⁰For with the heart man believeth unto righteousness; and with the mouth confession is made unto salvation.*

Please confess after me, *'Heavenly Father, I confess with my mouth right now that Jesus is now my Lord, and I believe in my heart that God raised Him from death. Lord Jesus, thank you for shedding your blood on the cross of Calvary to save me from my sin. I receive grace right now to be your disciple forever in Jesus' name.'*

CONGREGATION: Ameeeeeeeeeeeeeeeeeeen!

BISHOP JOHN BARNES: Friends, you are now born-again, and you are welcome to join Shekinah Pentecostal Church and join our believers' class and baptise, and then join a department and become a worker. Get a good study Bible and read it regularly and have fellowship with us regularly. The ushering department will take care of your registration after the service. All the first timers are welcome. You are also welcome to join us. God bless you all. He exits the podium.

TITHES AND OFFERING COLLECTIONS

It's now 12.25 pm and Pastor William Chapman goes up to the pulpit to lead the Church in the collections of tithes, offerings, and donations of the congregation. Pastor William Chapman holds a Doctorate degree in Economics from London School of Economics, and he is also a Chartered Management Accountant (CIMA). He is the head of Finance and Administration of the Church. He had his own Chartered Accounting Firm before God called him into full-time service in the church. He is 5 feet 9 inches tall with an extra-large waistline of 50 inches, and a protruding stomach like a heavily pregnant woman. This outlook seems to be a paradox considering the fact that he is given to serious fasting and prayers. One thing that is obvious about Pastor William Chapman is that he carries prosperity anointing. Anyone he prays for to prosper attracts money and becomes a success. So a lot of people go to him for prayers in order to connect to the prosperity anointing that he carries. The forty-five-year-old Pastor and millionaire is married to Dr. Tracey Chapman, who's got PhD in Anthropology, and is also an educationist, in charge of the children's department of the Church. They have three young children.

PASTOR WILLIAM CHAPMAN: Good afternoon Church.

CONGREGATION: Good afternoon Pastor William.

PASTOR WILLIAM CHAPMAN: Offering time!

CONGREGATION: Blessing time!

PASTOR WILLIAM CHAPMAN: It's time for us to honour the Lord with our substance. Please begin to package your tithes, offerings, and donations in your envelopes and write your giving details as requested at the front and back of the envelope. Please fill out your cheques properly and remember to sign them. For those of us giving with our debit cards or credit cards, please fill in the required account number details correctly along with your mobile phone details in case the accounts department needs to get in touch with you. Please open your Bibles to *Malachi 3:10* as I read:

> *"Bring ye all the tithes into the storehouse, that there may be meat in mine house, and prove me now herewith, saith the* LORD *of hosts, if I will not open you the windows of heaven, and pour you out a blessing, that there shall not be room enough to receive it."*

I am going to read one more scripture for the benefit of those who don't know that tithe is ten percent (10%) of your gross income, and that it is holy unto the Lord. The ten percent is not negotiable. Please open your Bible to the book of *Leviticus 27:30-32:*

30And all the tithe of the land, whether of the seed of the land, or of the fruit of the tree, is the LORD's: it is holy unto the LORD.

31And if a man will at all redeem ought of his tithes, he shall add thereto the fifth part thereof.

32And concerning the tithe of the herd, or of the flock, even of whatsoever passeth under the rod, the tenth shall be holy unto the LORD.

Let us pray. Heavenly Father, behold the tithes of your blessed people. I ask that you honour their obedience by opening the windows of heaven and releasing your abundant financial blessings to them, so much that they will not have room enough to receive it. The Bible says every seed produces after its kind. They are sowing money, let them also reap money in abundance. Let there be new jobs, promotions at work, business expansion and huge profits for your people in Jesus' name.

CONGREGATION: Ameeeeeeeeeeeeeeeen!

PASTOR WILLIAM CHAPMAN: Ushers, please go round with the offertory baskets and collect the envelopes. God bless you all. And with that he steps down from the podium.

BRIEF WORD ON TITHES AND OFFERINGS

Mary Jenkins and Alan Brown are indeed obedient workers in the vineyard of the Lord who truly desire to prosper greatly financially. Hence, they don't joke with their tithes and offerings to the Lord. As a matter of fact, they both have standing orders to their bank regarding their tithes and offerings every month and they do exactly what *Proverbs 3:9-10 says:*

9Honour the LORD with thy substance, and with the firstfruits of all thine increase:

10So shall thy barns be filled with plenty, and thy presses shall burst out with new wine.

What you sow is what you reap, and that is also applicable in the area of tithing and offerings. If you sow nothing, you will reap nothing. A farmer who decides to sow nothing during the planting season will definitely have nothing to harvest. A lot of Christians lack a revelation in the area of giving. Hence, they have resorted to making all manner of negative remarks out of ignorance about Men of God, and the Church of God regarding collections. Be careful! Abel gave God his best and God acknowledged it. Give God your best and He will also give you His best. When you sow bountifully, you will reap bountifully. When you sow sparingly, you will reap sparingly. The choice is yours.

SCREEN ANNOUNCEMENTS

MEDIA TEAM: Please note the following activities and events coming up in the Church.

1. There will be a Bible Study session every Wednesday evening from 6 pm to 9 pm, and a special praise and worship night every Friday from 6 pm to 9 pm here in the Church.
2. There will be a special anointing service on the second Sunday next month and special communion service on the third Sunday next month.
3. The singles night is coming up on the fourth Saturday of next month. All singles should be smartly dressed as they come and the Lord will divinely connect you to the bone of your bone, and flesh of your flesh in Jesus' name.
4. Please join a Bible study and prayer group near you.
5. Please continue to evangelise using the church leaflets and tracts to invite someone to church, and you can also use social media to send out electronic leaflets to your friends inviting them to church. Have a great week ahead. God bless you all.

BENEDICTION AND CLOSING PRAYER
It's 12.40 pm and the Man of God, Bishop John Barnes returns to the pulpit for the closing prayers for the next five minutes. There were no boring moments during this two hours forty-five minutes

service, and some people always wish it to continue. But it has to come to an end now.

BISHOP JOHN BARNES: Numbers 6:24-26:

24The LORD bless thee, and keep thee:

25The LORD make his face shine upon thee, and be gracious unto thee:

26The LORD lift up his countenance upon thee, and give thee peace.

This week is a week of peace and joy of the Lord for you and your family in Jesus' name.

CONGREGATION: Ameeeeeeeeeeeeeeen!

BISHOP JOHN BARNES: I declare God's protection over your life and entire household in Jesus' name. No evil shall befall you, neither shall any plague come near your dwelling in Jesus' name.

CONGREGATION: Ameeeeeeeeeeeeeen!

BISHOP JOHN BARNES: I declare you shall forever be compassed with the favour of God as with a shield in Jesus' name.

CONGREGATION: Ameeeeeeeeeeeeeen!

BISHOP JOHN BARNES: The grace.

CONGREGATION: The grace of our Lord Jesus Christ and the sweet fellowship of the Holy Spirit be with us now and forever. Surely, goodness and mercy shall follow us all the days of our life. And we shall dwell in the presence of the Lord forever.

BISHOP JOHN BARNES: Go in the peace of the Lord.

CONGREGATION: Ameeeeeeeeeeeeeen!

NEW LOOK GYM

It's now about 1 pm and Mary Jenkins and Alan Brown meet up in the car park.

"Hi Mary, I hope you enjoyed the service today?"

"Oh yes, and you?"

"It's great to be in God's presence. Let's be on our way to the New Look Gym at Waterloo."

And they got into their respective cars and drove off heading for the gym. In no time they are there because on a Sunday, the traffic is not as bad as on a working day.

The New Look Gym is positioned close to the River Thames with a wonderful view. It has a lot of modern facilities and activities, which include a restaurant and bar, a swimming pool, sauna rooms, showers and changing rooms, Aerobic classes, Judo and Taekwondo classes, and Yoga classes. Different working out machines including a Pec Dec Machine, Bench Press Machine, Seated Chest Press, Power Rack, Leg Press Machine, Hack Squat, Smith Machine, Leg Extension Machine, Leg Curl Machine, Leg Adduction Machine, Seated Calf Machine, Standing Calf Machine, Lat Pulldown Machine, Pull Up Bar, T-Bar Row, Seated Row Machine, Back Extension Machine, Preacher Curl Bench, Arm Curl Machine, Arm Extension Machine, Overhead Presses, Lateral Raises Machines, Ab Crunch Machine, Ab Roller, Medicine Ball, Stability Ball, Foam Roller, Rowing Machine, Treadmill, Recumbent Exercise Bike plus other little exercise items.[3]

They have instructors to train you on how to use the machines. They also have a mini-clinic with a nutritionist, first-aiders, a nurse, and a doctor. The rooms where people workout are brightly lit and air-conditioned with the temperature set at the right level, with televisions, and music playing constantly.

Straightaway, they went into their respective changing rooms and got ready to workout. As they came out, they got on the scale to find out their weights.

"What did you weigh Alan?"

He replies, "Exactly 100 kg. And you?"

And she said, "Whao! That's a huge weight. Don't you think that can break a woman up on the bed? I'm exactly 65 kg."

Alan replied, "You are a naughty girl."

They started laughing as they held hands going towards the treadmills. They got on the treadmill machines next to each other and started with walking.

"How long are we going to be here in the gym working out, Alan?"

"Roughly an hour, and then we will have our showers and go down to the restaurant and bar to refresh. Is that too much for you?"

"That's alright."

They both increased the speed of the treadmill machines so that they now started running moderately. And at exactly half an hour, the machines automatically started slowing down having obviously been programmed for half an hour. And they finally came to a stop, and proceeded towards the Recumbent Exercise Bikes next to one another. This time, they are already sweating and breathing heavily. Great cardiovascular exercise like this is good for the proper circulation of blood to and from the heart through the arteries and veins and that keeps the heart and entire body healthy. After fifteen minutes, they both got off again and moved to the Seated Row Machines next to each other and carried on working out. And after five minutes on this machine, they moved into the weights section and used different weights and body exercise for another fifteen minutes before they went straight to the showers to clean up, get dressed and go down to the restaurant and bar.

"See you at the restaurant darling, perhaps in the next thirty minutes."

"Hopefully I should be done by then as well. See you Alan."

In thirty minutes, Alan is already done and seated at the restaurant and facing in the direction of the River Thames, seeing the little boats and beautiful tower buildings in the direction of central London. He stood up, still looking in the direction of the River Thames and was visualising in his thoughts what life will be like marrying Mary Jenkins, his newfound, love, and she came in from behind and held him tight, while he struggled to turn round to see the person holding him.

"Whao!" He exclaims.

"That's a nice purple dress you've got on, and you smell nice too. I like your hairstyle as well. You are beautiful."

"Thanks Alan for the compliment. You are looking so smart as well. That's a nice view on the River Thames."

"Yes, it is. I have been feeding my eyes before you joined me."

"Shall we place our orders for food and drinks?" Alan asked.

The televisions are showing sports channels, and pop music is also playing on a low volume.

"Yes, let's make our orders."

And as they both sat at a table, through eye contact signal, one of the waiters approached them and took their order. While they waited for the order to arrive, she asked, "Alan, what is your ultimate plan for me as a man?"

"To marry you, if it turns out to be the will of God for us. And I was actually visualising that in my mind before you came down to join me."

"Have you told anybody anything about me in your family or at Church?"

"Not yet. I want to do three days fasting and prayers and seek the face of God about it before I speak to anyone. But for now, I can tell you categorically that you are beautiful and I really admire every bit of you. And he quoted to her, *Song of Solomon 3:7* that says, *"Thou art all fair, my love, there is no spot in thee."*

With a cheerful smile on her beautiful face she replies saying, "Thank you sweetheart." This is the first time she didn't call him Alan, and he noted it.

Here comes the waiter with the food, which he places on the table and leaves.

"Let's pray," says Alan.

They both bow their heads down as Alan prays, "Lord, thank you for another opportunity for us to be together today. We bless and sanctify the food and drinks. Let it nourish our bodies as we eat and make merry with our non-alcoholic French wine in Jesus' name."

"Amen!" she affirms.

Pouring the wine in two glasses, they turned to each other and made a toast to their health and prosperity saying together, "Cheers! Long life and prosperity" before they began to eat their delicious meals. This is their first meal of the day as they are supposed to be in Church on Sundays fasting as workers. And it's now exactly 6.30 pm. She calls out to the waiter.

And Alan said, "Why are you calling him?"

"I want to pay" She replies.

"Nooo!" said Alan.

"But you paid yesterday."

"But I asked to take you out. So I've got to foot the bill."

"That's fine sweetheart. Thanks for everything. Very much appreciated," she replies.

"You are welcome darling," and Alan paid the waiter. After the payment, they got up and went to their lockers, got their bags and left for their respective homes in their own cars.

This was a reflection of their first ever weekend together. Exciting, but unfortunately, Alan is no more. She wished Alan was still alive for her. She rolled from one end of the bed to the other trying to encourage herself, but the pain is obviously too much. The picture rolled off from her hand and fell down. She picked it up and placed it on the bedside drawers, and closed her eyes for a nap as she is now tired.

CHAPTER FOUR

ALAN BROWN'S FUNERAL

The CIA investigation into the events, and perpetrators of the attack on American Airlines Flight NY3351 that crashed into the Atlantic Ocean is still ongoing. However, significant progress has been made so far as forensic evidence reveals from the debris and the black box recovered that it was a terror-related attack, and the leader of the Hitman terrorist group from the Middle East region, Abdul Mohammed has confirmed their involvement in the attack. President Barack Obama of the United States of America has vowed to ensure Abdul Mohammed and others involved are brought to face justice. In view of this, the *Central Intelligence Agency (CIA)* is working tirelessly to catch the perpetrators. For this purpose, a high-powered computerised drone has been built with Abdul Mohammed's personal details programmed into it and specially launched to locate Abdul Mohammed and capture him alive from his residence in Ranya, a remote village in Iraq. Earlier on, Abdul Mohammed had boasted that he is invisible, and that the CIA will never capture him. Unknown to him, the CIA had been constantly tracking and monitoring him with sophisticated computerised equipment from a warship. As soon as he walked out to rest on his balcony on a hot afternoon, the drone was launched and within minutes it had located him, firing a tranquilizer at him, and he was nabbed by Special Forces. He was immediately taken to the United States to be charged and tried for the murder of one hundred and fifty souls that perished in the ill-fated NY3351 American Airlines flight.

As soon as Abdul Mohammed reached the United States of America, President Barack Obama was informed by the CIA. The President immediately held a press conference at the front of the *White House, 1600 Pennsylvania Avenue NW, Washington, D.C. 20500, U.S.* Scores of reporters and photographers were gathered with their video cameras, and other devices to cover the announcement.

PRESIDENT BARACK OBAMA: He said he was invisible, and boasted that we couldn't capture him, but I'm so excited to announce to the whole world that we captured him yesterday. I'm talking about Abdul Mohammed of the Hitman terrorist group, and he will be immediately charged with suspicion of planting an explosive device on the American Airlines flight NY3351 that led to the death of one hundred and fifty innocent souls on board. Meanwhile, the CIA is still working hard to capture any other accomplice of this heinous crime. I thank the CIA and the team of Special Forces officers who have worked relentlessly in this great operation. God bless America. Sorry, I will only take three questions from the press.

TONY FREEMAN OF INDIGO NEWS: Mr. President, will Abdul Mohammed face capital punishment when he is tried and found to be guilty?

PRESIDENT BARACK OBAMA: That's a decision that will be made by the court, and not me. If found guilty by the court, and capital punishment is imposed for the death of those one hundred and fifty innocent souls, and for causing Americans a lot of pain, then so be it.

JOHN FRANCIS OF THE NEW YORK DAILY UPDATE: Mr. President, will there be any form of compensation from the American government to families of the victims?

PRESIDENT BARACK OBAMA: Definitely, there will be compensation for the families of the victims from the government and from the relevant insurance companies. I have already set up a committee to look into that, and they will prepare a report.

GREG WILLIAMS OF TRANSPARENT NEWS: Mr. President, considering the fact that this is now the third attack on American Airlines by terrorists, what is the American government doing to stop this sort of attack in future?

PRESIDENT BARACK OBAMA: That's a very good question. As we all know, terrorism is not limited only to American Airlines or

America. We are seeing terrorism manifest in various other nations of the world and in different forms. Therefore, America will have to fight terrorism alongside other nations in order to effectively end it. And on our part, henceforth, there shall be tighter security by way of thorough searching of individuals boarding our airplanes and their luggage. And our airplanes will now be modernised and fitted with equipment that will ensure an explosion of any device will not be disastrous or lead to a crash. We will also be looking at banning suspected terrorist groups, and individuals from boarding our airplanes. Finally, I would like to let you know that I have already set up a committee and they are dealing with this matter. God bless America.

Mary Jenkins got to know this latest information as she switched on the television to hear the 8 pm BBC News.

"Of what benefit is this to me?" she muttered as she angrily switched off the television. "Capturing Abdul Mohammed or anyone else will not bring Alan Brown back to life." She said and started sobbing and crying out loud with tears flowing down her cheeks as she asked, "Lord why me?" And declaring, "My name is now Mara (meaning Bitter), and not Mary."

That was what Naomi called herself in Ruth 1:20 after she lost her family in the land of Moab. "I have lost everything with the loss of Alan. Is life still going to be worth living?" she asked herself. At this point, the Holy Spirit quickened her to remember this scripture, **2 Corinthians 12:9**: *"And he said to me, my grace is sufficient for thee: for my strength is made perfect in weakness. Most gladly therefore will I rather glory in infirmities, that the power of Christ may rest upon me."* This scripture comforted and strengthened her.

Thankfully, the battered corpse of Alan Brown was recovered and has been identified by the family and funeral arrangements made by them. Burial is fixed for tomorrow which is a Friday. Before Alan died, he took out an insurance policy to cover his funeral costs upon death. Now that he is no more, all the family did was contact the insurance company and the funeral directors to do the burial. There is absolutely no financial pressure whatsoever on anyone towards the funeral costs.

As early as 8 am, she received a call from her parents, Mr and Mrs Paul Jenkins in Manchester to cheer her up. They didn't meet Alan Brown in person before he died and Mary had only casually told her father about Alan, a week before death struck and cut his promising life short. The phone rang. "Hello Daddy."

"How are you darling? Your mum and I are with you in spirit in London as you mourn the death of Alan and go for the burial today. We have been praying for you for God to comfort you and fill your heart with peace in Jesus' name. If you need anything please let us know. We are also ready to receive you here in Manchester if that will help. We will talk to you again this evening after work to know how the burial went. God bless you, my dear."

"Amen! Thanks for the call Daddy and Mummy."

Her parents had placed the call on speaker while they spoke.

After speaking with the parents, she got into her car and drove off heading towards the location of the funeral directors at Finsbury Park. On getting there, she met with the entire Brown family, which included Alan's parents, Mr and Mrs Brown, flanked on their side by their ten-year-old grandson, Stephen Brown and their only daughter, Shirley Brown. A good number of people from the Shekinah Pentecostal Church were also present including Pastor Moses Elijah, head of the Outreach department Alan belonged to, and a few other members, Pastor Susan Edwards, the choir leader, and a few other members of the choir including Angela, Felicia, Deborah, and James, Deborah's brother. A few members of staff of Posh Cars Limited, the company Alan worked for, were also there including the Managing Director Dr. Jason Cooper. Everyone was dressed in a black outfit and also wearing a long face and talking about the horrible terrorist attack and the recent capture of Abdul Mohammed by the CIA which meant nothing to her.

She went straight and shook hands and embraced the Browns. She also greeted Pastor Moses Elijah, Pastor Susan Edwards, her choir colleagues and thanked them for coming. The funeral directors got the casket ready and they all got into their respective cars and drove off to the All Saints Cemetery on the outskirts of Finsbury Park where a service of songs will be held in a Church in honour of the late Alan Brown, before he will be finally laid to rest in perfect peace.

As they went into the Church for the service of songs, she kept staring at Stephen Brown, the ten-year-old grandson of the Browns. And the more she looked, the more she saw a striking resemblance between this boy and Alan. To start with, they have similar eyes, and lips. And as she was still trying to figure out who he was, the little boy started walking towards her. And she stopped him and subtly asked him, "Is Shirley your mum?"

And he answered in a tone similar to Alan's, "No, Shirley is my auntie. And I just lost my Dad." And he gently walked away. Immediately, her blood temperature rose up, and her countenance changed as she tried to control an outburst of anger within. Another bombshell for her, so to say, as she began to now think Alan Brown could have possibly been a trickster intending to deceive her.

"How come he didn't tell me he had a son?" She queried. "That was how Donald Bruce came into my life with lies and got away with it. All men are the same, I suppose." She thought. "I wish he was alive now, I would have challenged him to explain who this boy is."

And then she tried to calm herself down as she thought, "I think I'm being too emotional here by jumping to conclusions too soon. Alan didn't even have the chance to explain himself. It was a relationship that lasted only three months. I couldn't have possibly known everything about him in such a short time. After all, he doesn't know everything about me. Lord, forgive me for judging him and for my silliness." And she was right with her silly thoughts because she saw Shirley Brown coming towards her and said, "Sorry, I didn't introduce Stephen to you earlier. The little boy you just spoke to is Alan's son. His former girlfriend, Juliet Freeman, mistakenly got pregnant ten years ago and had him for my brother. They were not married. That's how Alan got Stephen Brown as a seed."

"Thanks for introducing Stephen to me." Mary replied.

Any time she ever remembers the name Donald Bruce, or that name is mentioned, she turns angry and bitter suggesting she has still not forgiven him for dumping her. Donald Bruce dumped her thirteen years ago after a two-year relationship she thought would have ended in marriage while she was a marketing undergraduate at Oxford University. That was the first ever, and only heartbreak she had suffered in a relationship because afterwards, she has always been on her guard and cautious about starting a relationship. The only thing Donald Bruce will never put up with a woman is for her to be domineering, and disrespectful. And Mary Jenkins towed that path unconsciously, perhaps because of pride, or maybe immaturity. They were constantly at loggerheads and eventually he called it quits. Mary felt terribly let down, and emotionally battered, brutalised, and bruised by Donald Bruce.

God commanded wives to respect their husbands in *Ephesians 5:22* saying: "*Wives, submit yourselves unto your own husbands, as unto the Lord.*" The phrase, "As unto the Lord" means to submit and respect your husband the way you will submit and respect Jesus. Unfortunately, not all women do this. The beauty of a wife lies in total respect for her husband. A woman who truly desires to be married to a man must also be humble, submissive, and respectful. This is what the Bible says, and this standard cannot be lowered in a Christian relationship or marriage. And you have to start practicing what this scripture says while in courtship with your fiancé as a woman.

Meanwhile, she was quickened and she remembered the powerful message preached by Pastor Moses Elijah a while ago on forgiveness. He thought that the phrase, 'Forgive and forget' is indeed a tough one but it's the standard for Christians. If you must forgive and not forget, then, by all means only remember positive things and not negative things about the so-called adversary or incident. Thirteen years is such a long time. Let go of all weights and move on light in life. Bitterness and grudges hinders only the bitter person. Jesus says in *Matthew 6:15*, "*But if ye forgive not men their trespasses, neither will your Father forgive your trespasses.*"

Bitterness defiles the body according to *Hebrews 12:15* which says, "*Looking diligently lest any man fail of the grace of God; lest any root of bitterness springing up trouble you, and thereby many be defiled;"* Apart from the Bible account, Medical Science research also confirms that unforgiveness and a root of bitterness is unhealthy as it can be a source of deadly diseases. Read below a few tips given by Pastor Moses Elijah on how to know if you have truly forgiven those who hurt you which Mary Jenkins dwelt on again.

HOW TO KNOW IF YOU HAVE FORGIVEN THOSE WHO HURT YOU

1. When you are no longer angry and bitter against them. – No more grudges.
2. When you no longer murmur or complain to anybody about what they did wrong.
3. When you no longer have the intention to seek revenge for what they did wrong.
4. When you no longer wish that some terrible evil will befall those who hurt you.
5. When you can experience the perfect peace of God when you remember what they did wrong or when you see them physically.
6. When you no longer bear malice against them, and you can communicate with them freely, fully reconcile with them as if nothing happened in the past. Tread with caution and apply **wisdom** and follow the leading of the **Holy Spirit** as you become friends with them again.
7. When you can still love them and pray for them as Jesus commanded in **Matthew 5:44** saying, *"But I say unto you, love your enemies, bless them that curse you, do good to them that hate you, and pray for them that despitefully use you, and persecute you:"* This scripture is the true test for forgiveness.

Completely *forget* what they have done wrong in line with the popular phrase, 'Forgive and forget'. If you must remember anything, it has to be only positive things about those who hurt you. Forget about the negatives completely. *Forgive them even when they do not say sorry.*

The benefit and beauty of forgiveness is that the peace, and the power of God will be released unto you abundantly, and the heavens will be opened unto you for unlimited overflowing blessings. Forgive!

SERVICE OF SONGS

The service of songs begins and Pastor Moses Elijah is the officiating minister.

PASTOR MOSES ELIJAH: Good morning everybody. For those of us who don't know why we are here, we are here because of our dear Brother Alan Brown who has translated to be with the Lord as a result of the terrorist attack on the American Airlines flight NY3351. May his soul rest in peace. I would like to call on Pastor Susan Edwards to come forward and lead us in a few Hymns. She will be supported by Pastor Jacob O'Brien on keyboard, Pastor Amanda Taylor on guitar, Brother Sylvester Smith on saxophones, and Pastor Stephen Thompson on drums.

PASTOR SUSAN EDWARDS: Good morning brethren. We will start by singing the Hymn: *"Amazing Grace,"* by John Newton – 1779; followed by *"Because He Lives,"* by Bill and Gloria Gaithers; and finally, *"Blessed Assurance,"* by Fanny Crosby - 1873. Please refer to your bulletin, or look at the screen. One, two, let's go.

AMAZING GRACE – By John Newton, Olney Hymns – 1779

1. *Amazing grace! How sweet the sound*
   That saved a wretch like me!
   I once was lost, but now am found;
   Was blind, but now I see.

2. *'Twas grace that taught my heart to fear,*
   And grace my fears relieved;
   How precious did that grace appear
   The hour I first believed.

3. *Through many dangers, toils, and snares,*
   I have already come;
   'Tis grace hath brought me safe thus far,
   And grace will lead me home.

4. *The Lord has promised good to me,*
   His Word my hope secures;
   He will my Shield and Portion be,
   As long as life endures.

5. *Yea, when this flesh and heart shall fail,*
   And mortal life shall cease,
   I shall possess, within the veil,
   A life of joy and peace.

6. *The earth shall soon dissolve like snow,*
   The sun forbear to shine;
   But God, who called me here below,
   Will be forever mine.

7. *When we've been there ten thousand years,*
   Bright shining as the sun,
   We've no less days to sing God's praise
   Than when we'd first begun.

The next hymn is:

BECAUSE HE LIVES – By William J. Gaither, & Gloria Gaither, 1971

Verse 1
God sent His son, they called Him, Jesus;
He came to love, heal and forgive;
He lived and died to buy my pardon,
An empty grave is there to prove my Savior lives!

Chorus
Because He lives, I can face tomorrow,
Because He lives, all fear is gone;
Because I know He holds the future,
And life is worth the living,
Just because He lives!

Verse 2
How sweet to hold a newborn baby,
And feel the pride and joy he brings;
But greater still the calm assurance:
This child can face uncertain days because He Lives!

Chorus
Because He lives, I can face tomorrow,
Because He lives, all fear is gone;
Because I know He holds the future,
And life is worth the living,
Just because He lives!

Verse 3
And then one day, I'll cross the river,
I'll fight life's final war with pain;
And then, as death gives way to victory,
I'll see the lights of glory and I'll know He lives!

Chorus
Because He lives, I can face tomorrow,
Because He lives, all fear is gone;
Because I know He holds the future,
And life is worth the living,
Just because He lives!

CONGREGATION: Sings.

PASTOR MOSES ELIJAH: May the soul of our Late Brother Alan Brown rest in perfect peace. Please open your Bible to *Ecclesiastics 3:1-2* as I read:

¹To everything there is a season, and a time to every purpose under the heaven:

²A time to be born, and a time to die; a time to plant, and a time to pluck up that which is planted;

From the scripture I just read, it's obvious that death is inevitable. Everyone born into this world surely has appointed time to also translate to be with the Lord. Death is an absolute must and no one can escape it.

Please open your Bible to *1 Thessalonians 4:13-14* as I read:

¹³But I would not have you to be ignorant, brethren, concerning them which are asleep, that ye sorrow not, even as others which have no hope.

¹⁴For if we believe that Jesus died and rose again, even so them also who sleep in Jesus will God bring with him.

I had to read this scripture to assure us that because our late brother Alan Brown, was born again, he had only translated certainly to be with the Lord. On the day of rapture when our Lord Jesus will appear again, even the Saints who died in Christ Jesus will rise up again with Him. Be comforted and know that the spirit of our brother Alan Brown lives on.

For those of us still alive, the Bible says in *1 Thessalonians 4:17:*

¹⁷Then we which are alive and remain shall be caught up together with them in the clouds, to meet the Lord in the air: and so shall we ever be with the Lord.

As a born-again Christian living a holy life, be encouraged and know that when the rapture comes, you will be caught up into the heavens to be with the Lord forever in Jesus' name.

CONGREGATION: Ameeeeeeeeeeeeeeeen!

PASTOR MOSES ELIJAH: The Bible says again in *Psalm 91:16,* *"With long life will I satisfy him, and shew him my salvation".* I pray that the Lord will satisfy everyone of us with long life in

Jesus' name. There shall not be premature death amongst us, and we shall surely fulfil our days on earth in Jesus' name."

CONGREGATION: Ameeeeeeeeeeeeeeen!

PASTOR MOSES ELIJAH: Please declare this scripture powerfully: *Psalm 118:17, "I shall not die, but live, and declare the works of the* LORD," in Jesus' name. Amen!

CONGREGATION: "I shall not die, but live, and declare the works of the LORD," in Jesus' name. Amen!

PASTOR MOSES ELIJAH: If you are here today and you have not given your life to Jesus, I would like you to come forward to the altar so that I can pray for you. Anybody? Nobody came forward. Thank God everyone is born again.

EULOGY – Shirley Brown

Alan used to be very economical as a little boy of about six years old. He hates wastage. He doesn't throw away his leftover food. He would put it in the fridge and eat it afterwards. And he was the one that initiated recycling in the family. At the age of seven, he became a newspaper vendor delivering newspapers to his customers at home and making some money. All I got from him was chocolates once in a while, so it didn't surprise me that he went on to study for a bachelor's degree in Economics, and a master's degree in Marketing in the University.

His favourite scripture in the Bible is Psalm 118:24 as a little Sunday school boy of about eight years. I used to pester him by calling him Psalm 118:24 as a nickname, but all he will do is rejoice and be glad, while it will amaze me that he is not angry. He will simply ignore me.

He loved me so much and would protect me from danger. I was once confronted by a big bulldog that frightened me almost to death as it charged at me ready to devour me as a child, but he came to my rescue by shielding me.

He loves God and cares for his family, colleagues, and friends. He was a very kind person. Once, all he had in his pocket was

£100 and a beggar approached him, and he gave the beggar the £100. Amazing! I have not seen anyone do that.

When he failed Mathematics in one of his secondary school examinations, he did not eat for a whole day. That's how bad he hated to fail in whatever he did. Anyway, I ate his portion of food that day. He was very successful in his academic work and career.

My greatest joy about my brother is that he gave his life to Jesus before death struck. He is with Christ Jesus now resting in perfect peace. God bless you all. And she exits the podium.

CONGREGATION: Laughing and clapping.

Immediately Shirley Brown finished reading the eulogy, Mary Jenkins stepped forward to read a poem in honour of Alan Brown. With tears in her eyes and handkerchief to dry them, she began to read with an unsteady shaky voice.

POEM – Mary Jenkins

You lived an exemplary life Alan
Caring, loving, and compassionate
But untimely death struck
And took away your precious life from me
My heart is full of sorrow
But dwelling on the good times
We shared together brightens it up
Death is cruel
O death, where is thy sting?
O grave, where is thy victory?
My Lord Jesus has defeated death on the cross
Alan, you have exited from the earth
But your spirit lives on
As you have only translated to be with the Lord
In your Father's house
There are many mansions, enjoy them
Rest in the bosom of the Lord
Till we meet again
Adieu Alan.
Rest in perfect peace my love

She exited the podium sobbing, shedding tears and in anguish, but pulled herself together as she quietly went to take her seat.

PASTOR MOSES ELIJAH: The grace…

CONGREGATION: The grace of our Lord Jesus Christ and the sweet fellowship of the Holy Spirit be with us, now and forever. Surely, goodness and mercy shall follow us all the days of our life. And we shall dwell in the presence of the Lord forever.

PASTOR MOSES ELIJAH: The service of songs has ended. Go in the peace of the Lord in Jesus' name.

CONGREGATION: Amen!
Immediately after the Service of Songs, the funeral directors moved the casket and proceeded to the burial ground. There was no need to lay him in state for people to view because he was badly battered in the plane crash and in a horrible state. The grave has been dug, and without any further delay, he was laid to rest in his own grave. Mary Jenkins was visibly shaken, crying and wailing uncontrollably. Friends gathered around her and Deborah was again on the ground to support her with her firmly built frame as an Olympic gold medallist weightlifter. They led her straight into one of the reception rooms comforting her with holy words. Afterwards, she had to say adieu to Alan Brown placing a wreath of flowers on his grave, thanked everyone for coming and bade them all goodbye. And she got into her car and drove off to East Dulwich where she lives.

At exactly 8 pm, her parents called again to find out how the funeral went, and how she is doing. And she said that it all went well. Thank God Alan is finally laid in his own tomb to rest in perfect peace.

CHAPTER FIVE

THE CAPTURE AND TRIAL OF THEOPHILUS ANDERSON, ALIAS COMMOTION

The investigation regarding the hacking of the financial computer systems of Apex Bank limited, and the subsequent disappearance of five hundred million pounds sterling (£500m) from the bank's accounts allegedly by Theophilus Anderson, alias Commotion is still ongoing. So far, information reaching the Manchester City Police Intelligence Unit indicates that Commotion has escaped from Britain to Barcelona, Spain as a fugitive. It's still a mystery to the police that he managed to infiltrate through the watertight police security and surveillance into Spain. A few days ago, Superintendent Paul Jenkins went to withdraw money from his Apex Bank account which serves as a secondary account and he discovered that his own account was also emptied and this was linked to the hacking of Apex Bank by Commotion. This infuriated him, and he vowed that he will do whatever it takes for Commotion to be caught and extradited back to Britain to face trial. The police in Britain are now working closely with their Spanish counterparts to capture Commotion.

Whilst they are busy drawing up plans as to how they can commence a more organised intensive search for Commotion, the Manchester City Police Station receives a phone call from Munich, Germany, and it was Theophilus Anderson, alias Commotion on the line teasing and taunting Superintendent Paul Jenkins and advising him to end his search for him because he will only succeed in wasting his time and taxpayers money. He claimed that he has more than enough money from Apex bank to enable him to leave the earth and go to another planet, possibly Mars where he would never ever be found. This made Superintendent Paul Jenkins more furious. And he decided to commence straightaway seven days of prayer and fasting and commit this matter to God to direct him on how to capture Commotion. That gave him peace. The Bible says in *Proverbs 3:5-6:*

> *⁵Trust in the LORD with all thine heart; and lean not unto thine own understanding.*

> *⁶In all thy ways acknowledge him, and he shall direct thy paths.*

Psalm 32:8 also says, *"I will instruct thee and teach thee in the way which thou shalt go: I will guide thee with mine eye."*

On the seventh day of his fast, at lunchtime, he sat down in his office chair and he switched off into a vision. The vision appeared so real. Behold, the man Theophilus Anderson was seen in the vision to be in Kingston, Jamaica. And the address given in the vision is 5, Macaulay Drive. This is one of the palatial mansions by the seaside for bourgeois and tycoons to enjoy the sunshine in the Caribbean. When he came back from the vision, he stood up and paced around his office in amazement. "How could he have sneaked out of Munich in Germany to be in Kingston, Jamaica?" He asked and wondered. Well for such a criminal, he can come up with any surprises. He was happy for the supernatural revelation and gave thanks to God and ended his fast that day.

Immediately after the supernatural revelation in a vision about Commotion, Superintendent Paul Jenkins contacted the Jamaican Police Intelligence Unit and they confirmed his presence at 5, Macaulay Drive. He started planning how the British Police officers from the Intelligence Unit will fly down to Kingston, Jamaica urgently. The two British Police officers arrived in Kingston from Manchester and hooked up with their Jamaican counterparts. Immediately, a high-powered surveillance was commenced to monitor Commotion at that address. And within hours, officers pounced on 5, Macaulay Drive and he was nabbed while he was sleeping at about 2 am in the morning sandwiched in between two beautiful ladies on a massive king-sized bed. A thorough search was conducted at that address and the following items were recovered which will also serve as useful evidence in court. One laptop computer, one computer tablet, two pistols loaded with bullets, seven thousand cloned Apex Bank debit and credit cards of customers, five international passports, twenty official letters from different organisations including one from the chancellor of the exchequer's office.

There was great excitement for Manchester City Police as soon as Theophilus Anderson was brought back to Britain. Superintendent Paul Jenkins immediately held a press conference with several journalists in attendance with their video cameras, and other devices to cover the announcement. He cleared his throat, and with beaming smiles of relief on his face, he spoke.

SUPERINTENDENT PAUL JENKINS: I am so excited to announce to the whole world that the search for Theophilus Anderson, alias Commotion, is finally over. We caught and arrested him in Kingston, Jamaica. He is back in Britain, and we will now charge him straight away based on our available evidence. Thank you, I will only take three questions from the press.

ANN CUNNINGHAM OF BBC NEWS: If Theophilus Anderson is found guilty, will he be asked to return the five hundred million pounds he allegedly stole from the Apex Bank?

SUPERINTENDENT PAUL JENKINS: I think that's a question for the court to decide. The police will not interfere with the due process of law. But I presume he might not get away with all that money.

SUE RIGBY OF TELL THE TRUTH: Can you tell us why it has taken the police such a long time to capture Theophilus Anderson?

SUPERINTENDENT PAUL JENKINS: The man is a highly organised and sophisticated criminal, always coming up with mysterious new ways of committing crimes. But thank God we finally caught him.

FREDRICK SIMPSON OF PACESETTERS MAIL: What do you think should be done to effectively deal with criminals like Theophilus Anderson?

SUPERINTENDENT PAUL JENKINS: Tougher laws should be promulgated to deter criminals. The police should also be given more powers and be provided with more sophisticated equipment, and training to deal with criminals. There should also be proper rehabilitation programmes for offenders. God bless you all.

The newspapers published the news with different captions. *Pacesetters Mail* caption read, *"T. ANDERSON ARRESTED BY POLICE"* and *Tell the Truth* caption read, *"NO MORE COMMOTION AS POLICE ARREST T. ANDERSON."* And *BBC BREAKING NEWS* read: *"Theophilus Anderson, alias Commotion, was finally arrested yesterday in Jamaica by the Police and brought back to Britain...."*

The capture of Theophilus Anderson was indeed a big relief for Superintendent Paul Jenkins. It helped to restore confidence in the general public, especially the customers of Apex Bank Limited, indicating that the police are still efficient. And in recognition of the efforts of the police to capture Commotion and for his immense role, Superintendent Paul Jenkins was promoted to the post of Chief Superintendent of the police.

Meanwhile, Apex Bank's financial system was crippled by the malicious virus allegedly released by Commotion to attack their systems. As a result, they have only been able to render very scanty services to their customers. The bank was just able to restore their system three days ago, and sent out letters to its customers informing them of what had happened. However, a huge number of customers already knew what happened to the extent that there have been protests by customers carrying placards to complain about missing money from accounts, shut down of online services, shut down of ATMs, and very scanty services at the branches, if not completely shut down. The bank is working tirelessly to restore full services. And when the news came about the capture of the suspected hacker, Theophilus Anderson, alias Commotion, this served as a relief both for customers and the bank.

Deborah heard it on BBC News that Apex Bank was hacked, and that the suspected hacker Theophilus Anderson has been arrested. She has an account with the bank. She quickly checked her account and found out that all her money was gone. All the money she received from the Olympics, and proceeds from her promotions. Gone! This is devastating for her. All her hope is centred on the money. She has worked so hard for the money, and she's got plans to invest it in a business. She picks up her phone and rings Mary Jenkins to tell her.

"Hello Mary, I just found out all my money has disappeared from my Apex Bank account. Theophilus Anderson had allegedly hacked into the bank's financial system."

"Oh dear, I'm so sorry to hear this," she sympathized with her.

When she hung up her mobile phone, Mary Jenkins checked her Apex Bank account which is her major bank account, and she discovered all the three hundred thousand pounds (£300,000.00) savings she had was gone.

"Everything!" She said, "That's it! I'm as good as dead. Jesussssssss! Where are you to help me now? I can't bear the afflictions anymore," she started crying uncontrollably in her closet with no one to comfort her. After a while, the scripture below came to her remembrance. *Malachi 3:11-12* that says:

> [11]*And I will rebuke the devourer for your sakes, and he shall not destroy the fruits of your ground; neither shall your vine cast her fruit before the time in the field, saith the LORD of hosts.*
>
> [12] *And all nations shall call you blessed: for ye shall be a delightsome land, saith the LORD of hosts.*

She said in anguish, "This is devourer. I give my tithe faithfully, and I always give a good offering along with it. This should not happen to me, Lord. Why did you not rebuke the devourer for me, Lord? With all my savings gone, can all nations truly call me blessed? Help me Lord."

MANCHESTER CITY CROWN COURT – CROWN SQUARE.

Before a case is committed to the Crown Court, it is first referred by the Police to the Crown Prosecution Service (CPS) to determine whether the case should go to court or not. The CPS is satisfied this case should be committed to court, based on the substantial evidence the Police have provided. Only very serious criminal cases are referred to the Crown Court otherwise the case is dealt with in a Magistrate Court.

All is now set for the trial – The Judge, Prosecutor, Defence Lawyer, Court Clerk, Defendant, IT Expert, and twelve jury members. Everyone is seated in the right place in court and set. Everyone in the court stands up as the judge enters the courtroom.

JUDGE BILL SAUNDERS: Good morning court. Please sit down. Case number MA9900 is before me for a verdict today. I understand all parties are present in court and I would like us to proceed straightaway.

PROSECUTOR ANDREW BLAIR: There are seven charges against the defendant Theophilus Anderson, alias Commotion. They are as follows:

1. Suspicion of hacking into Apex Bank Limited, and stealing five hundred million pounds sterling (£500m).
2. Suspicion of releasing a malicious virus which caused serious damage to the Apex Bank Limited financial systems.
3. Illegal possession of two pistol guns.
4. Attempted to cause serious bodily harm to police officers on the 45th floor of Howard William tower block with a gun when he fired four bullets at them.
5. Illegal possession of seven thousand cloned debit and credit cards of Apex Bank Limited customers.
6. Illegal possession of five international passports.
7. Illegal possession of twenty documents belonging to different organisations including one from the Chancellor of the Exchequer's office.

The evidence was presented in court for everyone to see. Theophilus Anderson, alias Commotion who is now under oath, having been asked to swear to tell the truth and nothing but the truth by the Court Clerk was questioned by the Judge:

JUDGE BILL SAUNDERS: Do you plead guilty or not guilty to these charges?

THEOPHILUS ANDERSON: I'm not guilty at all my Lord.

DEFENCE LAWYER ARTHUR BOLTON: Firstly, my client is a British citizen, and his current address is 10 Consort Way, Manchester City, M14 3JR. The house at 5, Macaulay Drive, Kingston, Jamaica does not belong to him as well as all the items recovered from that address presented in this Court by the Prosecutor. He just went there to visit somebody, and was woken up and arrested at about 2 am while he was sleeping. Therefore, none of those items were actually found in his physical possession. *Secondly*, two ladies were found in the house with my client when he was arrested, which means the evidence recovered from that address could be theirs, and the prosecutor has not proved to this court that the items are not for the two ladies. *Thirdly*, it was the police who first fired gunshots at my client to cause him bodily harm, and he fired back in self-defence. I therefore submit to this Court that my client is not guilty of any of the alleged charges and should be acquitted.

IT EXPERT JULIA PHILLIPS: Having examined the recovered computer laptop and tablet, I found out substantial evidence of links between these two computers and the financial systems of Apex bank. For example, the programming on the laptop shows that the laptop is the source of the special software used to hack into the Apex bank accounts, as well as send the malicious virus that crippled the bank's system.

PROSECUTOR ANDREW BLAIR: Examines Theophilus Anderson by asking him a number of questions. One of the questions he asked him was, "Where is all the money stolen from Apex Bank?" Unfortunately, he didn't get any answer from the hardened criminal as he remained silent.

THE TWELVE MEMBERS OF THE JURY: After listening to the case, the charges, and seeing the evidence provided by the prosecutor, and the defence lawyer's statement, all twelve jury members unanimously agreed that Theophilus Anderson was guilty of all the charges. Jury members are chosen at random from the community to represent as a juror in court. Unfortunately for Theophilus Anderson, it turned out to be that five of these jury members were also Apex Bank customers whose money was also stolen. They desperately want to see Theophilus Anderson locked up for life. He had no chance with them. Meanwhile, Theophilus has refused to disclose where the £500 million pounds is, claiming he doesn't have a clue about what they are talking about. He didn't even admit in court that he stole the money in spite of the evidence. He has safely banked the money in foreign bank accounts in different names. He has bank accounts in Barcelona, Munich, Kingston, and other unknown international cities. Attempts to freeze his bank accounts at home and abroad were unsuccessful as he has cleverly banked all his money in different fictitious names. Delivering a verdict, the Judge stated as follows:

JUDGE BILL SAUNDERS: From the evidence provided in this court, Theophilus Anderson is indeed a criminal, and a thief that must not be allowed to walk about freely because in my opinion, he is a dangerous fellow, and should undergo rehabilitation. I therefore sentence him to one year in prison. We don't know where you kept your loot today in order for us to confiscate it, but when we find out in the future, you still have to pay back all the money.

He was immediately taken away by the prison officers and he showed no sign of remorse. Rather he was smiling. As soon as the verdict was passed, there was anger, rage, and crying from Apex Bank customers in court to hear the proceedings. Deborah and Mary Jenkins among others were present in court. Mary Jenkins drove to Manchester City with Deborah, not just for the court case, but also to see her parents whom she had not seen since Easter. And she saw them briefly before going back to London the same day. There was a real outburst of anger. People were absolutely disappointed and disgusted that Theophilus Anderson will only serve one year in prison, and he is not even returning the £500 million pounds now. Some Apex Bank customers are already outside the court chanting abuses and carrying placards. One reads: *"JUDGE B. SAUNDERS IS CRAZY."* Others read: *"SACK JUDGE B. SAUNDERS NOW. HE IS A JOKE,"* *"ROT IN JAIL T. ANDERSON,"* *"GO TO HELL COMMOTION,"* *"APEX BANK IS STILL LIABLE TO PAY US OUR MONEY."*

WHAT THE BIBLE SAYS ABOUT FRAUD

This is one of Pastor Moses Elijah's teaching on fraud. The Bible says in **Exodus 20:15**, *"Thou shalt not steal."* Theophilus Anderson has acted contrary to what the Word of God says here, and there is usually a penalty for disobedience, except for where His mercy prevails.

The Bible says again in **Jeremiah 17:11**, *"As the partridge sitteth on eggs, and hatcheth them not; so he that getteth riches, and not by right, shall leave them in the midst of his days, and at his end shall be a fool."* When something is written in the Bible, then it is authentic and certain to happen. The five hundred million pounds fraudulently acquired by Theophilus Anderson was riches not by right. Therefore, in line with this scripture, he is certainly going to leave all the money in the midst of his days and end up as a fool in life. That's what this scripture says. He may be smiling now, but somehow, the Word of God has a way of coming to pass.

The Bible says again in **Proverbs 13:11**, *"Wealth gotten by vanity shall be diminished: but he that gathereth by labour shall increase."* (NIV) puts it this way, *"Dishonest money dwindles away...,"* And Amplified Bible says, wealth gotten **unjustly** will dwindle away. This scripture guarantees the fact that all the five hundred million pounds Theophilus Anderson got fraudulently will certainly diminish or dwindle away. It's just a question of time, and it will happen.

Proverbs 23:5 says, *"Wilt thou set thine eyes upon that which is not? for riches certainly make themselves wings; they fly away as an eagle toward heaven."* It's better to trust God, and not in fraudulent riches because such riches have a tendency of making themselves wings, and flying away. Theophilus Anderson may think he is clever having banked his loot in different fictitious names and in different banks and international cities of the world, but the truth is that all that money is sure to mysteriously disappear and fly away as an eagle toward heaven. That's what this verse says, and it is authentic.

Galatians 6:7 says, *"Be not deceived; God is not mocked: for whatsoever a man soweth, that shall he also reap."* This scripture says, if somebody sows fraud, he will also reap fraud. When you defraud somebody, somebody else will also defraud you. Theophilus Anderson defrauded Apex Bank, somebody else will also defraud him. What goes around comes around.

Finally, *Isaiah 57:21* says, *"There is no peace, saith my God, to the wicked."* It's wickedness for Theophilus Anderson to cause Apex Bank and all her customers pain and sorrow. Therefore, he can't have peace. Anyone committing fraud must know that the judgement of God is always the ultimate.

In another development, the trial of Abdul Mohammed has just ended in the United States of America. He was found guilty by the jury of planting the explosive device on the American Airlines flight NY3351 that crashed into the Atlantic Ocean killing all one hundred and fifty people on board including Alan Brown. The Judge sentenced Abdul Mohammed to die by electrocution for the murder of those innocent souls. Upon interrogation before he died, he named two other suspects who the CIA are still searching for.

CHAPTER SIX

MARY JENKINS IS HEALED OF FIBROIDS AND HER MONEY RESTORED

The affliction Mary Jenkins is going through has undoubtedly stretched her beyond limits. The thought of the fibroids, breast cancer, no job, no boyfriend, and now all her savings are gone. All these are indeed overwhelming, and quite unbearable for her. All day, she's in pain. Mary Jenkins keeps wondering how and when she will be completely healed and eventually be free indeed from the terrible afflictions she is going through. She needs amazing grace in abundance to triumph.

Now that all her savings with Apex Bank are gone, and with very little money left in her United Bank account, she's thinking, "There is no way I can keep this house anymore." She's had the beautiful house for nine years since she obtained her MBA and got her first big job at Elohim Cars Limited, London. She immensely prospered financially with this company with a fat salary, commissions, and bonuses before she was recently made redundant. The fat income she was getting gave her the courage to get a house of that kind in a posh area, East Dulwich. But it looks like all that, sadly, is coming to an end. She didn't bother at all with signing up for Social Security benefits when she lost her job because her bank account was fully loaded with money, and she believed she would get another job very soon. But sadly, she is seriously considering contacting them to commence signing on.

It's indeed looking gloomy but some scriptures are again fired up in her spirit, and she is quickened. The Bible says in *1 Samuel 30:6*, "*And David was greatly distressed; for the people spake of stoning him, because the soul of all the people was grieved, every man for his sons and for his daughters: but David encouraged himself in the LORD his God."* She personalised the scripture saying, *".....And Mary Jenkins encouraged herself in the Lord her God."* Great! King David is her favourite character and mentor in the Bible. She told herself she would have to step up prayers, praise and worship, Bible study, and fasting, and stop all mourning. It's going to be a case of strictly looking unto Jesus the author and finisher of her faith. She's going to effectively avoid all distractions in her mind by thinking, speaking, and acting positively. It's a case of being fully focused on Jesus, spirit, soul, and body. **Proverbs 18:10** says, *"The name of the LORD is a strong tower: the righteous runneth into it, and is safe."*

She is already a member of the choir department of the Shekinah Pentecostal Church, but now she also wants to join the outreach department, with a special mission to minister to sick folks in the hospital since she doesn't have a job now. That's what Alan Brown used to do, and he enjoyed it so much going to the hospital on Saturdays to pray for sick patients and encourage them. And he shared with her testimonies of how people are healed after he prayed. Now, it is her turn to follow the footsteps of the man she adored.

Straightaway, she joined the outreach department, received training, and she headed immediately for the Shalom University Teaching Hospital (SUTH) smartly dressed, with her Bible, and some tracts and pamphlets from the church to give to patients free. Her target is to minister to a minimum of ten people in a day at least twice a week. Just after three visits, having seen over thirty patients, spending between five to ten minutes per patient maximum, she soon discovered that many of them don't even have any family or friends that visit them. So they are greatly encouraged when she comes around to pray and encourage them with scriptures. She looks forward to seeing them, and they look forward to seeing her. Her attention is now shifting from the seemingly overwhelming challenges she's facing to helping others. On one occasion she went to visit a female patient called Kimberley Elliott, fondly called KE, with breast cancer in her late forties. She has already undergone a mastectomy, without improvement, and the doctors have given her only one month to live. She believed the doctor's prognosis of just a month to live and is now counting down the days. Mary Jenkins met her and shared two scriptures with her. The scriptures are:

Jeremiah 30:17, "*For I will restore health unto thee, and I will heal thee of thy wounds, saith the* LORD; *because they called thee an outcast, saying, this is Zion, whom no man seeketh after.*"

Psalm 118:17, "*I shall not die, but live, and declare the works of the* LORD.*"

"Are you born again Sister Kimberley?" she asked her. "Yes, I am."

"Declare this with me powerfully: Lord Jesus, thank you because I'm healed by your stripes. Heavenly Father, I believe your Word that you will restore health to me, and heal me of every wound. Therefore, I declare I am free from every trace of cancer. Cancer, I curse you and I say die now in Jesus' name. I will not die but live to declare the works of the Lord on earth. I shall surely live beyond one month, and fulfil my days on earth in Jesus' name."

Mary Jenkins laid a hand on her forehead while she lay on her bed, and she immediately started manifesting, stretching out and evil spirits crying out with her eyes wide open and suddenly calmed down as if she was dead. Mary held her hand gently and gave her a Bible and asked her to keep reading the scriptures at least twice daily. And to the glory of God, doctors saw her the next day, and expressed shock that her poor health has improved tremendously, being able to eat, and move about, as she was bedbound before. And she lived far beyond the one-month doctors predicted for her to die. Hallelujah!

In order to increase the fire of her prayers, which is mainly focused on healing both for her and the hospital patient visits she will be making, she got out her concordance and compiled healing scriptures for daily prayers and ministrations. After compiling the scriptures, she printed them, and started sharing and giving them out to the patients.

HEALING SCRIPTURES

Isaiah 53:5

But he was wounded for our transgressions, he was bruised for our iniquities: the chastisement of our peace was upon him; and with his stripes we are healed.

Jeremiah 17:14

Heal me, O LORD, and I shall be healed; save me, and I shall be saved: for thou art my praise.

Psalm 147:3

He healeth the broken in heart, and bindeth up their wounds.

Jeremiah 30:17

For I will restore health unto thee, and I will heal thee of thy wounds, saith the LORD; because they called thee an outcast, saying, this is Zion, whom no man seeketh after.

Matthew 4:23

And Jesus went about all Galilee, teaching in their synagogues, and preaching the gospel of the kingdom, and healing all manner of sickness and all manner of disease among the people.

Exodus 15:26

And said, If thou wilt diligently hearken to the voice of the LORD thy God, and wilt do that which is right in his sight, and wilt give ear to his commandments, and keep all his statutes, I will put none of these diseases upon thee, which I have brought upon the Egyptians: for I am the LORD that healeth thee.

Psalm 107:20

He sent his word, and healed them, and delivered them from their destructions.

Jeremiah 8:21–22

²¹For the hurt of the daughter of my people am I hurt; I am black; astonishment hath taken hold on me.

²²Is there no balm in Gilead; is there no physician there? why then is not the health of the daughter of my people recovered?

1 Peter 2:24

Who his own self bare our sins in his own body on the tree, that we, being dead to sins, should live unto righteousness: by whose stripes ye were healed.

Mark 6:13

And they cast out many devils, and anointed with oil many that were sick, and healed them.

Acts 19:11–12

¹¹ And God wrought special miracles by the hands of Paul:

¹² So that from his body were brought unto the sick handkerchiefs or aprons, and the diseases departed from them, and the evil spirits went out of them.

Isaiah 10:27

And it shall come to pass in that day, that his burden shall be taken away from off thy shoulder, and his yoke from off thy neck, and the yoke shall be destroyed because of the anointing.

Isaiah 33:24

And the inhabitant shall not say, I am sick: the people that dwell therein shall be forgiven their iniquity.

Joel 3:10

Beat your ploughshares into swords, and your pruning hooks into spears: let the weak say, I am strong.

3 John 1:2

> *Beloved, I wish above all things that thou mayest prosper and be in health, even as thy soul prospereth.*

Psalm 107:2

> *Let the redeemed of the LORD say so, whom he hath redeemed from the hand of the enemy;*

John 8:36
If the Son therefore shall make you free, ye shall be free indeed.

It's Friday morning and she receives a letter from Dr. Joseph Moore informing her she will be having a surgery to remove the fibroids next week on Monday. The letter gave details of the things she has to get ready. She was not even scared, or moved like before. She just remained calm while the peace of God within filled her up to overflowing. The Holy Ghost is at work. God always moves ahead of the devil.

She picks up her mobile telephone and calls her father, Chief Police Superintendent Paul Jenkins to inform him of the contents of the letter, and to request for special prayers. It's a video call. The phone rings, "Hello Daddy"

"How are you darling?"

"Dad, I just got a letter from Dr. Joseph Moore telling me I will be in for the surgery to get rid of the fibroids on Monday."

"Alright darling. Just last night I had a dream and I saw you rejoicing and jubilant that you were healed from fibroids. I woke up from the dream and I thanked God so much because it's indeed a good thing to see you healed. My dreams always come to pass. So I believe this will certainly come to pass that you are healed. And now you called me."

"I believe in your dream Daddy."

"Cheer up then. Just remain confident, and put all your trust in the Lord that the surgery shall surely be a success. I am praying for you. I love you sweetheart."

"I love you too Daddy."

After she hung up, he became so emotional and started sobbing and tears started flowing down his face. He couldn't hold it back, in spite of the fact that he was on duty in his office. She is his only daughter, and he loves her dearly. A knock on the door by one of the officers got him to immediately wipe the tears completely dry. "Yes, come in."

"Sir, I just want to let you know Commander Emmanuel Hughes called earlier on from London, and he says you should ring him back immediately."

"Thanks. I will do that right away."

There will be a special evening service that day from 6 pm to 9 pm called, "Praise and worship night." She immediately got ready and went to church full of expectation, believing in the miraculous move of God to touch her and heal her. Pastor Susan Edwards and the choir team got on stage to lead the congregation in a solid two hours of praise and worship. The instruments, singing, and clapping started and reached a crescendo and the whole auditorium seemed to be filled with cloud.

2 Chronicles 5:13–14 says:

> [13]*It came even to pass, as the trumpeters and singers were as one, to make one sound to be heard in praising and thanking the* LORD; *and when they lifted up their voice with the trumpets and cymbals and instruments of musick, and praised the* LORD, *saying, for he is good; for his mercy endureth for ever: that then the house was filled with a cloud, even the house of the* LORD;

> [14]*So that the priests could not stand to minister by reason of the cloud: for the glory of the* LORD *had filled the house of God.*

Evil spirits were crying out and loads of people were slain under the anointing. The anointing was so strong to the extent that Deborah's brother, James, who had once boasted that he will never fall down under the anointing fell down and slept for about half an hour on the floor without realising it. The superman fell down that day.

As Pastor Susan Edwards continued to minister, a word of knowledge came forth from her by the inspiration of the Holy Ghost as follows: "God is performing divine surgery on a woman right now, to heal her of fibroids. Receive your healing right now in Jesus' name."

When Mary Jenkins heard that, she quickly keyed in and screamed out loud, "I receive my total healing from fibroids right now in Jesus' name!" And she fell down violently to the floor so much that two ushers quickly came to her and covered her partly exposed spotless, attractive smooth skin with a cloth. Bishop John Barnes was not in the house that night to minister because he travelled to New Delhi, India to minister on a crusade. Hence, Pastor Moses Elijah got behind the pulpit as soon as Pastor Susan Edwards exited, and he called more fire from heaven as he led the congregation to pray in *tongues* for a solid half hour. Whao! Shekinah Pentecostal Church was on fire as the Holy Ghost's consuming fire descended more and began to consume everything not of God from the lives of the people of God. Glory! He also led more prayers in *understanding* for another fifteen minutes on health, finance, marriage, career, and general welfare of the people. And after collection of the tithes and offerings, he came back to the podium and delivered the closing prayers and at exactly 9 pm the meeting was closed.

Below is a teaching given a while ago by Pastor Moses Elijah on the benefits of praying in tongues.

BENEFITS OF PRAYING IN TONGUES

As a Christian who truly desire to keep growing, and keep doing exploits, then praying or speaking in the language of the Holy Ghost is necessary.

Let's look at some of the benefits of praying in tongues.

1. When you pray in tongues, you can pray for a longer period of time. You will be able to have a good prayer exercise.
2. When you pray in tongues, you are communicating with God, and not men. See 1 Corinthians 14:2.

3. When you pray in tongues, you are edifying yourself. To edify is to teach yourself in a way that will improve your mind or character. See 1 Corinthians 14:4 & 26.
4. When you pray in tongues, you are speaking mysteries, and unknowingly praying for things you are not even aware of. Mystery language unveils mysterious things. 1 Corinthians 14:2.
5. Praying or speaking in tongues will profit you more when you are able to interpret. Therefore, desire to also interpret the tongues you speak. See 1 Corinthians 14:13&27. When you interpret your tongues, you will have understanding of what God is saying, and what to do.
6. When I pray in an unknown tongues my spirit prayeth, but my understanding is unfruitful. Praying in tongues will launch you into the spiritual realm. Hallelujah! See 1 Corinthians 14:14.
7. To pray in tongues will build you up in the most holy faith. You will be charged up like a battery. *Jude 1:20* says, *"But ye, beloved, building up yourselves on your most holy faith, praying in the Holy Ghost,"*
8. To pray in tongues will strengthen you with might.

Ephesians 3:16
That he would grant you, according to the riches of his glory, to be strengthened with might by his Spirit in the inner man;

Ephesians 6:18
Praying always with all prayer and supplication in the Spirit, and watching thereunto with all perseverance and supplication for all saints;

9. Praying or speaking in tongues is a heavenly language that confuses and destroys the works of the devil.
10. To pray in tongues will help sharpen you, and cause you to be filled with the Holy Ghost.

Ephesians 5:18-19
[18]And be not drunk with wine, wherein is excess; but be filled with the Spirit;

¹⁹Speaking to yourselves in psalms and hymns and spiritual songs, singing and making melody in your heart to the Lord;

11. To pray in tongues is further proof that you are indeed born again.

   Acts 19:2 & 6:
   ²He said unto them, have ye received the Holy Ghost since ye believed? And they said unto him, we have not so much as heard whether there be any Holy Ghost...

   ⁶And when Paul had laid his hands upon them, the Holy Ghost came on them; and they spake with tongues, and prophesied.

What a great lesson for some Christians who because of immaturity, would only come to church when the Senior Pastor or Founder is around. For your information, it is God you are coming to church to meet and for His Word, and not any man. Bishop John Barnes was not around, yet the church was packed full, and the Holy Spirit still manifested in full measure like when the Bishop was around. That is God for you. Don't despise anybody because God will use the foolish and despised things of this world to confound the wise and mighty. Take every service serious in your local church because Sunday is not the only day you will find the presence of God in church. That was a Friday service, and great testimonies abounded from the meeting.

It's 6 am Monday morning. Mary Jenkins woke up and did her morning devotion which lasted one and a half hours. She prepared her bag, ticking off one by one all the items on her list to ensure nothing was missed out. She drove off to the SUT Hospital for the surgery. She had already had a pre-surgery assessment which confirmed she was alright to have the surgery. On getting there, she went to the reception for a brief registration. All the while, her heart has been at peace and calm. Dr. Joseph Moore and two other medical consultants were there. One of the Medical Consultants suggested one more check before she would be wheeled away in a trolley into the operating theatre for the surgery. As she moved into the special *Computerised Tomography*

(CT) Scan machine, which uses x-rays to operate, the indicator showed there were no fibroids anywhere in or around her uterus. A second check revealed the same result. (*Magnetic Resonance Imaging (MRI) Scan* is an alternative test, and it uses radio waves to function.)

"Incredible! I find this embarrassing you know. Maybe this scanning equipment is faulty. Let's take her to another scanning machine for another check," declared Dr. Joseph Moore as he spoke to the two consultants. Upon checking her on another scanning machine, they found out that there was no trace of any fibroids in her body. Miracle! They asked her to get dressed and go home because she won't be having any surgery. It's a mystery to the doctors, but she knew what happened to her in Church on Friday, and the dream her father had. She immediately got up and started rejoicing in jubilation for real. There was no point telling the doctors because they may not understand unless they are believers. All they know is medical science and physical surgery, and not divine surgery like this. Doctors care for you but only God heals.

The Bible says in **Psalm 107:20**, "*He sent his word, and healed them, and delivered them from their destructions.*" The word of knowledge spoken by the servant of the Most High God, Susan Edwards, and wholeheartedly received by Mary Jenkins has effectively destroyed the monstrous fibroids and healed her. This goes to show that the Word of God carries anointing, and power to perform divine surgery to heal. The Word of God heals when you receive it by faith. I prophesy to you as you read this book that the power of God will also be made tremendously available to you to heal you as you open your heart to receive the Word of God by faith in Jesus' name. Amen!

She immediately got on the phone to the dad, "Daaaaad!"

"Yes, my love," answered the dad. "Your dream has come to pass. I had no surgery today because the fibroids have been removed supernaturally by Doctor Jesus."

"Whao! This is excellent news, and my soul is indeed filled with joy."

She then shared her last Friday experience in church with her dad and ended the call. She also rang her mum almost immediately to share the testimony.

What a good God we serve! She didn't even have to see Bishop John Barnes as she intended before the surgery and the Most High God still healed her of the fibroids miraculously. She burst into tongues, singing and praising God, and thanking Him for the healing miracle.

"Lord, I thank you for healing me completely of fibroids. I praise and honour you Jehovah for this great deliverance you have wrought in my life, for putting the devil to shame and delivering me from fibroids pain, and reproach." She put on her praise and worship music and started dancing all to the glory of God.

After a while, she sat down and began to think about what she has to do regarding her accommodation. She doesn't have much money left in her United Bank account anymore.

"I have to sell this three-bedroom mortgaged house now, and downsize," she reflected. While she was pondering on this her phone rang, and it was Deborah on the line.

"Whao! It's good to have you on the line. I have just been cleared of fibroids. Jesus healed me supernaturally. I didn't have the surgery after all. The doctors found out from a last-minute scan check that the evil monstrous fibroids had disappeared, and I am free and free indeed to the glory of God."

Deborah answered saying, "This is great testimony. I am very happy for you. I have some other great news for you my dear"

"Go on and share it darling. I'm all ears."

"It's been on the BBC News since this morning that Apex Bank Limited has restored back the money of all the customers whose accounts were hacked by that bloke Theophilus Anderson, alias Commotion. I have checked my account and all my money has been fully paid back."

"Really?"

"Yeah!"

"Praaaaaaise God!" She began to sing the song, *The Lord has given me victory.* They began to sing the song, *What a mighty God we serve* together.

As she sang, she was also dancing. They both rejoiced over the phone, until they ended the phone call. And straightaway she logged online and found out that Apex Bank online services are up and running again after the malicious virus crippled their online services. And she found out that all her money had been fully paid back. That is a double miracle and victory for her. She felt like somebody who's just won a lottery jackpot. She is highly delighted and began to thank, praise, and worship the Lord with a loud voice, uncontrollably all night long. It's been a long time since she praised God like this. She flowed so easily in the anointing, and she could feel the strong presence of God filling her and the whole house. Amazing grace is in abundance to praise and worship God.

These are some of the songs she played as she sang and danced. Don Moen – Celebrate Jesus; Sinach – Way Maker; Matt Redman – 10,000 Reasons (Bless The Lord); VaShawn Mitchell ft. Bebe Winans, Tasha Cobbs - Nobody Greater; William McDowell – I Give Myself Away; Donnie McClurkin – Only You Are Holy & Agnus Dei; and Eben – Victory. She was filled with the joy of the Lord after the praise and worship. Awesome!

CHAPTER SEVEN

PRISCILLA JENKINS' WEDDING

The next morning, she woke up feeling so strong. After her morning devotion and shower, she decided to give herself a treat by having a full English breakfast consisting of bacon, mushrooms, sausage, egg, tomatoes, beans, toast, with tea to flush it down. After the delicious breakfast, she immediately became drowsy while seated on the sofa watching television. She rested for a good while, and then got dressed and set off to the hospital to go and start ministering to the patients there.

Autumn is gradually coming to an end, and also paving way for the chilly freezing weather of the winter months to commence. December is fast approaching and her cousin, Priscilla Jenkins' wedding is drawing near. They have not spoken for a while now.

"I need to call her to find out how she is doing, as well as Barry Evans her fiancé," she thought. Mary grabbed her mobile and made the call. As she got through she said, "Prisco! Prisco!! How are you doing?"

"Ah! Longest time, *Hotdog!*"

"Hey! Don't start again with that nickname."

"What are you going to do to me? Chill! Hooooooootdog!"

They both burst into loud laughter remembering their childhood days. They used to play together with toys, ride bicycles together, play in the park together, and went to Primary and Secondary School together. They were inseparable, and some thought they were twins as they look alike a bit, and are just three months apart in age, while Priscilla is senior. Priscilla is the daughter of Chief Superintendent Paul Jenkins' elder brother, Thompson Jenkins.

Mary Jenkins was given the nickname 'Hotdog' because she used to like hotdogs a lot. *They both go down memory lane and*

remembered their silly adventure in the city of Liverpool when
they were both seventeen years old after their secondary education.
It was a hot summer day, and both of them caught a coach just for
three quid each and headed for Liverpool to hook up with two
teenage boys who had been professing their love for them for a
while in London. They put on torn jeans, T-shirts partly exposing
their breasts, baseball hats, with conspicuous make-up, and dark
glasses. They didn't tell anyone their destination. They turned
their phones off so that no one could reach them.

As soon as they arrived in Liverpool they headed straight for
"The Wheelers Pub," established 1850, their meeting point.
Everywhere was filled with the smoke of tobacco, like a chimney,
so much that you can hardly see people. The walls and top of the
Public House have all turned black because of the smoke. The
music was on a full blast, so much that you had to shout for
the person next to you to hear what you said. They went to the
barman and lied, saying they were over 18 years old and ordered
Budweiser beer, and *Benson & Hedges* cigarettes, and started
puffing and drinking while they waited for their dates to show up.
Unknown to them, Police Inspector Andrew Reynolds was in the
pub. He spotted them and recognised them. Seeing the way they
were dressed, drinking, and smoking he approached them and
asked, "What are you two doing in Liverpool City?" They were
speechless because they didn't expect him to be there.

They stammered together, "To to to to see our friends."

From that answer alone, and their stern countenance, he
knew they were lying and that they were up to some mischief.
They tried to be rude by saying, "Leave us alone and mind your
own business." But he stamped his authority over them and
subdued them. Straightaway, he ordered them to board the next
available coach back to London. They were visibly shaken as they
made their way straight back to the coach station and back to
London without seeing the two teenage boys. Police Inspector
Andrew Reynolds was a colleague of Chief Superintendent Paul
Jenkins at that time. He had attended Mary's fifteenth birthday
party just a couple of years earlier and met her and Priscilla. That
was how he recognised them. Before they got to London, Andrew

Reynolds had already phoned their parents to tell them what happened. They thanked him, and expressed great shock at the girl's stinking behaviour. The parents told them off seriously when they finally got home. That was the first and the last time they ever embarked on such an escapade. What a day of madness for well-brought-up children!

A woman can actually dress in the attire of a harlot, and such women are loud and stubborn. *Proverbs 7:10-11* confirms this saying:

> [10] *And, behold, there met him a woman with the attire of an harlot, and subtle of heart.*

> [11] *She is loud and stubborn; her feet abide not in her house:*

The Bible says again in *Proverbs 9:13*, *"A foolish woman is clamorous: she is simple, and knoweth nothing."* *The Living Bible* puts it this way, *"A prostitute is loud and brash and never has enough of lust and shame."* It's a shame that two teenage girls had to dress seductively, and leave home without taking permission from their parents, and go wild in a binge drinking and puffing on cigarettes, while waiting to hook up with their dates. That, kind of portrays the lifestyle of a prostitute – Loud and brash in dressing, words, and attitude! This is not the lifestyle of a born-again Christian. *1 Corinthians 14:40* says, *"Let all things be done decently and in order."*

They carried on with their conversation after that momentary recollection of the past.

MARY: How are you preparing for the wedding?

PRISCILLA: I'm fine my dear. I was going to call you earlier to tell you I would like you to be my Chief Bridesmaid.

MARY: Meeeeeee!

PRISCILLA: Yes Oh!

MARY: Alright oh! You know I can't say no. How's Barry Evans your fiancé?

PRISCILLA: He's there oh. Just a fortnight ago, he came to see me. While he slept, I grabbed his mobile phone, and rummaged it. I made some awful discoveries in his WhatsApp communication with a lady called Anna Murray. I saw several romantic pictures of both of them kissing, holding each other, and erotic communication. I was saddened by what I saw. I challenged him, but he was angry that I secretly checked his phone. He denied having anything serious with the lady. I almost called it quits with him. And then I thought about the ten-year courtship. To pack it up and start afresh with another man was something I couldn't even think of. I guess I have to put up with him. All men are the same anyway.

MARY: I thought Barry claims to be a born-again Christian. This is not looking good at all. Have you prayed about him again? And have you told your Pastor to pray about him? I think it's still better to get it right before you tie the knot with him. What you just told me is a bad sign that needs to be dealt with, except you think you can bear the pain of sharing him with Anna Murray.

PRISCILLA: My greatest problem now is where can I find another man as good as him if I decide to kick him out? You know he's been good to me especially in the area of financial support. And one is not getting any younger anymore.

MARY: Well, hand over the matter to God in prayers to help you. I will also support you in prayers.

PRISCILLA: Thanks. I really need your support in prayers.

MARY: It's important to note that generally, some people don't change for good, but they tend to manifest in a greater measure what they really are. For example, someone who cheats in a relationship may not stop, but will rather cheat more because cheating in a relationship is inherent in them. Again, whatever people manifest during courtship, they are likely to also display in marriage. Perhaps the best thing to do is to terminate any relationship which is against your core values during courtship. But there is again the danger of some people pretending to be nice during courtship, and subsequently revealing their true evil self after marriage. They had an ulterior motive during courtship. The main question to ask here is, is any person perfect for marriage? Everyone comes into marriage with their baggage, and as work in progress to be worked upon, and over time, they may become perfect if there is anything like that. The safest thing to do before marriage is to ask for God's direction and guidance as you hook up with a life partner. Does that guarantee there will be no challenges in the marriage? No! In Genesis 24, Isaac married Rebekah, and there was God's leading regarding the divine connection between the pair. In Genesis 25:19–26, we see that Isaac was forty years old when he married Rebekah, but they did not give birth to Esau and Jacob until he was sixty years old because Rebekah was barren. That's a big challenge, to marry without children for twenty years. How many Christians can be patient for that long in this generation without calling it a day? And mind you, God's leading was in the marriage. Anyway, I have to go now.

PRISCILLA: Thanks a lot for your wise counsel. Bye love.

It's Saturday morning, and she decided to go down to the Classic Food Store to pick up a few groceries. She likes her salads and food very fresh. Hence, she shops for groceries frequently to avoid the food spoiling. She quickly made her list to avoid forgetting anything, and she got into her Lexus car and drove off. She got there and went straight to pick up cereals, fruits, vegetables, chicken, fish, spices, snacks, and drinks.

Driving back home, her mind picked up the breast cancer challenge she's going through. The lump is still there on her left breast and gradually enlarging, so she has been taking her medication according to the doctor's prescription. She has heard of aggressive malignant cancerous cells which have the ability to spread so fast and invade a person's body uncontrollably in a very short time. The fear of that happening made her mind blank out and she swerved on the road, which was narrow due to road parking. In a twinkle of an eye she hit the kerb of the road and suddenly came back to her senses again. She applied the brakes and brought the car to a standstill. Fortunately, there was no other car involved, no pedestrian, and her car was still in perfect condition. She was only doing 20 miles per hour in the residential area of Brooks Estate, on Harrison Road, Peckham with her seat belt well fastened, so she had no whiplash.

As soon as she brought the car to rest, she came down and looked around the car. There was no damage. A fully bearded Caribbean bloke with long dreadlocks stretching down to his shoulders and beyond who saw what happened approached her and said, "Hey, woman, I hope you're alright? Were you sleeping on the steering or drunk to let that happen? You've got to give Jah the praise it was not worse than that, and be careful."

She replied, "I'm alright. Thanks."

With mixed feeling of shame, fear, and gratitude that it was not worse than that, she got back into the car and made a short prayer with thanksgiving. "Lord, I thank you for your love and kindness, not allowing this incident to be worse than this. I am grateful for your protection. Help my mind from not dwelling on this breast cancer anymore in Jesus' name, I pray. Amen!"

After praying, she drove away. She has taken this to be a warning to concentrate and be fully focused spirit, soul, and body while driving. The Bible says in *Proverbs 4:23,* "*Keep thy heart with all diligence; for out of it are the issues of life.*" We need to constantly guard our hearts from being polluted by negative thoughts, worries, and fear. *2 Timothy 1:7* says, "*For God hath not given us the spirit of fear; but of power, and of love, and of a sound mind.*" Fear crumbles people, and interestingly, most things we fear never get to happen. It's just the devil bombarding the mind with false evidence appearing real (FEAR). The devil is a liar. Be in faith through the Word of God and fear will flee.

When she got home, she discovered her mail had been delivered, and behold, one of the letters was from Dr. Joseph Moore explaining to her that there had been a long queue of women waiting for breast cancer surgery. That's why there has been a delay in contacting her with a surgery date. However, she will be having a surgery to remove the lump from her breast in six weeks' time. She will be contacted again before the surgery. She had a sigh of relief after reading the letter, and said, "Lord, over to you. You healed me from fibroids, heal me from this breast cancer supernaturally and take all the glory as you perfect all that concerns me in Jesus' name."

She got online and sent her curriculum vitae to five companies whose advertisements for the position of Senior Marketing Officer she had seen, and she also completed an application form for the vacant position of a Marketing Manager she had seen responsible for the marketing of building materials in North London. The salary and fringe benefits were alright, but the job will involve much travelling, and supervision of staff. She sends off the application for the job online.

Mary got dressed and headed for the hospital to minister to patients. Her target is to minister to a minimum of ten patients. As she got to the John Atkinson male ward, she saw one of her former students while she was at Oxford University and recognised him straightaway. His name is Dominic Lloyds. He was in the department of Business Administration, while she was in the Marketing department in the same faculty. He belongs to two cult groups and claims to be an atheist. He used to make a mockery of Christian fellowship groups on campus then and that's how he caught her attention. Loads of people have preached to him to accept Jesus as his Lord and Saviour, but he snubbed all attempts to do this.

MARY JENKINS: Hello Dominic, how are you? It's been a very long time. I recognised you immediately I saw you.

DOMINIC LLOYDS: I'm not too good. I still recognise your face, but I have forgotten your name. I remember you were at Oxford.

MARY JENKINS: I'm Mary Jenkins. I was in the Marketing department.

DOMINIC LLOYDS: Oh yes! That's it! I remember now. What are you doing here?

MARY JENKINS: I'm here to minister to sick patients. Pray and encourage them in the Word, and get them to receive salvation if they are not born again. What brought you here?

DOMINIC LLOYDS: I'm ashamed to tell my story, but I have to open up and tell you because I definitely need you to pray for me.

I'm facing a desperate situation of near death. As I'm talking to you now, I have had an unstoppable erection for the past three days. I slept with a Caribbean lady I met in a nightclub here in London, but did not make good my promise to her in full, and she inflicted me with voodoo, and since then, I've had a continuous erection. The doctor who is going to perform the surgery has told me I may be impotent afterwards if the surgery does not go well, and that is scaring me to death. Please pray to God to have mercy on me and heal me.

MARY JENKINS: "Oh dear! I really sympathise with you. I will pray for you now." She found it hard to believe that a cultist atheist like Dominic is now asking for prayers from her. Surprising! The situation must be really desperate for him. She laid her hands on his forehead, and being filled with Holy Ghost power, she burst into heavy tongues until he began to manifest and evil spirits started to cry out while on his hospital bed, and she intensified her prayer in tongues, and as this happened he felt the tremendous power of God and his erection immediately began to shrink and became normal. "Father, thank you because by your mercy and your stripes, your son is receiving his healing right now. Holy Spirit, touch him and heal him from this erection challenge and make him whole in Jesus' name."

DOMINIC LLOYDS: Ameeeeeeeeeeen! The erection came down while you were praying for me. I am healed. Oh my God! This is a miracle. Thank you, Jesus.

MARY JENKINS: Thank God for the miracle. Are you ready to accept Jesus now as your personal Lord and Saviour?

DOMINIC LLOYDS: Of course yes! I'm very ready.

MARY JENKINS: Please say after me, 'I believe in my heart that God raised Jesus from the dead, and I confess now with my mouth that henceforth, Jesus is my personal Lord and Saviour forever. I renounce every other god in my life now. Lord Jesus, I ask that you forgive me of all my sins as I repent right now in Jesus' name. Amen!' I am inviting you to Shekinah Pentecostal Church where

I worship. This bulletin gives you details of our opening times and activities. You can also log in online and find out more about the church. This Bible and tract is for you. Have a blessed day.

DOMINIC LLOYDS: Thank you very much for the prayers and everything. Very much appreciated. I will surely be there on Sunday.

Dominic Lloyds is now a Chartered Accountant and has his own firm. He is married to Heather Lloyds. He is a habitual womaniser with many girlfriends. His wife Heather has given up on this matter after so many bust-ups with him. She keeps praying she doesn't contract a disease from him, and that one day he will give his life to Jesus. He kept this erection ordeal secret from her, but he has made up his mind to share the testimony with her, and never to commit adultery again. When people claim to be atheists, do they really mean it? When they face a serious problem they cry out for help from God. The Bible says in *John 4:48*, *"Then said Jesus unto him, except ye see signs and wonders, ye will not believe."* Dominic experienced a miracle and gave his life to Jesus. Praise God!

The Doctor came in to find that Dominic's erection has gone down and normalised after examining him.

"What happened?" He asked.

"A Christian lady I knew when I was at University came here and prayed for me, and the erection came down and my penis became normal again to the glory of God."

The Doctor said, "That's a miracle! Anyway, I will have to discharge you now."

Dominic arrived home and shared the testimony with his wife, who was absolutely delighted that at last, he has given his life to Jesus.

It's about 4 pm and Mary decided to take a walk down the road and to a nearby park just to receive some fresh air, and stretch her legs, and connect to nature in the park. She dressed up casually, pulled her hair together properly, and stepped out just walking steadily along the road as the light wind blew pleasantly and cars drove past. She reached the park and walked round it while appreciating the plants and flowers, and the birds flying about. She sat down on one of the benches and started watching children playing in the park as well as some dogs. The whole atmosphere was indeed refreshing as she breathed fresh air, not polluted with car fumes. She can also smell the freshness of the plants. After half an hour the weather started getting a bit nippy, so she decided to start walking back home when her mobile phone rang. A female voice came through saying, "Hello, is that Mary Jenkins?"

"Speaking," she replied.

"This is Jennifer Rhodes, and I'm calling from the Quick Move Employment Agency. I saw your CV online, and your profile matches what we are looking for. Would you be interested in a Marketing Manager's position in Birmingham?"

She replies, "Sorry, I am based in London and I wouldn't like to relocate to Birmingham. Thanks for the offer."

"Bye," replied Jennifer, and they both ended the call. She is so connected to the headquarters of Shekinah Pentecostal Church in London that she would not like to relocate to another city now for any reason whatsoever, even if they were going to pay her twice her old salary. Her spiritual life means a lot to her. Besides, she is fully established in London in other areas.

December is finally here with its chilly cold and London and most parts of Britain are already experiencing a heavy fall of snow and at times it gets really foggy. Meteorologists are forecasting a white Christmas. She is also gradually getting ready for Priscilla's wedding as she is going to be the chief bridesmaid. Mary has already got her dress ready from Magnificent Superstore. Her parents and the entire Jenkins' and Evans' family and friends are sure to attend to grace the occasion. The wedding is taking place in Edinburgh on Christmas Day, which happens to be Barry Evans' birthday. So it's going to be a double celebration. She has decided not to drive because of the long distance and bad weather due to frost and snow, which is likely to result in slippery roads. She goes online and books a return flight ticket, plus five days' hotel accommodation in the 5-star Hilton Palace Hotel, Edinburgh from the 22nd to 26th December. This will give her enough time to assist her cousin with preparations before the wedding as well as time for them to chat as they have not seen each other for a long while.

She rings up her parents and tells them of her plans to be at the wedding. They also confirm they will be there. She rings her cousin, Priscilla and informs her she will be coming to Edinburgh on the 22nd of December to stay in the 5-star Hilton Palace Hotel.

The 22nd December arrives and all her clothing has been properly packed so she calls a cab to take her to Stansted Airport from where she will take off to Edinburgh. The weather is bad as predicted. The temperature has gone down into the negatives, below freezing point with frost on the roads. The cab driver arrives and they set off. From the man's appearance and accent, she can tell he is from Somalia.

"Do you like this job you do as a cab driver?"

"Not really. To be able to make a bit more money, I have to put in so many hours. There are a lot of expenses to take care of to remain in this business. I just like the flexibility, and the fact that I am my own boss." He laughs. "What do you do ma?"

"At the moment, I'm unemployed. However, I used to work for Elohim Cars Limited as a Senior Marketing officer."

"Ah! I know the company."

"I'm not surprised you do because you taxi drivers know everywhere," they both laughed.

"What religion are you sir?"

"I'm a Muslim, but I have a strong desire to become a Christian."

"Why do you want to change your religion?"

"Simply because I'm embarrassed how Muslims are associated with violence and terrorist attacks."

Immediately he said that, the painful memories of Alan's death awaked within her, and her belly rumbled, and tears rolled down her cheek, which she wiped off with her handkerchief.

"Have you heard of Shekinah Pentecostal Church?"

The driver replied, "Yes of course. Bishop John Barnes is the leader, and a lot of miracles happen there."

"That's right. That's the Church I attend, and I would like to invite you to come and worship with us one Sunday. This is our bulletin and our opening times and our activities are all in there."

He pulled up and parked the car. She paid and gave him additional five pounds tip.

He says, "Thank you very much for the tip ma."

"Oh! Please don't mention it. You know you can give your life to Jesus now. Are you ready to do that?"

"Yes ma."

She leads him with the confession to be born again and said, "Congratulations! You are now a born-again Christian. See you in Church soon."

"Thank you and safe journey with your flight."

She goes ahead and checked in her luggage and boarded her flight to Edinburgh.

Mary boarded the plane and fastened her seat belt, and they took off and quite soon landed smoothly in Edinburgh in spite of the terrible weather. As soon as she came out of the arrivals area, Priscilla and Barry were there waiting to pick her up. Immediately they set eyes on each other, there was wild excitement as she shouts out, "Priscoooooh!" Full of smiles and laughter she replies, "Hooooooootdog!" They embraced one another so tight exchanging pecks, and gazing at each other with great admiration as Barry Evans looks on in a seemingly ignored mood.

Mary and Priscilla gently disengaged from embracing each other, and she turned to Barry and embraced him while he gave her a peck on both of her cheeks and said, "It's good to see you Mary. I hope you had a nice flight?"

She answered, "Yes I did. How are you two doing?"

They both answered, "Great!"

Barry took Mary's luggage and started moving in the direction of the car park while the two excited cousins followed behind still holding hands and chatting while people at the airport looked at them in a manner suggesting they may be lesbians. They all got into the car and Barry drove off straight to the 5-star Hilton Palace Hotel.

As soon as they got to the hotel, she registered at the reception desk and checked into her room.

"Whao! It's beautiful in here." They all commented almost simultaneously.

After a few minutes, the happy couple signified they were going back home, which is just a stone's throw from the hotel. "What would you like to have for dinner Mary darling? Let me go and get it ready so that you can come over and eat after you have showered and settled down."

Mary said, "Prisco sweetheart, you know my favourite food." And Priscilla jokingly asked "Hotdog?"

They both started laughing again, and Mary said, "Roast potatoes, mixed vegetables, roasted chicken, gravy, and seafood salad will be absolutely fine."

"That's alright, just come over as soon as you are done with your shower and settling down."

They both embraced one another very tight again and exchanged pecks before the couple headed for the door and left.

When they left, Mary started praying in tongues, banishing every spirit not of God out of her hotel room, and pleading the blood of Jesus on all items. She laid hands on the bed, and pillows, and cast out by faith every spirit of immorality, and sexual perversion that may be there, and sanctified them in the name of Jesus. She got out her anointing oil and anointed the bed, pillows, wardrobe, and entrance door. The human traffic in a hotel room is high, and people can come in and leave behind their spirits which may be evil and can possibly be contracted if this kind of exercise is not performed to take authority over such evil spirits. Satan is a spirit and it can enter a person. The Bible says in **Luke 22:3**, *"Then entered Satan into Judas surnamed Iscariot, being of the number of the twelve."*

Looking round at the hotel room decoration and the amenities provided, she had a feeling of satisfaction that she is having good value for the money she paid. She immediately unpacked her shoes and clothes and hanged them in the wardrobe, and went straight into the bathroom for a shower. As she got close to the mirror, she viewed her left breast comparing the size with the right one. She felt the lump on the left breast and said, "Lord, have mercy on me and heal me in Jesus' name." She quickly had her shower and dressed up and dashed out to see Barry and Priscilla, just a stone's throw away.

She got there and went straight for the doorbell, and Barry was there to open the door for her. "Whao! You are looking absolutely beautiful." He declared as he reached for her and wrapped his arms round her upper frame and gave her a peck while he breathed in the pleasant welcoming *Fahrenheit* perfume she wore.

She says, "Thanks Barry."

He replied, "You are welcome."

Mary started walking towards the kitchen as she says in a loud voice, "I'm getting a strong aroma of food in this house," and Priscilla dashed out of the kitchen to welcome her. They hugged one another with smiles radiating on their beautiful faces. Barry sat on the sofa looking at both of them and he could see a resemblance between the two cousins. While he gazed at them, Mary noticed it and asked, "Why are you looking at us like that?" And he answered and said, "You two look alike." And she said, "Oh! We hear that all the time." They both burst into laughter.

"The food is ready," says Priscilla as she calls out to Barry to come to the dining table for dinner. She brought out the food to the table and they all sat down.

"Barry, please pray for us," says Priscilla.

"Lord, we thank you for providing this food for us. Replenish our strength, and refresh our soul as we wine and dine in Jesus' name."

They all affirmed by saying "Amen!"

Priscilla dished her own portion of food and the rest did the same while Barry opened the non-alcoholic *Pierre Zero* French red wine and filled everyone's glass. They all raised their glasses for a toast and simultaneously said, "Cheers!" Then Mary said, "And to the couple about to be married, long life and prosperity."

They started eating and Mary commented, "My cousin is the best chef in the world. This food is lovely. I bet Barry loves your cooking too."

Barry agreed, "Oh! Surely I do. She's absolutely fantastic when it comes to cooking."

Priscilla answered and said, "Thanks, to both of you for the compliments."

They all finish their meal and went to sit down in the living room. "Oh! It's nice in here. I like the decorations. How many bedrooms do you have here?" Mary asked.

"Three," replied Barry.

After a brief conversation Mary said, "Prisco my love, I beg to leave now. I'm all yours tomorrow. Let me go and get ready for sleep. I will see you 10 o'clock in the morning after my breakfast at the hotel."

Priscilla got up and reached for her cousin and held her again while Barry looked on. "I'm so glad you are here for my wedding. I really appreciate you. Have a good night rest and see you in the morning."

She takes her leave and she closes the door behind her.

Mary got back to her hotel room and changed into her nightgown and wished she was married and had her own husband with her in that nice hotel room to have real good time together. She said, "Lord, when will it happen that I have my husband? You said in **Genesis 2:18**, *'And the* LORD *God said, it is not good that the man should be alone; I will make him an help meet for him.'* It's not good that a woman should be alone Lord. I'm overdue for the blessing of a good husband. Lord help me." She got out her Bible and read a few scriptures at random focusing more on the book of Isaiah. She went on and sang praises and prayed and got into the comfortable hotel bed and slept.

She woke up in the morning and as she opened her eyes, it dawned on her she was not in her East Dulwich apartment but at the Hilton Palace Hotel in Edinburgh. She quickly did her morning devotion, got into the bathroom and had a shower, dressed up and went to the restaurant to have her breakfast, which is included in her hotel accommodation bill, and already paid for. It's a buffet, so she went ahead and served herself a full English breakfast with a cup of tea, and water. She sat down and was seated beside a gentleman who got into a conversation with her.

"Hi, I recognise your face. You work for Elohim Car Company in London," the man said.

And she replied, "I no longer work for the company."

He said, "My company bought three cars from Elohim Car Company, that's how I got to meet you. You were in charge of the Marketing department. I remember you signed the document giving us clearance to remove our cars from Elohim premises."

"How long ago was this?" She asked.

"It must have been about seven years ago."

"Well, I'm sorry I don't remember you. Please pardon me. I deal with so many customers, and it's been a long while now."

"Are you based in Edinburgh now?" he asked.

Mary replied, "No! I'm here for my cousin's wedding, and I'm sorry I've got to leave you because I need to join her now."

"This is my business card. Please give me a ring, if not I can get your number and call you."

"That's alright. Cheers!" She took her leave, and as she walked down the hallway of the hotel, she looked at the card and saw that the man's name is Shaun McGregor. She immediately remembered her horrible male colleague at Elohim with the same surname. Shaun McGregor also has a very strong Scottish accent and that was a put off for her. He looked smart outwardly though. She just put the card in her wallet and carried on walking down the street with its colourful Christmas decorations.

She arrives to see Priscilla and Barry, and rang the doorbell, and Priscilla opened the door for her.

"Good morning, Mary my darling. I hope you slept well?"

"Good morning Priscilla."

They both embraced and she gave Priscilla a peck and said, "How's Barry doing?"

"Oh! He has just gone into the bedroom."

And Mary said, "Let's talk Prisco honey. What things have you got ready so far for the wedding, and what things have you got left? I hope you made a list so that you don't forget anything. Have you both sorted out your dresses and the clothes for the best man, and all the bridesmaids?"

"Yes! Barry got me a special elegantly made *Yves Saint Laurent* white wedding dress, and I like it."

"Great! Have you sorted out the wedding rings, invitation cards, cake, flowers, church, and hall for reception?"

She replies, "Yes! All done. What we've got left to do is attend our last marriage counselling class tonight, rehearse tomorrow for the wedding at Shekinah Pentecostal Church, and finalise the fees for the events planner, Top Class Events Company. She is charging us fifteen thousand pounds (£15,000.00) just for church and hall decorations, music, video, photographs, food, and drinks for a hundred guests. Seventy pounds (£70.00) per person for food and drinks comes to seven thousand pounds. That's a lot. We are bargaining for fifty pounds (£50.00) per person."

Mary asked, "What's Barry saying on that?"

"Barry has tried so much. I believe he will pay. He has spent so much, and he is still spending. This wedding by my estimation is going to cost a total of about thirty-five thousand (£35,000.00) pounds, and he is the one spending for nearly everything."

"No! That's not fair. You've got to support him as well."

"He has much more money than me," Priscilla replied.

"Even at that, you still have to do something tangible."

"I've spent about two thousand pounds on a few bits and pieces," Priscilla answered.

Barry Evans is a bank manager with National Bank Limited, at the Edinburgh branch. He is a Chartered Management Accountant, and also holds a BSc degree in Economics and Statistics. He has worked for National Bank, since he graduated from university. He is financially loaded, and that's part of the reason why Priscilla has stayed with him for ten years in courtship, while he also had concubines.

It's Christmas evening and also bachelor's evening for the wedding. All is set for the wedding. Barry has paid Eleanor Campbell, owner of Top Class Events Company the fifteen thousand (£15,000.00) pounds bill she charged for her services. They have completed their marriage counselling at the church, had the rehearsals for the wedding, and members of both the Evans' and Jenkins' families have arrived. Barry's parents, siblings, uncles, cousins, nephews, and friends have arrived and most of them are lodging at the Hilton Palace Hotel. Paul and Brenda Jenkins, the parents of Mary Jenkins have also arrived and they are also lodging at Hilton Palace Hotel. The Evans' organised a small party in their home which extended into the garden for the bachelor's evening. The whole house is full of family, friends, and children running up and down in excitement. People even defied the chilly winter cold that's now gone into minus figures and stayed in the garden, which had a nice well-heated canopy for the evening while music played and food and drinks are being served.

As soon as Paul and Brenda came in, Mary went straight to her daddy and hugged him and he gave her a peck, and she also embraced her mummy and gave her a peck. They all settled down and enjoyed the evening while they shared jokes together. Perhaps the most interesting part of the joke of the bachelor's evening was when Benjamin Scott, Barry's colleague at work asked the couple to tell their guests how they first met. Barry asked Priscilla, "Do you want me to speak or you want to speak?" And she said, "Speak, but make sure you are accurate."

He cleared his throat and started. "I and my wife-to-be first met at the National Bank where I work. She came into the bank and asked me how to open an account with our bank. I told her and she left to come back the next day. I liked her when I first saw her, so I started working out in my head how I could indicate my intentions to her. Luckily, she came back the next day, and also met me. I took her into one of the special interview rooms for customers where I collected her completed form, and mobile number. From there on, we started communicating."

While he was still speaking, a rascally-minded fourteen-year-old teenager heckled him from among the guests and asked, "Have you made love to your wife-to-be? We are taught in the Sunday School that it is a sin to commit fornication."

As soon as he was asked the question, Barry stopped speaking as he was interrupted and stunned by the boy's question and the loud laughter that ensued among the guests. People gathered in small groups discussing the boy's question and what the correct answer should be. And on that note, the bachelor's evening was brought to an end. It was a lot of fun. Most people left to their various homes, and the Jenkins' walked down to Hilton Palace Hotel. The wedding commences at 11 am in the morning immediately after the normal Christmas service at Shekinah Pentecostal Church.

It's a beautiful Sunday morning, and also Christmas Day. The streets of Edinburgh are filled with Christmas decorations, and it's indeed a white Christmas as predicted by the meteorologists. Barry and Priscilla arrive in their luxurious Limousine car elegantly dressed along with Mary Jenkins, Bob Lee the best man, and a few others. Everyone is now gathered in the Church gorgeously dressed and exchanging 'Happy Christmas' warm greetings, handshakes, and embracing one another while O Come All Ye Faithful, Jingle Bells, and Silent Night by *Jim Reeves,* and Mary's Boy Child (Jesus Christ) by *Boney M* Christmas carols were softly played. People are now seated at their appropriate positions inside the Shekinah Pentecostal Church.

At exactly 11 am, the officiating Minister-in-charge stepped forward to the pulpit. His name is Reverend Dr. Lawrence Nduka Chukwuemeka, a Nigerian born from Igbo tribe, and now a British citizen. He migrated to the United Kingdom after his secondary education in Nigeria at Kings College, Lagos, and proceeded to Oxford University in the United Kingdom where he obtained a first class Bachelor of Arts degree in Philosophy and Theology, and later also obtained his MA and PhD from the same University. He joined the Shekinah Pentecostal Church in London a little over a decade ago, and was recently transferred to the Edinburgh branch. His evangelical prowess earned him speedy promotion as a black man winning white souls into the kingdom of God. Bishop John Barnes has great admiration and respect for him. He is the only one Bishop John Barnes allowed to use the title, Reverend instead of Pastor so far in the ministry. He is an eloquent man full of the Holy Ghost, with great signs and wonders following his evangelical ministry. Since he took over the leadership of SPC, Edinburgh branch a year ago, the Church has more than tripled in membership, and the whole city of Edinburgh is experiencing a great revival. He is married to Pastor Esther Chidinma Chukwuemeka who is also in charge of the choir and they have two young children.

REV. DR. L. N. CHUKWUEMEKA: Good morning Church, and happy Christmas to you all. We are here in the presence of God the Father, the Son, and the Holy Ghost to witness the joining together in holy matrimony of our Brother Barry Evans and Sister Priscilla Jenkins. I would like to call on Pastor Esther to lead us with the hymns. She will be supported by Sister Rose Fergusson on keyboard, Pastor Robert Walter on guitar, Pastor Wayne Jones on saxophone, and Brother Joseph Henderson on drums.

PASTOR ESTHER CHUKWUEMEKA: It's time for us to take our hymns. Shall we rise up on our feet? Please refer to your bulletin or the screen for lyrics of the hymns. We will start by singing the hymn, *"All things bright and beautiful,"* by Cecil Frances Alexander. This will be followed by, *"Trust and Obey,"* by John Sammis. One, two, let's go.

ALL THINGS BRIGHT AND BEAUTIFUL – By Cecil Frances Alexander, Published 1848

1. *Refrain:*
   All things bright and beautiful,
   All creatures great and small,
   All things wise and wonderful:
   The Lord God made them all.

2. *Each little flow'r that opens,*
   Each little bird that sings,
   He made their glowing colors,
   He made their tiny wings.

3. *The purple-headed mountains,*
   The river running by,
   The sunset and the morning
   That brightens up the sky.

4. The cold wind in the winter,
   The pleasant summer sun,
   The ripe fruits in the garden,
   He made them every one.

5. The tall trees in the greenwood,
   The meadows where we play,
   The rushes by the water,
   To gather every day.

6. He gave us eyes to see them,
   And lips that we might tell
   How great is God Almighty,
   Who has made all things well.

The next hymn is:

TRUST AND OBEY – By John Sammis, 1846–1919

Stanza 1
When we walk with the Lord
In the light of His word,
What a glory He sheds on our way!
While we do His good will,
He abides with us still,
And with all who will trust and obey.

Refrain
Trust and obey, for there's no other way
To be happy in Jesus, but to trust and obey.

Stanza 2
Not a burden we bear,
Not a sorrow we share,
But our toil He doth richly repay;
Not a grief or a loss,
Not a frown or a cross,
But is blest if we trust and obey.

(Refrain)

Stanza 3
But we never can prove
The delights of His love
Until all on the altar we lay;
For the favor He shows,
For the joy He bestows,
Are for them who will trust and obey.

(Refrain)

Stanza 4
Then in fellowship sweet
We will sit at His feet,
Or we'll walk by His side in the way;
What He says we will do,
Where He sends we will go;
Never fear, only trust and obey.

(Refrain)

CONGREGATION: The rest of the choir and congregation join in.

REV. DR. L. N. CHUKWUEMEKA: I would like to deliver a short admonition on marriage before I join the couple. This is very important so that you will have a fair idea of what you are about to go into, and if you decide to do a *lastminute.com* pull out, you can still do so, because once you are joined together, you cannot pull out. It's a serious vow and business, that you are about to undertake. Please open your Bible to the book of **Genesis 2:24** as I read:

> ²⁴*Therefore shall a man leave his father and his mother, and shall cleave unto his wife: and they shall be one flesh.*

Once both of you are joined together in this union, you become one flesh. It's indeed a mystery established by the Most High God.

And the Union is meant to be until death. No divorce is permitted. A revelation of the fact that you are now one flesh means that you are not allowed to say or do anything that will hurt your partner because you will indeed be hurting yourself if you do so. You are expected to do most things together. Sleep together, eat together, have fun together, and most importantly, your mode of communication has to change from singular to plural. For example, it has to be our, we, us instead of I, me, and mine. It has to be *our* money, car, house, and not *my* money, car, or house.

The Bible says again in ***Amos 3:3***: *"Can two walk together, except they be agreed?"*

Henceforth, you are expected to always be in agreement regarding your affairs. Quickly always agree together in matters affecting both of you. Do most things jointly in agreement including having a joint bank account, and joint mortgage – that's the spirit of oneness, unity, and absolute trust in marriage. Always ensure you are transparent, true, and honest to one another. Also bear in mind that where there is agreement, there is always peace and progress. I would like to add here that there should be constant communication between both of you. Be quick to admit your faults, forgive one another, saying sorry when you ought to do so, and genuinely repent for your mistakes.

Ephesians 5:22 says, *"Wives, submit yourselves unto your own husbands, as unto the Lord."*

Note that as a wife, you ought to respect and submit to your husband in all things as you will do it to Jesus, especially when what you are meant to do is not evil, illegal, or contrary to the Word of God. The preceding verse 21 of this same chapter says submission should be to one another in the fear of the Lord. Hence, the husband also has to submit to the wife especially when the wife is right. Both of you have to drop your ego and pride and allow the Holy Spirit to rule in your affairs. I would like to drive this point home by making reference to *1 Corinthians 11:3* which says, *"But I would have you know, that the head of every man is Christ; and the head of the woman is the man; and the head of Christ is God"*. This means that the man is to lead as the head and the woman is to follow. The woman must not try to usurp power through stubbornness and rebellion. That's witchcraft spirit in operation according to *1 Samuel 15:23*.

Ephesians 5:25 says, *"Husbands, love your wives, even as Christ also loved the Church, and gave himself for it;"* Ensure you love your wife wholeheartedly. Make love to her regularly, and ensure you provide for her spiritually by sharing the Word of God with her, as well as providing for her material needs, and protecting her. The commandment of love is for all Christians, hence, as a wife you also have a responsibility to love your husband.

Proverbs 14:1, *"Every wise woman buildeth her house: but the foolish plucketh it down with her hands."*

You've got to be a wise wife always building your home. This means that you will make the Lord and His Word the centre of your life. Avoid idleness and gossips, and always ensure you do good and not evil to your husband. See *Proverbs 31:10-31* for qualities a good Christian wife should possess in order to run a good home. This is my short admonition to both of you this morning.

I will now proceed further by asking the entire congregation this important question: Does anyone present here in the congregation know of any reason why this couple should not be lawfully joined together as husband and wife? Declare it now or hold your peace forever.

CONGREGATION: Immediately the Man of God finished asking the question, Anna Murray, Barry's girlfriend stormed out of the congregation and declared vociferously, "Yes! I know why they should not be married, and I have reasons and evidence to prove it. Barry lied to me he was going to marry me and even got me an engagement ring."... And she flashed the ring for the congregation to see. She continued, "These are pictures of us kissing one another and having fun. He fornicated with me. He is a bloody liar. They should not be joined together."

The whole congregation immediately turned and focused on her. She was casually dressed in jeans, a jumper, and trainers, and her countenance clearly suggests she is in a mood to fight. She continued to scream down the walls of the Church like crazy. No shame at all. There was pandemonium. What an embarrassment for Barry Evans and Priscilla Jenkins! Anna Murray apparently planned this to distract, disrupt, and spoil this joyful long-planned and awaited moment for this couple. Barry did not tell Anna he was getting married, so he kept on wondering how she could have known about the wedding. It turned out to be that Anna Murray got to know through Top Class Events promotions in an events magazine. The company's advertisements listed Barry's wedding as one of the events lined up for the day.

While this was going on, Barry was speechless and apparently in a shameful solemn mood. And Priscilla Jenkins was busy flogging herself in her thoughts saying, "I should have effectively called it quits when I saw those pictures of him with Anna Murray on his WhatsApp social media page. I knew he was lying when he said he didn't have anything serious with her and my cousin Mary warned me to pray more about Barry, and to also tell the Man of God to help me in prayers, but I didn't listen to her. It's my fault entirely. Oh, Lord, help me."

While Priscilla thought about these things, she slumped down to the floor falling flat as one whose spirit had left, not minding about her beautiful white wedding gown. Immediately, Barry and two other men came close to her and lifted her up and put her back on her feet again, and took her to her special seat, and sat her down while her Mum and Dad, Mary, and Barry came beside her to comfort her. By this time, she has become emotional, and tears were flowing from her eyes, and her beautiful make-up was wearing out because of the tears and the wiping out with her handkerchief. Her thoughts went back and dwelt on the sermon the Man of God, Reverend Dr. Lawrence Chukwuemeka just preached saying, "...and if you decide to do a lastminute.com pull out, you can still do so, because once you are joined together, you cannot pull out. It's a serious vow and business, that you are about to undertake." Those words hunted her and she seriously thought on calling it quits right there.

Meanwhile, Anna Murray was on one side of the church still screaming, while some people crowded the visibly heartbroken woman who felt terribly jilted by Barry Evans. Barry did indeed get her an engagement ring, but he was just making a fool of her. Barry saw her as a gold digger. She makes monetary demands from Barry with impunity. Barry gave money to her in large amounts, as if he had been bewitched. The kind of money he has never given to Priscilla, his parents, siblings, or God as offerings. This is idolatry! He lavished money on her buying her expensive clothes, jewellery, shoes, bags and a car and he realised she was faking her love to him so he decided to dump her. Anna Murray is forty-one years old and she has turned down many suitors mainly on the grounds that they were not rich. She has never been married, and she doesn't have any child. To marry Barry would have been a dream come true for her to marry a rich man, but behold, that dream is quashed, and she is in tears and gutted.

While she sat down screaming and crowded by a few people, the Man of God, Reverend Dr. Chukwuemeka approached her and declared with all authority while pointing to her, "Satan, I bind you, and I command you right now to come out of her, and be quiet in Jesus' name." She immediately ceased to scream and mellowed down, and she was led out of the Church peacefully. And he and the rest of the congregation came back to have their seats to continue the wedding.

REV. DR. L. N. CHUKWUEMEKA: I'm so sorry for the interruption we had. Thank God the situation is now under control and peaceful. Before I carry on, I would like to ask the couple right now if they still wish to be joined in holy matrimony, and they both gave a positive affirmation. He now asked the father of the bride to present the bride to the whole congregation.

THOMPSON JENKINS: He goes to her daughter Priscilla, and they held hands together and walked majestically to the altar facing the congregation.

REV. DR. L. N. CHUKWUEMEKA: Do we have people who know her in this congregation? And do you know her to be a born-again Christian?

CONGREGATION: A few hands were raised up, and a few people among her family and friends said, "Yes!"

REV. DR. L. N. CHUKWUEMEKA: The Groom, Barry Evans was also up on the altar, and the same questions were put to the congregation by the priest. Do we have people who know him in this congregation? And do you know him to be a born-again Christian? When he finished asking the two questions, there was another interruption.

CONGREGATION: A fourteen-year-old teenager lashed out from where he was seated to cause another disruption saying, "Yes! I know him to be a fornicator, and a liar. He messed my auntie up and dumped her. I want him to swear on the Bible now that it is true or false."

Barry immediately turned and recognised the face and voice, and his jaw dropped in awe, and his heart was pounding heavily, while it seemed as if his feet were stuck with glue to the ground unable to move. This was the same boy who asked Barry Evans the nerve-racking question the previous night at the bachelor's evening that ended the party. He is Anna Murray's nephew, Jeremy Park, alias *'Wonder boy.'* Anna told him what Barry did to her, and he is not happy. He loves his auntie so much and hates to see her in pain. So he is there at the wedding to seriously mess Barry up.

REV. DR. L. N. CHUKWUEMEKA: This time around, Reverend Chukwuemeka and the entire congregation did not give the teenager any breathing space. The priest himself and most members of the Evans and Jenkins family and friends immediately circled him and gently ordered him out of the Church while he was praying in tongues arresting every evil spirit against the wedding. The interruption lasted only about three minutes. The priest returned to the Pulpit, and apologised again for the interruption and continued.

I would like to emphasise to both of you that the vows you are about to take are in the presence of God and all men in this congregation as witnesses and it is not a joke. Therefore, you must take it seriously and do it wholeheartedly. If there is any known reason to either of you as to why you should not be lawfully married, please disclose it now. There was silence indicating they had nothing to disclose. He turned to the bridegroom, Barry

Evans and asked him, 'Will you take Priscilla Jenkins to be your wife, to love her, cherish her, comfort her, honour and protect her, forsaking all others by remaining faithful to her till death?'

BARRY EVANS: Yes, I will.

REV. DR. L. N. CHUKWUEMEKA: He turns to the bride and asked the same question. 'Will you take Barry Evans to be your husband, to love him, cherish him, comfort him, honour and protect him, forsaking all others by remaining faithful to him till death?'

PRISCILLA JENKINS: Yes, I will.

REV. DR. L. N. CHUKWUEMEKA: He turns to the congregation and asked them, 'Will you the families and friends of Barry Evans and Priscilla Jenkins support this couple in marriage now and in the years to come?'

CONGREGATION: We will.

REV. DR. L. N. CHUKWUEMEKA: The Priest invites the couple to face each other and the Bridegroom to hold the Bride's right hand and declare as follows:

BARRY EVANS: I, Barry Evans, take you, Priscilla Jenkins, to be my wife, to have and hold from this day forward. In all circumstances, to love and to cherish you, till death do us part, according to God's holy law and I make this vow in the presence of God.

REV. DR. L. N. CHUKWUEMEKA: The Priest invites the Bride to hold the Bridegroom's right hand and declare as follows:

PRISCILLA JENKINS: I, Priscilla Jenkins, take you, Barry Evans, to be my husband, to have and hold from this day forward. In all circumstances, to love and to cherish you, till death do us part, according to God's holy law and I make this vow in the presence of God.

REV. DR. L. N. CHUKWUEMEKA: The Priest receives the rings and prays, "Heavenly Father, I ask that you add your blessings to these rings and let it be a symbol of everlasting love and faithfulness, to remind this couple of their vow and covenant which they make this day in Jesus' name."

CONGREGATION: Ameeeeeeeeeeeen!

REV. DR. L. N. CHUKWUEMEKA: The priest invites the bridegroom to place the ring on the fourth finger of the bride's left hand and make the following declaration:

BARRY EVANS: I, Barry Evans, hereby give you this ring as a sign of our marriage. With my body I honour you and all that I am I give you, and all that I have I share with you in the name of God the Father, Son, and the Holy Spirit.

REV. DR. L. N. CHUKWUEMEKA: The priest invites the bride to place the ring on the fourth finger of the bridegroom's left hand and make the following declaration:

PRISCILLA JENKINS: I, Priscilla Jenkins, hereby give you this ring as a sign of our marriage. With my body I honour you and all that I am I give you, and all that I have I share with you in the name of God the Father, Son, and the Holy Spirit.

REV. DR. L. N. CHUKWUEMEKA: The priest held the hands of the couple and declares, "By the authority bestowed on me as a servant of the Most High God, I hereby pronounce you two married in the presence of God the Father, Son, Holy Spirit, and among these witnesses in Jesus' name. *Matthew 19:6* says, *"Wherefore they are no more twain, but one flesh. What therefore God hath joined together, let not man put asunder."* The Priest turns to the Bridegroom and says, "You are married, and you may now kiss the Bride."

MR & MRS EVANS: They got together and he removed the veil from her face which now reveals the face of his beautiful wife Priscilla, and he held her tight and planted his lips straight into her succulent moist mouth while he sticks out his salivating tongue into hers and he felt a strong sudden erection in his penis. And the congregation was also very much drawn into this kissing moment as they let loose laughter, shouts of joy and approval, cheering, and thanking God, while the camera and video men quickly moved closer to capture this wonderful moment.

REV. DR. L. N. CHUKWUEMEKA: The newly married couple now goes on their knees and the Man of God prays for them declaring: "No weapon formed against you and this marriage shall prosper, and any tongue that rises up against thee in judgment I condemn right now. I declare fruitfulness in this marriage. You shall produce both males and females in Jesus' name. I declare a hedge of protection over your lives in Jesus' name. I declare a prosperous and blissful marriage forever in Jesus' name. He burst into heavy tongues for a while and now said in Jesus' name. Amen!"

CONGREGATION: The couple and entire congregation shouted a big 'Ameeeeeeeeeeeeeen!'

REV. DR. L. N. CHUKWUEMEKA: The grace.

CONGREGATION: The grace of our Lord Jesus Christ and the sweet fellowship of the Holy Spirit be with us now and forever. Surely, goodness and mercy shall follow us all the days of our life. And we shall dwell in the presence of the Lord forever.

REV. DR. L. N. CHUKWUEMEKA: The wedding service has ended. Go in the peace of our Lord Jesus.

CONGREGATION: Amen!

As soon as the wedding service was over, there was sighing of great relief radiating on the faces of the couple that seems to be saying, "Thank God we are now lawfully married in spite of the enemy's attacks." They started receiving congratulatory greetings from family and friends as they came shaking hands and embracing them. Mary Jenkins also came to them along with his parents to say congratulations.

The photographer requested the people to come outside for pictures in different groups. The couple, the couple and the priest, the couple and both parents, the couple with the Evans' family, the couple with the Jenkins' family, the couple with both families, the couple with families and friends, the couple with the chief bridesmaid, the couple with all the bridesmaids, the couple with best man, the couple with the groomsmen, the couple with all attendees, and so on.

As soon as they finished with the photographs, they moved on to the wedding reception hall which is also on the Church premises. Top Class Events Company has done a great job decorating the hall.

WEDDING RECEPTION PROGRAMME

1. Wedding guests arrive.
2. Assorted drinks, snacks, nuts, biscuits, and sweets are on table for guests to serve themselves.
3. Short opening prayer.
4. Introduction of special guests.
5. Bride and groom's entry and introduction.
6. Best Man delivers his speech.
7. Toasts.
8. Cutting of the cake.
9. Couple first dance.
10. Bride's dance with her father.
11. Menu! Menu!! Menu!!!
12. Receiving of gifts.
13. Photographs.
14. Dance! Dance!! Dance!!!
15. Going away ritual.
16. Single ladies assemble for the bouquet throwing.
17. Single men assemble for the garter throwing.
18. Circle is formed for farewell.
19. Bride and groom leaves for their honeymoon.

The wedding guests were so timely, arriving almost at the same time. Eleanor Campbell and her great team from Top Class Events Company have done a marvellous job decorating the hall to a very high standard as this will also help showcase her company. Most men appeared smartly dressed in their tuxedos to grace the occasion, and a few of them wore the traditional Scottish highland dress, which consists of a tartan full plaid kilt, tartan socks with garters, and a jacket. The ladies are also gorgeously dressed in their smart suits, and a few ladies also dressed in the traditional

Scottish highland tartan, with bodice and jacket, alongside children, bridesmaids, groomsmen, family, and friends, all looking great.

Straightaway, the Master of Ceremony walked onto the stage, and the party began as stated in the programme. When it was time for the Bride and Groom to come in, they were ushered in with loud shouts of approval that got them smiling and laughing, and it's now obvious from their faces that the pain of the church wedding service interruptions had all disappeared, paving way for enjoyment time. The couple were ushered in behind the Bridesmaids and Groomsmen all dancing in a well-organised choreographed manner that caught the attention of the entire audience of guests at the reception and made them ecstatic. Exciting!

The toast was proposed after the Best Man's eloquent speech which caught Mary Jenkins attention, and the couple moved ahead to cut the gigantic, well-decorated, traditional stack cake with nice icing to top it up. After cutting the cake, they got on stage to dance to the romantic love song, *'Endless love'* by Lionel Richie and Diana Ross, which was immediately followed up with Bob Marley's *'One love'*. As they danced, they twisted round and round so flexibly and he lifted her up so well into the air in the manner that they rehearsed. She is now visibly overwhelmed with excitement, full of joy, smiles, cheers, and laughter while all the guests joined in and sang the songs along with the couple. The atmosphere is indeed captivating as the next music comes up and the Bride and her father Thompson Jenkins took to the stage and danced very well by shaking their bodies down to the ground.

It's Christmas Day, and to lively up the special wedding occasion, the DJ played the popular Spanish Christmas carol, **"Feliz Navidad"** meaning, "Merry Christmas" or "Happy Christmas" by José Feliciano.

This song got the whole audience into a great excited mood as they sang, clapped, and danced to the song, shaking hands, and embracing one another. The newlyweds, Mr and Mrs Evans, also joined in to enjoy the Christmas carol.

They all had to take a break to feed on the sumptuous meal prepared by one of the top caterers in the city and hired by Top

Class Events Company. They served their food on one plate remembering the preaching of the Man of God, to do things jointly. Barry made a short prayer and he took a small portion of fish and fed her saying, "I love you darling," and rubbed her back gently and she replied, "I love you too." Soon after the meal, they both got up and started going round the tables greeting their family and friends one on one, with handshakes, hugs, and pecks while the gifts are pouring in. The gift comprises mainly kitchen items, clothing, and decorations. Mary Jenkins got her cousin a set of nice gold jewellery made up of *Gucci* bracelet, *Dior* necklace, and a lovely pendant to go with it. She also got her a nice piece of art with a scene of the seaside with lovely plants and boats with the occupants displaying their fishing nets and oars under a beautiful blue sky. And another framed work of Psalm 23. Lovely! She got Barry two sets of *Dolce & Gabbana* designer ties and cuff links to go with it.

They quickly joined in the various group photographs, and she led the bouquet throwing for the single ladies. The struggle for it after she threw it was too much and it was ripped apart. Oh no! The guests formed a circle and got ready to wish them farewell for their journey to their honeymoon location, and after that they head straight to Edinburgh Airport for a flight to Mallorca, the very beautiful Spanish Island for their honeymoon. Bob Lee, Barry's best man drove the couple to the airport. He dropped them, and bid them goodbye.

They checked in their luggage and boarded the plane. And shortly after they took off, Barry remembered the ugly scenes Anna Murray and her nephew Jeremy Park created at the wedding, and his conscience was pricked knowing it was his fault. He also remembered the preaching of Rev. Dr. Lawrence Chukwuemeka saying, "*I would like to add here that there should be constant communication between both of you. Be quick to admit your faults, forgive one another, saying sorry when you ought to do so, and genuinely repent for your mistakes.*"

With a heart full of conviction he immediately turned to her and said, "Priscilla my love, I just want to say I am deeply sorry for the interruptions at the wedding today by Anna and Jeremy.

It's indeed my fault and I am so sorry for what happened. Please forgive me."

With a pure forgiving heart, and broad smiles on her beautiful face, she turned to him and said, "Barry my sweetheart, I forgive you wholeheartedly."

They both meant it. The remorse was genuine, and the forgiveness was also genuine. No faking! This is what is truly expected of Christians. That was the only time they ever mentioned the incident. They went ahead and had a fantastic honeymoon without a single disagreement or row.

CHAPTER EIGHT

MR AND MRS EVANS' HONEYMOON

They arrived at Palma de Mallorca Airport on the Island of Majorca, Spain safely and took a cab straight to the Champion 5-star hotel on the seaside. The temperature has gone far below freezing point with heaps of snow and ice everywhere, hampering the car's access. Champion is an exclusive hotel mainly for the bourgeois, tycoons, and celebrities. Barry specially chose it as a surprise for her. They both have positive surprises for each other that will take them over the moon in this once-in-a-lifetime honeymoon. As they arrive at the Champion Hotel, they alighted from the cab and went straight to the reception with their luggage and registered and went to their lavishly furnished suite. Everything in this suite is massive, classy, and unique. The decorations and artwork displayed on the walls caught her attention, and then the amenities.

"This suite is breathtakingly beautiful and I like it. You must have spent a fortune on this. Thanks sweetheart." she purred.

He answered and said, "You are welcome."

Once a couple is legally married, that gives them full licence to have sex. Sex is a very important aspect of a married couple's marriage. Apart from the purpose of procreation, sex refreshes the soul. Have sex often, and if you've got the strength, do it daily. Whenever the word 'sex' is mentioned, some Christians frown on it as if it's a taboo to do so, and they do so perhaps out of pretext or ignorance. *Of what use is a honeymoon without talking about sex or having sex?* Many marriages are no longer exciting, and some others are as good as dead because romance, love, and constant sex have been excluded. Rekindle the fire in your marriage by engaging in serious romance, love, and sex. God created sex for married couples to enjoy. Therefore, enjoy it.

The Bible says in *1 Corinthians 7:1-5*:

¹Now concerning the things whereof ye wrote unto me: It is good for a man not to touch a woman.

²Nevertheless, to avoid fornication, let every man have his own wife, and let every woman have her own husband.

³Let the husband render unto the wife due benevolence: and likewise also the wife unto the husband.

⁴The wife hath not power of her own body, but the husband: and likewise also the husband hath not power of his own body, but the wife.

⁵Defraud ye not one the other, except it be with consent for a time, that ye may give yourselves to fasting and prayer; and come together again, that Satan tempt you not for your incontinency.

Every married couple should look forward to a time to render due **benevolence** to their partner. And it's best to render it wholeheartedly, without reservations, being fully involved spirit, soul, and body in order to derive maximum satisfaction. It should be a time nothing else should matter to you in the world but you and the one you truly love. Verse 4 in the above scripture says you don't have full power over your own body anymore as your partner also has rights to it. Therefore, it's of no use denying your partner sex by making flimsy excuses. And the next verse reiterates this point by saying, *"Defraud ye not one the other..."* Create a fascinating honeymoon paradise world just for two of you in your imagination.

Genesis 1:27-28:

²⁷So God created man in his own image, in the image of God created he him; male and female created he them.

²⁸And God blessed them, and God said unto them, be fruitful, and multiply, and replenish the earth, and subdue it: and have dominion over the fish of the sea, and over the fowl of the air, and over every living thing that moveth upon the earth.

157

According to the above scripture, God created Barry and Priscilla in His own image. And God blessed them for holy matrimony on Christmas day saying, *"Be fruitful, and multiply, and replenish the earth..."* How will a couple multiply and replenish the earth? By making love!

Barry has made marriage vows to be a good husband to his wife, and turn over a new leaf, especially now that he has dumped Anna Murray. He calls out to her to come and join him for a short prayer and thanksgiving for the success of their wedding and safe journey to Spain, and she joined him.

"Please turn off your mobile phone," says Barry, and both of them turn off their phones to avoid unnecessary disturbance from people calling and sending messages to congratulate them.

He starts praying, "Heavenly Father, we thank you for the success of our wedding, and smooth flight down to Mallorca. Lord, we thank you for quenching the enemy's attack to spoil our marriage. It is by your mercy that we are joined together as husband and wife, and we appreciate your mercy. Lord we thank you for all our guests. We ask that you protect all of them, and lead all of them safely back to their respective homes. Thank you Lord, for all the gifts we received from our family and friends, and we ask that you bless them more in Jesus' name." And they both say, "Amen!"

Immediately after the prayer, she held her husband and said, "I love you sweetheart. Thanks for everything."

And he replies, "You are welcome."

He wanted to have a shower before making love, but her tender touch was irresistible. He held her firmly and gazing at her face, they both had eye contact, and she lowered her smiling face gently. She held his face close to herself and went straight for a kiss and they started panting with their eyes closed as they hurriedly begin to undress. He was determined to ensure they both reached orgasm, so he started by gently fondling her and giving her a good massage, kisses, and fingering, to kick-start her and get her wet before intercourse, which sent both of them out of this planet, and they landed over the moon. What a honeymoon! She had earlier gone on the internet to explore new ways and styles of making love in order to reach orgasm, and also as a surprise for him.

Some of the new sex styles she discovered are, the Erotic Accordion, The Pinwheel, Electric Slide, X Marks the Spot, The X-Rated, Ladder Loving, Passion Propeller, Backstairs Boogy, Deep Impact, and the Bootyful View.[4]

She concentrated more on the Bootyful View style because it allows for great control over speed, depth, and intensity of stimulation. She also tried the Jockey positions especially the straight one that allows her to be on top of Barry giving her full control to manoeuvre things the way she likes. As she tried some of these styles, Barry was absolutely dazzled. The beauty of trying some of these new styles is that most parts of the body are moved flexibly and it feels like taking exercise. In order to derive full pleasure and satisfaction from sex, it's vital to try a lot more styles apart from the traditional missionary style and these styles should be tried in the bedroom, living room, bathroom, or wherever that is convenient. This gives the honeymoon variety, and makes it memorable.

She is also determined to satisfy him sexually if that will help permanently keep his attention away from Anna Murray or any other woman that may want to compete with her for her husband. They got together again to have carnal knowledge of each other and she participated fully by being involved in spirit, soul, and body as she twisted her body flexibly, rather than just laying down like a log of wood and leaving him to do everything. She made very good romantic utterances which turned him on and helped him to be fully charged and energized with a lasting erection. Barry was indeed dazzled at her surprising new lovemaking techniques. It's soul-refreshing. Barry was quickened to remember the scripture below and he spoke it to her saying,

The Living Bible (TLB) says in *Song of Solomon 4:10-12:*

> [10]*How sweet is your love, my darling, my bride. How much better it is than mere wine. The perfume of your love is more fragrant than all the richest spices.*

[11] Your lips, my dear, are made of honey. Yes, honey and cream are under your tongue, and the scent of your garments is like the scent of the mountains and cedars of Lebanon.

[12] My darling bride is like a private garden, a spring that no one else can have, a fountain of my own.

These loving words from the Bible ignited more fire in her and she held him saying, "I love you darling. You are the sweetest. I'm all yours forever."

Barry replied, "I love you too honey."

She immediately positioned herself for the pretzel style which allows for deep penetration. And afterwards, she also positioned herself for the cowgirl style, as well as the reverse cowgirl style and they had intense sex until they were fatigued.

After making love, they headed straight for the Jacuzzi for a bath. Before their bath, they washed their teeth and tongues thoroughly to enhance dental care, fresh breath, and also make kissing more enjoyable. They washed one another's bodies while they laughed and shared jokes.

"You are sweeter than honey my darling," says Barry and continued, "I enjoyed every bit of you. I like the way you held me tight and responded with kisses, and screams of approval, when we were making love. I hope you will do this to me forever."

"Sure! I will even do much more," she replies. And that statement that she will even do more ignited another fire in him and he held her again in the massive Jacuzzi and they held each other tight and they made love again.

As they carried out their fantastic love sessions, they had Lionel Richie love songs playing gently. When they finished in the bathroom, they put on their night gowns and sprayed a bit of their charming perfumes. She went straight to him and put both arms round his neck with a little box containing a lovely birthday jewellery present she got for him and kissed him and said, "Happy birthday to you sweetheart. This special jewellery is for you."

He took the little box from her and held her tightly again and with their eyes closed, they engaged in a very soul-refreshing kiss and as they disengaged from holding each other he opened the box and found a golden bracelet, necklace, and wristwatch. And he said, "Thanks a million for this. This is very much appreciated. I love you darling. I wish every day was birthday for me so that I can get more presents from you."

Priscilla replied and said, "You are welcome," and they started laughing. They got into the bed and under the thick quilt to keep warm while they held each other and kissed and slept.

It's important to mention here that honeymoon is not just a western culture thing but that it's also biblical. The Bible says in *Deuteronomy 24:5* that:

> *"When a man hath taken a new wife, he shall not go out to war, neither shall he be charged with any business: but he shall be free at home one year, and shall cheer up his wife which he hath taken."*

The Bible says here that a man should take one whole year off and be on honeymoon cheering up his new wife. And for a man to effectively cheer up his wife on a honeymoon there has to be loads of romance, love, and sex.

It's Boxing Day and they woke up and made their morning devotion. They proceeded straight to the bathroom for a bath after the devotion. They put their music on while they got dressed and afterwards they walked down to the restaurant for breakfast, which could have been served to them in their suite, but they chose to go to the restaurant as it will enable them to see a bit more of the hotel. They got there and went for cereal, and complete English breakfast served on one plate for both of them. Barry got coffee, fresh orange juice, mango juice, and water. Barry cut out some of the scrambled eggs and fed her while rubbing her back gently and she responded saying, "Thanks honey."

Barry answered and said, "You are welcome sweetheart."

They retired to their posh hotel suite after their breakfast and proper relaxation in the restaurant. When they got back he held her gently and then more closely fondling her succulent breasts and planting a sweet loving kiss on her, and that fired her up. The Bible says in *Proverbs 5:18-19*:

18Let thy fountain be blessed: and rejoice with the wife of thy youth.

19Let her be as the loving hind and pleasant hoe: let her breasts satisfy thee at all times: and be thou ravished always with her love.

The word *'ravish'* also means to **intoxicate** or **enrapture** as used in NKJV. He gently grabbed her breasts and continued to caress and kiss her and he got intoxicated with her love as they got euphoric and then got into the mood to copulate, which went so intense and wild emotionally, and really satisfactory. They got into the bathroom and clean up, and came out and carried on listening to their favourite love songs. He got out their chess game and they started playing. She used to be the champion before that day, but in a twist, he won the game and she joked and said, "I let you win because it is Boxing Day, and it was your birthday yesterday."

And he replied and asked, "What has all that got to do with my winning you darling?" She was silent.

He went to her and said, "You are so beautiful, and I love you."

She replied, "I love you too."

They got ready to go to the gym to work out and use the swimming pool. When they got to the gym within the Champion Hotel premises, the attendant asked for her name and she said, "Priscilla Jenkins," and the attendant said, "I haven't got Priscilla Jenkins here on the computer. What I've got is Priscilla Evans," and Barry said, "Please pardon her. You are right. It's for for Mr and Mrs Evans. We just got married yesterday; I guess it hasn't sunk in well yet."

And she said, "I'm sorry sir. It hasn't registered well on the brain properly yet." And that got all three of them laughing. They went past the entrance and got into the gym with the issued pass.

They got on the treadmills next to one another and started walking and then increased the speed a little bit for moderate jogging which they did for fifteen minutes and got off to use the recumbent exercise bike for another fifteen minutes. They went on to do other light exercises for another fifteen minutes and left the gym to go to the swimming pool. They got into the swimming pool and noticed that the water was well heated in spite of the chilly winter cold. Everywhere was also very clean. They stayed at the shallow part of the pool for a while holding one another so tightly and kissing before they dived in swimming. They stayed in the pool swimming for half an hour before they finally left for their suite. They immediately got dressed smartly and left for the Champion Hotel restaurant and bar for some food and drink. They ordered their food. Barry always liked to have alcoholic red wine in the past, but she was surprised to see him order *Botonique* non-alcoholic Spanish red wine for both of them. She was thrilled because that's an indication of a new regime with a positive life-changing lifestyle that will help their marriage. They settled down on one of the beautiful upholstered sofas.

When their food and drinks arrived, they prayed and he fed her with some of the chicken breast and she said, "Thank you sweetheart," with a broad smile of approval. He leaned towards her and held her soft hand squeezing it gently to feel her warmth. They concentrate and began to eat and he asked, "I hope you are having a good time so far on this honeymoon?"

Priscilla excitedly replied in the affirmative saying, "Of course sweetheart and I wish it would go on forever."

Barry said in a very gentle romantic tone, "I'm glad you are enjoying yourself."

They finished their meal, and he opened the non-alcoholic Spanish wine, filled their glasses, and they held up their glasses and said, "Cheers!" together.

Barry sipped a little, and held her around her waist to bring her closer, and gave her his glass to sip from.

Priscilla had a couple of gulps and said, "This is a nice wine. I like it."

They had their wine and relaxed very well until she was feeling sleepy resting her head on his side with her breast pressing on him closely, and he was stimulated and had a strong erection. And when he could no longer resist the erection, his thought focused on making love again, and he requested that they should return to their suite.

They immediately dashed out, and in a twinkle of an eye, they were back in their suite. He immediately held her and undressed her, unfastened her bra and they got together again digging it out and fabulously lost in love, as they head again out of this planet to somewhere over the moon, perhaps landing on the stars. They made love energetically like crazy, yet soul-refreshing and as they ended this session, she held him tight and whispered into his ear and said, "I enjoyed the sex. You are fantastic. I reached orgasm again and again on this honeymoon and I wish it could last forever."

Those complimentary words of approval set him on fire again as he got a full erection and they set off on another hot round of sex in this wild romance. As they ended this session, he saw tears of joy flowing ceaselessly down her cheeks. And she said again, "Honey, you are the sweetest. I'm all yours forever," as she said this she remembered Anna Murray, and with a cringed face she thought to herself, "If she ever dares to come near my husband again she is as good as dead, because she can't spoil my joy again." That's just an expression of a momentary surge of emotions of jealousy. They got into the bathroom and had a bath in the Jacuzzi, dressed up in their nightgowns, sprayed a bit of their perfumes, and got under the quilt, kissed and fell asleep.

They woke up on the third day of their honeymoon, which is going well so far. They had their morning devotion, and got into the Jacuzzi for a hot bath, and they got dressed, and went down to the restaurant for their breakfast. They finished having their breakfast and came back to the suite. Their phones have remained off for most of the time except that occasionally they will put it on and check their messages.

As they came back, they decided to do Bible study on the subject: **WHAT IS LOVE?** The scripture below taken from The New International Version (NIV) gives a summary of what love is. Barry read *1 Corinthians 13:4-8 (NIV)* which says:

> *⁴Love is patient, love is kind. It does not envy, it does not boast, it is not proud.*
>
> *⁵It does not dishonour others, it is not self-seeking, it is not easily angered, it keeps no record of wrongs.*

⁶Love does not delight in evil, but rejoices with the truth.

⁷It always protects, always trusts, always hopes, always perseveres.

⁸Love never fails. But where there are prophecies, they will cease; where there are tongues, they will be stilled; where there is knowledge, it will pass away.

TYPES OF LOVE

1. *Erotikos* is a Greek word. And it is the root word of the English word erotic. Erotic has to do with sexual passion or love. It is characterised by sexual desire. This is the kind of love that is so common in the world, and it is mainly of the flesh. This type of love does not last because it is mainly based on sex! Sex!! Sex!!! Usually, people who engage in this kind of love don't have much connection with the things of God, and a condition may be attached to love. If you are in this kind of relationship, make the decision today to start rebuilding your love life based on the Word of God and not mainly on sex.

2. *Philanthropia* is also a Greek word. It is the origin of the English word philanthropy. This is love of mankind shown by practical kindness and help to humanity. We have charity organisations like the Red Cross giving this kind of love. We also have individual philanthropists who love mankind and give donations to worthy causes.

3. *Agape* is another Greek word. This is unselfish brotherly love. It is the unconditional love of Jesus Christ. This is the kind of love we ought to express towards one another as Christians. Be mature in love to the point that the love of God is shed abroad in your heart by the Holy Ghost – Romans 5:5. Graciously shower your spouse with unconditional amazing abundance of love to help their soul refresh and keep prospering.

Their Bible study lasted just an hour but it gave them the opportunity to exchange views with an open heart and lovingly without any argument. Afterwards, they got dressed and went out into the snow holding hands and chatting outside as they took a walk along the seaside to see the beautiful blue sky, with the mild sun radiating down to the earth, and fishes occasionally springing up from the waters and boats and ships passing through. They were outside playing and running along the bank of the great waters and having fun together as a few other tourists look on in admiration.

They moved on and got onto their special booked coach to take them round Mallorca Island for sightseeing. They got on the coach, and a tour guide was onboard showing them important landmarks in the city and countryside of the beautiful island while they took photographs with their camera and mobile phones. They saw the glorious Cathedral de Mallorca, Bellver Castle, Royal Palace of La Almudaina, the Drach caves, and Serra de Tramuntana Mountain.

The Tour Guide gave them information about the Cathedral de Mallorca saying, "This is one of the most exciting tourist attractions. It is 121 metres long, 55 metres wide, and its nave is 44 metres tall. The Cathedral covers 6,600 square metres of land, and has a capacity of 18,000 people. The building of the Cathedral was begun in 1229 by King James 1 of Aragon, but finished in 1601. It was designed by famous Catalan architect Antonio Gaudin in the Catalan Gothic style but also has Northern European influences. It was built of sandstone blocks or ashlars. The cathedral is a magnificent piece of art considered to be the fourth most beautiful church in the world."[5]

They cruised through seeing the beautiful handwork of God embedded in nature, now being unravelled as a result of this great adventure called their honeymoon. It's indeed exciting and the memory will live with them forever. Barry held her gently close to himself and put his hands round her soft waist and reached for her lips and they close their eyes as the tender kiss started pulling some chords in their nerves and sending message of copulation to the brain to satisfy the soul. They finished the sightseeing of the beautiful island, and went straight to the Champion Hotel restaurant and bar to have their meal, after which they went to their suite to relax.

After relaxing for a while, they got out their scrabble game and started playing. Barry used to be the winner in the past, but on this occasion she won. He said, "I let you win because it will be boring for me to keep beating you," and she quipped, "Really? Men and their ego," and she went close to him and held him from behind resting her breasts on him and said, "I love you sweetheart."

He felt a transmission of a current of love from her into his calm body and he replied with a deep emotion of love, "I love you too." Turning round to see her beautiful face, he said again, "I have a poem from the Bible written by King Solomon I would like to read to you honey."

Priscilla said, "Please read it to me. I need the Word of God to thrill me," and they opened to the Song of Solomon in The Living Bible, chapter four and he read verses one to seven to her in a romantic tone.

The Living Bible (TLB) says in *Song of Solomon 4:1–7:*

King Solomon:

> [1]*How beautiful you are, my love, how beautiful! Your eyes are those of doves. Your hair falls across your face like flocks of goats that frisk across the slopes of Gilead.*

> [2]*Your teeth are white as sheep's wool, newly shorn and washed; perfectly matched, without one missing.*

> [3]*Your lips are like a thread of scarlet – and how beautiful your mouth. Your cheeks are matched loveliness behind your locks.*

> [4]*Your neck is stately as the tower of David, jewelled with a thousand heroes' shields.*

> [5]*Your breasts are like twin fawns of a gazelle, feeding among the lilies.*

> [6]*Until the morning dawns and the shadows flee away, I will go to the mountain of myrrh and to the hill of frankincense.*

> [7]*You are so beautiful, my love, in every part of you.*

Immediately he finished reading it, she said, "Thanks Love, you have made me wet again!" and grabbed him firmly close to herself and planted her lips on him and saying, "I love you."

Barry responded, "I love you too darling."

The kissing went on for a long while, as they close their eyes and caressed one another. They carried on enjoying a lot more activities and having fun together for two solid weeks, which was like two minutes to them as it went so fast in their own eyes. They left and went back to Edinburgh and three weeks later she missed her menstrual cycle, and they went ahead and had a bouncing baby boy exactly nine months from their memorable honeymoon. They have joy, and their joy is indeed full and overflowing. They are both radiant and flourishing with amazing grace in abundance, full of love, peace, and joy in this blissful marriage.

Finally, we see here that Mr and Mrs Evans had just a two-week honeymoon. And *Deuteronomy 24:5* referred to earlier, says a man should take one full year off cheering up his new wife in a honeymoon. But King Solomon takes it further by stating that honeymoon should be every day forever for a couple. This is how he put it in *Ecclesiastics 9:9*, *"Live joyfully with the wife whom thou lovest all the days of the life of thy vanity, which he hath given thee under the sun, all the days of thy vanity: for that is thy portion in this life, and in thy labour which thou takest under the sun."* To live joyfully with your lovely wife all the days of your life simply implies everyday is a honeymoon forever. Enjoy your honeymoon every day forever in Jesus' name. Amen!

For full details of the story of this exciting honeymoon, get the sequel book titled: *MR AND MRS EVANS' HONEYMOON ON THE ISLAND OF MAJORCA, SPAIN.*

CHAPTER NINE

MARY JENKINS IS HEALED OF CANCER

On Christmas Boxing Day, Mary Jenkins and her parents, Paul and Brenda Jenkins, woke up to breakfast at the Hilton Palace Hotel restaurant. It's so nice that the family can get together to dine. It was a reminder of old memories for all three of them when they used to sit together for their meals before their daughter left home after her education. And while they were having their delicious English breakfast, Shaun McGregor turned up. He came close to where the family were seated and greeted them saying, "Good morning to you all," and they all answered and returned his greeting.

Mary turned to him and said, "Hello Shaun, please meet my parents, Mr and Mrs Jenkins."

Shaun shook hands with Paul, and hugged Brenda giving her a peck, and also embraced Mary and planted a peck on her cheek. She smelt his nice *Hugo Boss* Cologne and that immediately reminded her of Alan Brown.

Shaun said, "It's a pleasure meeting you all," and he turned to Mary and said, "I expected your call."

She answered and said, "I'm sorry but I was busy with my cousin's wedding. That's why my parents are also here."

Shaun asked, "Can I get your mobile number?"

Mary was not sure what to say because her parents were also listening to the conversation and she got eye contact with her mummy suggesting approval, and she reluctantly gave him her mobile number. Shaun left them to go and serve his own buffet breakfast.

After he left, she spent a few seconds thinking of Bob Lee, and the eloquent speech he delivered at the wedding reception. She liked the handsome man's English accent and phonetics, and she was attracted to him for that, and wished it was him that was making a

MICHAEL NWADUBA

pass at her. Shaun's Scottish accent is still not pleasing to her. As he left her, her parents asked to know who he was, and she said he is just an acquaintance at the moment, and they indicated they like him.

Mary asked them, "Can't you hear his strong Scottish accent?"

To which her father said, "I can't hear any accent."

Brenda agreed with her husband and said the same thing and she said, "Maybe it is me."

Paul told her bluntly, "Take him if you like him."

Her mummy said the same thing.

Priscilla her cousin has just married and they want their daughter to also marry. After relaxing for a while, the Jenkins went back to their hotel rooms. Mr and Mrs Jenkins packed their things and took a taxi down to Edinburgh Airport from where they flew back to Manchester. Much later in the evening Mary Jenkins also took a taxi to Edinburgh Airport from where she flew down to Stansted Airport before taking a taxi back to her East Dulwich house.

When she got home she discovered that her apartment had become dusty, so she immediately began to dust, hoover, and tidy her apartment. After doing that, she sat down and reached for her wallet and pulled out Shaun McGregor's business card to read it because she didn't actually read it the day he gave it to her. All she did that day was see the name. While she still had the card in her hand and in what seemed to be telepathy, her mobile phone started ringing and she answered it to hear Shaun McGregor on the line saying, "Hello, is that Mary Jenkins?"

She answered and said, "Speaking."

Shaun continued and said, "This is Shaun McGregor and I'm just calling to say hello."

"Oh! That's so nice of you. I just got back to London and it was a smooth flight."

"Welcome back. Anyway, it's nice to hear your lovely voice. I will leave you for now."

Mary said, "Thanks and bye."

Shaun McGregor is a Scot from Edinburgh. He graduated from Glasgow University with a first class Bachelor of Science degree in Chemical Engineering. He also holds a Master's degree in Chemical Engineering from Oxford University. He is an Oil and Gas magnate

170

and owns his own company called Unique Oil and Gas Company. His business is well established and his company and Bishop John Barnes Global Oil and Gas Company have done business together a few times, so he knows Bishop John Barnes. He is a handsome man of average height, slightly taller than Mary, a single man in his late thirties, and he had admired Mary right from when his company bought three cars from Elohim Car Company. So it is a good thing he is reconnecting with her and who knows, it might turn out well this time.

It's now 31st December and she is ready for the special crossover anointing service commencing from 8 pm to 12.30 am at the Shekinah Pentecostal Church. Bishop John Barnes will definitely be there to anoint people and she will be there full of expectation to receive her healing. She is determined to enter the New Year cancer-free and has written her goals for the next year because she strongly believes in setting and achieving goals.

Mary is also a highly principled Christian. Therefore, she is committed to the following core values: To always put God first, honour God, love, integrity, loyalty, diligence, excellence, giving, and adventure. Adhering strictly to these values has greatly helped her character transformation. No compromise!

The powerful evening service commenced with the auditorium full to maximum capacity and they also had overflows outside the main auditorium. Pastor Moses Elijah got onto the podium and led the congregation in an opening prayer that got the entire congregation fully involved and visibly activated the strong presence of the Holy Spirit in the auditorium. This powerful thirty-minute ministration session focused on thanking God for the present year, and praying for a better next year which will roll in in the next few hours. And as he prayed, evil forces began to depart, and deliverances and healings also started happening.

As soon as he exited the podium, the anointed Woman of God, Pastor Susan Edwards stepped forward and took the stage and led the congregation in a powerful praise and worship session, for half an hour. The whole congregation erupted with shouts of joy and praises to the Most High God especially for the gift of life for the current year as they look forward to a more glorious New Year. As she ministered, you could feel the strong presence of God, and evil spirits started crying out of the life of the people of God, and some went down as the anointing flowed through.

As soon as she left the pulpit, the highly anointed Man of God, Bishop John Barnes mounted the stage. He has been on a fourteen-day fast to usher him into the New Year, and there has been a corporate seven-day fasting for the whole church. As soon as he got behind the pulpit, even without saying a word, very serious manifestations of evil spirits began to take place among the congregation. He cleared his throat and began.

BISHOP JOHN BARNES: Hallelujah! Will somebody in the house give our marvellous God some praise? Let there be shouts of praise for a year well spent. Thank Him for His love, protection, provisions, excellent health, your job, business, and family.

CONGREGATION: The whole congregation opened their mouths and burst into thanksgiving in the way each individual knew best and for what He has done for that person.

BISHOP JOHN BARNES: In Jesus' name. As we prepare to start a new year, it's important for us to start well so that we can end well. Hence, I will share with you tonight one important thing we all have to do in order to have a successful new year. The title of the topic is:

HOW TO SET AND ACHIEVE GOALS

Please open your Bible to the Book of **Habakkuk 2:2-3** and I will read:

> 2And the LORD answered me, and said, Write the vision, and make it plain upon tables, that he may run that readeth it.

> 3For the vision is yet for an appointed time, but at the end it shall speak, and not lie: though it tarry, wait for it; because it will surely come, it will not tarry.

From the scripture I just read, you can see that it's important for us to write our visions, dreams, or goals down. When you write it down, it's no longer guess work, but it becomes concrete. The essence of setting goals is to give direction and guidance in order to achieve desired targets. Goals stop us from living life aimlessly.

A goal or a vision is simply a blueprint clearly set out in writing to be achieved for a specific period. What satellite navigation is to a car driver is what your goal is to you. It helps to guide you to get to your desired destination. When you set out to build a house, you draw a plan. Similarly, you also have to carefully design your life and set out to live out your dreams by putting one block upon another until your life appears as you have planned it to be. You can truly be the architect of your own life today by clearly writing your goal.

To live your life without a goal, is to live life without direction, or aimlessly. It's like playing football without goalposts. Therefore, you have no target to aim at, and no goal will be scored. This sort of life is clearly a life of defeat, and failure. Thank God for this timely message as you take advantage of it and write your goals. It's important to note the following when you set goals.

THINGS TO NOTE ABOUT GOALS

1. Your goal must be specific.
2. You have to write your goal in a present continuous way. For example, I am losing weight. You can also write it in an affirmative way.
3. Your goal must be measurable in order to monitor progress. For example, my target is to lose weight from 100 kg down to 80 kg.
4. Your goal must be time-bound or have a deadline. The weight-loss goal should therefore be written as – My target is to lose weight from 100 kg down to 80 kg by the 31st of December next year.
5. You must work on your goals daily like a ritual. Continue to do even little things daily that will help you achieve your goals. Your brain responds to your goal as you work on it daily.
6. Your goal must be clear and precise.
7. You must have strategies, tactics, and a workable process for your goals. Therefore, develop a plan of action to follow through in order to achieve your desired goals.

8. You must be committed to your goals.
9. You must break off from habits that act as a barrier to achieving your goals, and develop the right new habits, beliefs, and values that will enable you achieve your goals.
10. You must continually focus on positive things that will help you achieve your desired goal.
11. You must surround yourself with the right positive people who will support your goals rather than negative people who will tell you your goals are not achievable to discourage you.
12. Meditate, affirm, declare, and visualise your goals daily.
13. You must get rid of all fears, doubts, and unworthiness regarding your goals.[6]

As a guide, your goals can contain the following: Health targets, financial targets, family targets, spiritual targets, academic targets, and career targets. Set your goals today, and set yourself up on the path to greatness.

Mary believes a lot in setting goals. She has written her goals for next year. In fact, she has her goals displayed on the wall by her bedside for her to gaze at regularly. She is connected in to the Spirit, and this teaching comes to her as confirmation that she is doing the right thing.

Bishop John Barnes continued and said, "Today is a special anointing service, and I will now move on and share on the topic:

THE PURPOSE OF THE ANOINTING OIL

The anointing oil will do the following things:

1. The anointing removes burdens and destroys yokes. The Bible says in *Isaiah 10:27*, *"And it shall come to pass in that day, that his burden shall be taken away from off thy shoulder, and his yoke from off thy neck, and the yoke shall be destroyed because of the anointing."*
2. The anointing brings forth healing. *Mark 6:13* says, *"And they cast out many devils, and anointed with oil many that were sick, and healed them."* And *James 5:14-15* also says:

14Are any sick among you? let him call for the elders of the church; and let them pray over him, anointing him with oil in the name of the Lord:

15And the prayer of faith shall save the sick, and the Lord shall raise him up; and if he have committed sins, they shall be forgiven by him.

3. The anointing strengthens and establishes. The Bible says in **Psalm 89:20–21:**

   20I have found David my servant; with my holy oil have I anointed him:

   21With whom my hand shall be established: mine arm also shall strengthen him.

   1 Samuel 16:13 also says, *"Then Samuel took the horn of oil, and anointed him in the midst of his brethren: and the Spirit of the LORD came upon David from that day forward. So Samuel rose up, and went to Ramah."*

4. The anointing teaches. **1 John 2:27** says, *"But the anointing which ye have received of him abideth in you, and ye need not that any man teach you: but as the same anointing teacheth you of all things, and is truth, and is no lie, and even as it hath taught you, ye shall abide in him."*

After the preaching by Bishop John Barnes which lasted exactly one hour, from 9 pm to 10 pm, he requested that all the Pastors present in the auditorium should come forward to the altar to assist him with the anointing exercise, and two hundred Pastors turns up on the massive altar. The ushers had already prepared for this exercise as this is not the first time the church had to carry out this sort of exercise. About thirty-five thousand saints are about to be anointed for strength and protection for the coming year. That number includes those outside the auditorium in the overflow.

A big drum of fresh olive oil was brought to the altar while the Ministers formed a circle holding hands for the oil to be blessed. Bishop John Barnes began praying saying, "Heavenly Father, I present this anointing oil before you and I ask that you infuse it with your supernatural power to deliver, transform, and heal your people. Let there be instant removal of burdens, destruction of yokes, and bondages as written in your Word to set your people free and make them free indeed in Jesus' name." The Bishop dips into the drum of oil a brand new King James Version Holy Bible so that all the promises of God from Genesis to Revelation will be infused in the anointing oil.

CONGREGATION: They shout a thunderous, "Ameeeeeeeeeeeeeeeeeen".

BISHOP JOHN BARNES: I declare that as you use this anointing oil it will bring forth all-round healing and victory for you and your entire family in the name of Jesus.

CONGREGATION: Ameeeeeeeeeeeeeeen!

BISHOP JOHN BARNES: This anointing will bring to an end every form of disease known and unknown to man including diabetes, fibroids, cancer, malaria, lupus, kidney diseases, liver diseases, deafness, cataract, epilepsy, leukaemia, bareness, high blood pressure, hypertension, HIV diseases, hepatitis, multiple sclerosis, flu, etc. in Jesus' name.

CONGREGATION: The whole congregation shouted a deafening, "Ameeeeeeeeeeeeeeen!" And Mary shouted with her whole energy from where she was in the choir, "I receive it in Jesus' name. Ameeeeeeeeeen!" And the two people on her left and right turned and started looking at her but she was speechless, and she simply ignored them. You see, when you are desperate for the healing power of God, you will shout like blind Bartimaeus not caring about what anyone around you thinks or says.

BISHOP JOHN BARNES: This anointing will destroy every yoke, madness, witchcraft, stagnation, poverty, failure, retrogression, and curses in Jesus' name.

CONGREGATION: Ameeeeeeeeeeeeeeen!

BISHOP JOHN BARNES: This anointing will bring forth promotion, new jobs, new businesses, financial prosperity, and open doors of favour unto you in every area of your life in the New Year and forever in Jesus' name.

CONGREGATION: Ameeeeeeeeeeeeeeeen!

At exactly 10.15 pm, the Bishop now instructs that the oil be shared among the Pastors while the ushers organise how people should come forward to the altar in an orderly manner to receive the anointing. Straightaway, the Saints of God started coming forward as directed by the ushers, and it turned out that Mary Jenkins is in the queue of the Man of God, Bishop John Barnes, and that was what she prayed for. As soon as Bishop John Barnes laid hands on her forehead with the fresh anointing oil saying, "I anoint you in the name of the Father, Son, and the Holy Ghost," she felt a sudden Holy Ghost fire transfer from the crown of her head to the soles of her feet which felt like an electric current flowing through her, and that brought her down. Bishop John Barnes has been fasting for the past fourteen days, so his anointing power is on high voltage to destroy anything not of God.

Mary Jenkins was immediately moved aside by the ushers and covered with a cloth while she lay on the carpeted floor. She got up after about seven minutes and lay her hands on her forehead and contacted some of the anointing oil and laid it on her two breasts and immediately the anointing touched her left breast, she cried out so loud, and was again brought down violently as the ushers rallied round her again to offer help. She finally got up again after about five minutes and went back to her seat believing in her heart that that is effectively the end of breast cancer in her life. Meanwhile, there are many other manifestations by other people in the congregation as they were anointed and many received their deliverances and healings.

The anointing exercise for the people of God finished 11.45 pm. Pastor William Chapman came to the pulpit to lead the congregation in the collection of the tithes and offerings of the Saints of God. Mary Jenkins completed an envelope for a bank transfer of seven thousand pounds sterling (£7,000.00) as her special seed into the church account to God in appreciation of what she believes is a healing for her and also towards her all round victory in her finances and love life in the new year, regarding a new job, and a husband, the bone of her bone and flesh of her flesh. Seven stands for perfection.

"That's a heavy seed that will yield a massive harvest," she thought as she prays on her envelope using *Malachi 3:10* and *Psalm 138:8* for God to perfect all that concerns her. Afterwards, the Ushers collected the envelopes.

It's now exactly 12 midnight and Bishop John Barnes shouted out to the congregation in a loud voice saying, "Happy New Year," and the congregation responded, "Same to you."

The Bishop continued, "Lord, we thank you that we made it to see another glorious year. We have seen the beginning of the year and we shall also see the end by your special grace. Lord, I ask that you see us through, protecting, and providing for us and our entire families in Jesus' name. Please go round and extend greetings to those around you."

And the Congregation says, "Amen!" and starts going round greeting people and exchanging pleasantries through handshakes, hugs, embracing, pecks, and kisses, for about three minutes. Pastor Susan Edwards came back on stage with the choir to minister to the church in a special New Year song. After that, a few announcements were made, and Bishop John Barnes did the benediction and the meeting ended.

She got into her Lexus car and drove off straight to her East Dulwich home, feeling happy that she is alive to see the New Year. She went through Oxford Circus, Piccadilly Circus, Trafalgar Square, Parliament Square, Westminster Bridge, Elephant & Castle, Peckham route to East Dulwich. As she drove, she saw the beautiful street decorations, spectacular fireworks, and people celebrating because of the New Year. Exciting!

Immediately she got home, she undressed and went straight to the bathroom, and before she got into the bath she started pressing her left breast searching for the lump, but it was not there anymore and she came close to the mirror to compare the pair and, behold, they both look exactly the same.

"This is a miracle!" she says and started rejoicing and dancing giving all the glory to God. She got into the bath and had a quick bath and came out, dressed up, and started dancing and praising God for the New Year and the miracle. She is now feeling perfect peace. She went to sleep at 3 am.

She woke up in the morning feeling very light and refreshed. She did her morning devotion, and went straight into her bathroom to have a wash. And she dressed up smartly and put on her *Fahrenheit* perfume. She got into the kitchen and prepared her English breakfast. She quickly ate and put on her praise and worship songs. As soon as she finished eating, her mobile phone started ringing, with people calling to wish her happy New Year. The first call came through and it was her friend Jane Foster calling from Australia. She has not spoken to her for ages. So as soon as her number appeared on her mobile screen, she screamed saying to herself, "This is a good year indeed for Jane to remember me."

She picked the call and answered saying, "Hello Jane, Happy New Year to you. It's great to hear your voice after such a long time. How is your family doing?"

Jane answered and said, "Happy New Year to you. I'm great, so is my family. I just thought I should call and say hello to you on this New Year."

"Oh! That's so nice of you. I will definitely keep in touch. Thanks for calling, and my regards to your family," and they both end the call.

Jane used to be her colleague at Elohim Car Company before she got married and moved on to join her husband in Australia after a series of arguments between her and her husband, Brian Foster, about who should join who. Before they got married in London they both agreed that after the marriage they will move together to Australia where Brian lives. However, when they agreed to this, Jane didn't mean it. All she simply wanted was to first get married to the husband and then say no afterwards, but Brian Foster put his foot down claiming it's too early for such deceit and rebellion. They were apart for over two years, before she finally moved down to Australia after the husband had threatened to divorce her. After the marriage she started claiming she has a good Job in England as a Marketing officer and therefore,

Brian should be the one to move from Australia and join her in England. Brian also claimed he has a good job in Australia. So they both got stuck not moving forward. It was Mary Jenkins who settled the matter for them by speaking to Jane Foster using the Word of God to convince her to go and join the husband in Australia.

Mary Jenkins gave Jane Foster the following reasons to convince her to move to Australia. *Firstly,* the Bible clearly recorded in the marriage between Isaac and Rebekah in Genesis 24 that it was Rebekah who left Mesopotamia to join Isaac in the land of Canaan. *Secondly,* the Bible says in 1 Corinthians 11:3 that the man is the head of the woman. Therefore, the man is to lead, and the woman to follow. *Thirdly,* Ephesians 5:22 says, wives should submit to their own husband in all things as unto the Lord. *Fourthly,* a husband marries the wife by paying her dowry. This shows that you belong to Mr Foster. Hence, she is the one that changed her maiden name from Jane Maguire to Mrs Jane Foster. Brian didn't have to change his name. These points effectively ended the two-and-half-year dispute and Brian Foster was grateful to Mary Jenkins for those words of wisdom.

She picked up her phone and called her parents. She got through and spoke, "Happy New Year Daddy and Mummy." The phone is on speaker so they can both hear. And they both replied saying, "Same to you sweetheart. How are you doing?"

"I'm fine. I just called to hear your voice and wish you two a Happy New Year. Take care."

She didn't tell them the lump has disappeared from her left breast until she sees Dr. Joseph Moore next week for the surgery and for him to test her with the hospital equipment and confirm that she is cancer-free before she will tell anyone.

She picked up her phone and called the Evans'. She got through and said, "Hello Barry, this is Mary, Happy New Year. How are you and my cousin doing? I hope you two are enjoying your honeymoon?"

He answered and said, "Happy New Year to you too. We are great, still enjoying our honeymoon. We have one more week left and we will go back to Edinburgh. Please hold on for her."

"That's fine."

He passed the phone to his wife Priscilla.

"Prisco! Prisco!! Happy New Year. How is the honeymoon going?"

"I wish you the same darling. Everything is going perfectly fine. My husband has been great and loving to me."

"That's great. I just called to wish you a happy New Year. Bye for now."

They both hang up.

As she sat in front of the television watching praise and worship ministration on *Trinity Broadcasting Network (TBN)* Christian channel, her phone rang and behold, it was Shaun McGregor. He was full of vibrant energy as he got through to her and spoke these words, "Happy New Year to you Mary. I pray this year will turn out to be a much more prosperous year for us in Jesus' name."

And she replied saying, "I wish you the same Shaun. Amen!" And she processed his statement, "In Jesus' name. It looks like he is a Christian." She thinks. "Are you a Christian Shaun?"

"Of course, I am a Christian. I serve and worship the Most High God. He has been good to me."

That gladdened her heart and she now asked, "Where do you worship?"

"I worship at Shekinah Pentecostal Church."

And she asked, "Which branch?"

"Edinburgh and London branches, depending on where I am."

"Are you a worker in the Church and which department are you?"

He said in a very pleasant tone, "I am a worker, and I am in the Choir department. I am a Saxophonist."

"Whao!" she exclaimed. She loves the saxophone instrument a lot. And she is thrilled by the fact that he is in the choir department. "How come I haven't seen you in the choir?"

"You know it's a very big department and I'm not always in London."

"Do you have a house in London?"

"Yes, I have houses in London, Edinburgh, and Birmingham."

"By the way, What do you do for a living?"

He answered in a very modest tone, "I am a business tycoon. I have my own well-established Oil and Gas Company."

She replied, "That's great."

Shaun continued, "This is a new year, and I will like us to get together and have some good times together."

"That's fine," she replied.

Shaun says, "Thanks. I will keep in touch. Enjoy the rest of the first day of the year."

As she hung up, she started dwelling on his words, *"Of course, I am a Christian. I serve and worship the Most High God. He has been good to me... Yes, I have houses in London, Edinburgh, and Birmingham... I am a business tycoon. I have my own well-established Oil and Gas Company..."* Business tycoon, and owns a well-established Oil and Gas Company. That sounds great she thought. Hearing all this about him seems to gradually erode the strong Scottish accent. She is beginning to convince herself that the Scottish accent is not noticeable. After all, her parents told her the same thing.

The postman delivered her letters and she received a reminder letter on Thursday about her surgery next Monday to remove the lump from her left breast. After reading the letter she said, "Satan, you are a failure. My God has gone ahead of you again and put a stop to your evil works. Shame! I am victorious and healed in Jesus' name."

She was not even moved as she read the letter. Instead, she rose up, singing praises unto the Lord for her healing. The lump has already disappeared supernaturally. There is nothing to remove. She remained very calm as she remembers **Psalm 46:10** that says, *"Be still and know that I am God: I will be exalted among the heathen. I will be exalted in the earth."* She shouts out, "Be thou exalted in my life and on this earth in Jesus' name. Amen!"

Not allowing anything to distract her or shift her focus from God, she continued her evangelism to sick patients at the hospital in the New Year. She took some of the laminated healing scriptures she prepared and a few tracts and bulletins and set off for the hospital and went straight to John Atkinson male ward and met her first patient to minister to in the New Year. "Happy New Year to you sir," she greeted the young man and he answered back in a low tone conveying pain with a grimaced face, "I wish you the same."

"My name is Mary Jenkins, and I'm here to cheer you up, and minister to you spiritually."

"Oh! That's very kind of you. My name is Adam Pearce, and I really need that ministration from a beautiful lady like you. In fact, I'm already motivated seeing you right now. I hope there are no charges for your service," he joked.

"The service is absolutely free of charge. Do you have any specific prayer request?"

He said, "Yes! Please pray that the Lord will heal me from HIV disease."

She read two scriptures to him – Jeremiah 30:17 and Jeremiah 17:14 and began to pray, "Lord, I commit your son into your hands and ask that you heal him instantly by your stripes. I command every trace of HIV disease to be supernaturally destroyed right now in Jesus' name."

She switched over and began to speak in tongues, and concluded the prayer by saying in Jesus' name.

And Adam Pearce said "Amen!"

Mary asked him, "Are you born again?"

He replied, "Yes! I am a born-again Christian."

She said, "That's fine. These healing scriptures are for you to read regularly, and this is my Church bulletin and tract. I'm inviting you to join us at Shekinah Pentecostal Church."

"Thank you for the ministration, and I look forward to see you again."

She said, "I will come again. God bless you. Bye for now."

She woke up Monday morning feeling strong, and at peace and ready for her morning devotion. After that, she went straight to the bathroom, and before getting into the bath, she stood close to the mirror and compared the size of her two breasts and pressed the left breast repeatedly and she could not find any lump. It has disappeared forever. 'Thank God this demon of breast cancer has been banished. I'm free indeed," she said.

She packed her bag and set off to the hospital to see Dr. Joseph Moore for the surgery she believes will not happen. When she got to the reception, they registered her for the surgery. While she waited for her turn she kept speaking in tongues silently.

When it was her turn, Dr. Joseph Moore appeared.

"Good morning Dr. Joseph," she greeted.

"Good morning to you Mary," said Dr. Joseph and continued, "Last time you came for the fibroids surgery, I was highly embarrassed about what happened. Based on that experience, I would like to check for the lump before we do anything."

"That's fine Doctor," she didn't want to disclose anything to him. She was taken to a special room for a check-up with one of the scanning machines, which revealed there was no more lump on her left breast or any trace of cancer in her body. Dr. Joseph Moore's jaw dropped in awe.

"The result is negative. There is no lump or any trace of cancer. This is a miracle. Will you please tell me what is going on here, because the same thing happened last time?"

"Doctor, Jesus is at work. He has removed the lump through a divine surgery, and I am forever grateful for the victory over breast cancer and fibroids," she said.

Dr. Joseph congratulated her and asked her to get dressed and go home because she is free from cancer. She immediately got dressed, thanking God she is free from cancer and that she will never again have to expose her breasts for any male doctor to see or touch and left and went home. She got home and phoned her parents and gave them the good news and went on a long session of thanksgiving, praise, and worship unto the Lord while she danced like King David danced with all her might. Exciting!

The Bible says in *Isaiah 10:27*:

"And it shall come to pass in that day, that his burden shall be taken away from off thy shoulder, and his yoke from off thy neck, and the yoke shall be destroyed because of the anointing."

It came to pass that on the 31st of December during the crossover service into the New Year that Mary Jenkins received the anointing oil, and the burden and yoke of breast cancer was destroyed through divine surgery. This again goes to prove that the anointing oil carries tremendous power of God to heal. Praise God! Hallelujah!

CHAPTER TEN

THE GLORY OF GOD MANIFESTS FOR MARY JENKINS

It's Tuesday, about midday and while she was relaxing in her beautiful apartment with a glass of French *Bordeaux* non-alcoholic red wine her phone rang. She picked it up, and a pleasant female voice spoke, saying, "Hello, this is Jennifer Rhodes from Quick Move Employment Agency on the line. Can I speak to Mary Jenkins?"

Mary replied and said, "Speaking."

Jennifer continued saying, "There is an excellent Marketing Manager's position with fantastic salary and fringe benefits that needs to be filled urgently at the National Bank Headquarters in London, and your profile is a good match. Is this a position you would like to consider?"

Mary replied, "Of course, I'm interested. What is the basic salary per annum for this job?"

Jennifer answered and said, "Two hundred thousand (£200,000.00) pounds per annum plus other benefits. Can I arrange an informal chat for you with the Marketing Director of the bank?"

"Yes please!" she replied.

"I will arrange for him to call you tomorrow by 2 pm. Bye for now."

Immediately she ended the phone call she screamed out loud out of excitement saying, "Two hundred thousand (£200,000.00) pounds sterling. Whao! This is a jackpot." Her basic salary at Elohim was ninety thousand pounds (£90,000.00) per annum plus fat commissions and bonuses. Now, the basic salary for this job is more than double. She remembered the seven-thousand-pound seed (£7,000.00) she sowed at the crossover night and believes the harvest is manifesting already, and she thanked God.

She got into the kitchen to prepare her lunch. She wants to have cod, roast potatoes, mixed vegetables, and gravy sauce with it. She prepared her lunch and sat down to enjoy her meal while she watched the BBC News on television. The newscaster read, "According to figures released by the Office for National Statistics, inflation figures for the last quarter of last year rose again, and experts are predicting further rises in this New Year. In an official statement by the Prime Minister, David Cameron, from his official residence, *10 Downing street, London,* said the government is set to announce new measures to curb this rising trend in inflation."

After the news she said, "I am a heavenly citizen. I'm above inflation in Jesus' name. When men say there is a casting down, I'm saying there is a lifting up. I have more than enough money, and this is my time to shine in Jesus' name."

While she sat down after her lunch with a second glass of the French *Bordeaux* non-alcoholic red wine, her phone rang, and it was Shaun McGregor on the line with a very lively tone, so much that she didn't even notice the much emphasised Scottish accent, as he said, "Good morning Mary. How are you doing today?"

With a merry heart, perhaps because of the red non-alcoholic wine, she answered and said, "I'm excellent!"

Shaun noticed the vibrant energy in her voice and quickly said, "I would like you to join me for a special dinner and outing this Saturday. Is that okay?"

Excitingly, she said, "Yes. That's fine with me."

"Is 5 pm alright for you?" he asked.

"Yes," she answered.

"Can I have your address because I will come over to pick you up?"

So Mary gave him her East Dulwich address and they both ended the call. Immediately after the conversation, she spent a while analysing his good qualities and convincing herself that he is alright. However, she still needs to find out more details about him as time goes on.

It's exactly 2 pm Wednesday afternoon and her phone rang and when she picked it up Dennis Graham, the Marketing Director of National Bank Limited, was on the line. They had an informal chat about the job which went very well, suggesting the bank is very keen to hire her. She is due to be at the Bank for a formal interview on Friday.

Early Thursday morning after she had her breakfast, she heard a knock on the door, and it was a special delivery from the postman that she needs to sign for. She signed for the parcel and got back inside her apartment wondering who had sent the parcel, and what the content should be. She went ahead and immediately opened it, and behold, it was a beautiful red teddy bear with the inscription, 'I LOVE YOU'. And there was an accompanying beautiful card with a handwritten note that says, "I LOVE YOU MORE THAN WORDS CAN EXPRESS." –Shaun McGregor.

She immediately held the teddy bear tight, gave it a peck, and went emotional with tears of joy spilling down her beautiful tender cheeks as she remembers *Philippians 1:6* that says,

> *⁶Being confident of this very thing, that he which hath begun a good work in you will perform it until the day of Jesus Christ:*

And she said, "Lord, you have begun a good work in my life, perfect all that concerns me and Shaun McGregor in Jesus' name. Amen!"

She immediately picked up her phone and rang Shaun McGregor for the first time, and as she got through, she said, "Good morning Shaun, I'm calling to acknowledge the receipt of the beautiful teddy bear and card you sent to me. Very much appreciated."

He replied and said, "Good morning to you Mary. You are welcome honey. I thought I should reach out to you in love in my own little way. See you 5 pm Saturday by God's grace."

They both end the call.

After the conversation with him, she decided to get a few things ready for her interview scheduled for the next day. She got out and arranged all her certificates, special awards, and her most recent curriculum vitae properly as part of her portfolio. She got ready her smart leather *Louis Vuitton* briefcase and put all the documents inside. She also got ready her best *Christian Dior* business suit. Mary proceeded to read through again the Job Description and Person Specification for this position which

Jennifer Rhodes sent to her. She went onto the internet to find out essential company information about National Bank. She checked to know when the company was established, their major objectives, achievements, products and services, number of employees, company turnover and assets from their financial statements, and the structure of the organisation. She was satisfied with what she found out.

Before Mary went to bed on Thursday evening, she set her alarm for 5 am the next day.

She woke up Friday morning and said her prayers. She used the following scriptures to pray. *Isaiah 45:2* that says:

> ²*I will go before thee, and make the crooked places straight: I will break in pieces the gates of brass, and cut in sunder the bars of iron:*

Matthew 10:19-20 also says:

> ¹⁹*But when they deliver you up, take no thought how or what ye shall speak: for it shall be given you in that same hour what ye shall speak.*

> ²⁰*For it is not ye that speak, but the Spirit of your Father which speaketh in you.*

She prayed, "Heavenly Father, thank you because you have gone ahead of me to make the crooked places straight regarding this interview. Thank you, Lord, because you have already cut in pieces anything that may be a barrier. Holy Spirit, take over my mouth and speak words of wisdom through me that the enemy will not be able to gainsay at the interview in Jesus' name. Amen!"

She immediately went into the bathroom to shower and she wanted to check her left breast for any lumps and suddenly remembered the Lord had delivered her from that sickness. Mary said, "Thank you, Lord, for my permanent healing," and had her bath, after which she came out and had a light breakfast and got dressed, anointed herself with her special anointing oil, and drove off.

She got to the interview venue twenty minutes before the 11 am scheduled time. As soon as it was 11 am, she was called into the

Bank's special executive boardroom where she met Dennis Graham, the Marketing Director, plus the Head of Human Resources, Kenny Powell, and the Bank's Chief Strategy Officer, Andrew Bailey. As soon as she entered the room, the head of human resources commented that she was looking very professional in her appearance, and others concurred. The glory of God is already radiating around her by reason of the anointing. The interview panel was very friendly and they only asked just a few simple questions. "What background information do you know about National Bank?" She told them the things she found out from the internet about the company. "Why do you think we should hire you for this post?" She told them about her qualifications, experience, skills, and knowledge in a relaxed manner. At the end of the interview they asked her if she has any questions for them. And she asked about career prospects in the organisation, training, and benefits attached to the two hundred thousand pounds per annum basic salary. They gave her the answers and the interview ended. They told her they would give her a feedback within the next few days. The Holy Spirit really took over her mouth and spoke through her as she prayed. And the fact that they all liked her meant that the Lord went ahead of her to make the crooked places straight by removing all obstacles.

She had just returned home when her phone rang, and it was the head of National Bank Human Resources, Kenny Powell on the line. When she answered the call he spoke saying, "Hello, can I speak to Mary Jenkins?"

Mary replied, "Speaking."

"This is Kenny Powell, Head of Human Resources of the National Bank Limited. Congratulations, I would like to offer you the job as the Bank's Marketing Manager, and a first-class letter has been sent out to you to this effect."

A very happy Mary replied, "Thank you very much for offering me the job. I will wait to receive my appointment letter to know what to do next. Thank you very much. Bye."

They both hang up and Mary excitedly jumped for joy in her living room and her head almost touched the ceiling. "Two hundred thousand (£200,000.00) pounds sterling basic salary!" she exclaimed. She immediately commenced thanksgiving, praise, and worship unto the Lord. She intended to go to the hospital to minister to some sick folks, but she cancelled it in order to carry on with her praise and worship.

Looking through her wardrobe, she couldn't find anything suitable for her outing with Shaun McGregor, so she decided to go to Magnificent Superstores shopping complex at Oxford Circus in central London to get another designer black dress for the outing, as well as have her hair styled plus a manicure and pedicure. Her heart is full of joy and overflowing because of the job offer and other great things the Lord has done for her. She is grateful to God.

Early Saturday morning after her devotion, bath, and light breakfast, she dashed out to Magnificent Superstores where she bought a black *Louis Vuitton* beautiful designer dress, had her hair styled and a manicure and pedicure to match. She is really excited, looking forward to having a great time with Shaun. She's indeed glad that her parents had met him in Edinburgh.

She got dressed in her beautiful outing dress, put on her *Gucci* makeup which matched her dress, handbag, shoes, and manicure and pedicure colours. Spraying on her *Fahrenheit* perfume, she went to the mirror to see what she looks like, and she is indeed satisfied. At exactly 5 pm Shaun McGregor appeared in his luxurious *Rolls-Royce Phantom* car. He got out of the car and went straight for the doorbell.

She opened the door for him, and he came close to her full of smiles and they went straight for a hug and he gave her a peck and they both smelt the sweet smell of one another's perfume. They now gently disengaged from holding each other and he said, "You look absolutely gorgeous in that black dress, and I like your jewellery and hairstyle. Thanks for agreeing to go out with me today darling."

Mary replied, "Your bespoke tuxedo is superb, and I like your smart haircut."

They held hands and moved into the living room. He gazed round the living room and commented, "This is a nice apartment with nice artwork and decoration."

"Thanks Shaun. What can I offer you?"

Shaun answered, "Absolutely nothing! We are going out shortly."

After a while he asked, "Can we get going sweetheart?"

And she said, "Yes! I'm ready."

They stood up holding hands and walked towards the front door and left the apartment, walking straight to his car. Shaun opened the door for her before he got into the driver's seat and drove off.

"I like your Rolls-Royce Shaun." She commented.

He replied, "Thanks darling."

Meanwhile, instrumental music by Kenny G was playing softly.

Mary asked, "Is that Kenny G playing?"

"Yes!"

"I like it," said Mary.

"Thanks," said Shaun as he drove her straight to Kings 7-Star Hotel in Marble Arch, central London. This is not far from the historical landmark triumphant arch designed by John Nash in 1827 to be the state entrance to the *cour d'honneur* of Buckingham Palace.

Kings 7-Star Hotel is an exclusive hotel for royals, tycoons, top government officials, and celebrities. The hotel exudes majesty and splendour in every way. Right from the front of the hotel, the exterior decoration portrays royalty and the interior decorations, art, statues, plants, and flowers placed in strategic places are magnificent. In the entrance lobby the ceiling is more than three times the height of a normal house and has very thick walls. The assorted brilliant chandelier ceiling lights caught her attention and she said, "Splendid!"

The upholstered chairs and a massive table is covered with carvings of ancient faces, crowns, swords, knights in armour, houses and places with fantastic lights. They walked through to the restaurant for their dinner, where a smartly dressed waiter was already waiting to take their order which was swiftly served. As soon as they got in there, a feeling of utter awe ran through her. She was absolutely amazed at what she saw, to the extent that her jaw dropped. Awesome! What she saw transcended what she had ever seen in her entire life in glory. The only place that could possibly compare with this seemingly out-of-this-world hotel is perhaps Buckingham Palace. It's indeed a state-of-the-art hotel. The cutlery was unique and golden. The dishes were uniquely designed, and the glasses came with a diamond finish. Everything is regal indeed! She took in all this beauty and admired Shaun McGregor. By this time, she has completely forgotten about Shaun's Scottish accent.

When the food and drinks arrived, he prayed and they said, "Amen!" He served the *Dom Perignon* non-alcoholic champagne in two glasses and they raise up their glasses for a toast and said, "Cheers!" in unison. While she was still dazed by the magnificence of what she was seeing, she calmly and nervously began eating her food, starting with her favourite salads. As she took a few bites, she noticed that even the food is really sumptuous and she commented, "This is delicious Shaun. I love it." Shaun said, "Please go on and enjoy it sweetheart."

Shaun is a man of few words hence he didn't get chatty with her. Besides, the lifestyle of a millionaire is mostly a question of 'Money talks.' Anyway, he is also trying to gradually know who she is. Therefore, there is no rush. When they finished their meal and relaxed, he took her to a special live jazz theatre and instrumental musical performance, just for two of them as the audience right there at the Kings 7-Star Hotel. The musical is scheduled to last for exactly forty-five minutes, and that alone cost Shaun McGregor forty-five thousand pounds sterling (£45,000.00) to book at the rate of one thousand pounds per minute. And that's peanuts for him anyway as a multi-millionaire.

As they come in, more of the auditorium's special lights were turned on and they dazzled her whilst the instrumentalists took their places. The professional saxophonist, pianist, drummer, trumpeter, guitarist, and violinist all took their seats. They all introduced themselves by simply saying their names and commenced playing. They are now in their own paradise world just for two of them. The instrumentalists performed popular songs which included many she is familiar with so she was really thrilled. At the end of the performance, she was so overwhelmed by what she saw, experienced, and enjoyed that she didn't know what triggered her and she dropped her guard and turned to

Shaun McGregor and held him tight and said, "I love you honey," and they both looked at each other lovingly while they both wrapped their arms around each other, and he gave her pecks on both sides of her cheek, and replied, "I love you too darling."

Under normal circumstances, Mary Jenkins will never tell a man, "I love you" or address the man as "Honey" on her very first date. For her, it's a question of why should a Holy Ghost filled, tongue talking, well-worded Christian do a thing like that? Perhaps it could be linked to the excessive power of money. Money answereth all things!

They left together to pick up the car, and he drove her straight to her East Dulwich house. They got inside the house and sat next to one another on the sofa, and he asked her, "I hope you enjoyed your first date with me?"

She answered in the affirmative, "Of course I did. Thanks a lot honey."

Shaun said, "You are welcome, and thanks for honouring my invitation to go out with me today. Please let's pray before I go."

He prayed and thanked God for the outing and they said, "Amen!"

Shaun got up and ready to go, and they held one another tight feeling each other's warmth as he gave her a peck and bade her goodbye.

She now said, "Sweetie, please call me when you get home."

And he answered and said, "I will." Shaun left for his Kensington mansion, and in forty minutes he was at home. He undressed, and had a shower, and changed into his nightgown and called her to say he's back home and goodnight.

After he left, she went into the bathroom for a bath before putting on her nightgown. She prayed and got into her bed and with her eyes open she started reflecting on all that happened in that evening outing with Shaun McGregor and she went into a soliloquy saying, "He is gentle, smart, wealthy, and loving. He is all I need in a man. I love him wholeheartedly."

She turned round in the bed and grabbed the red teddy bear he got for her and held it so tight and in her imagination it was him she was holding and gave it a peck and unconsciously said, "I love you

Shaun," and tears of joy started flowing down her cheeks. And she held the teddy bear more tightly again and it was as if she perceived in her subconscious the *Hugo Boss* perfume Shaun McGregor wore and that increased her emotions intensely as she continued sobbing and went for her handkerchief to wipe her tears of joy. She lay on the bed with the teddy bear beside her and she dosed off.

She woke up the next morning with her thoughts flooded with the previous day's outing as she smiles with exceeding great joy and thought, "Is Mary Jenkins in a dreamland or what?" and she pinched herself to test if it's real. She got her Bible out and went straight to read the four chapters in the Book of Ruth and came back and read the love story of Ruth and Boaz in chapter three twice. This fuelled her emotions immensely as she prayed, "Lord, I commit this relationship into your hands, and I ask that you perfect all that concerns me and Shaun as you perfected Ruth and Boaz in Jesus' name. Amen!" The Bible described Boaz in **Ruth 2:1** as, "*...A mighty man of wealth...,*" and that's how she sees her dear Shaun.

She went ahead daydreaming of the exceedingly great life she desires to have with Shaun in the future after having a foretaste and concluded as written in the Bible in **Song of Solomon 8:7** that, "*Many waters cannot quench love, neither can the floods drown it: if a man would give all the substance of his house for love, it would utterly be contemned.*" She declares, "I will submit to him, and respect him, honour, love, and cherish him wholeheartedly and no force of hell or flood can quench this love." And she was also quickened to remember and reflect on the **Amplified** Version of **Ephesians 5:33** that says,

> "*However, let each man of you [without exception] love his wife as [being in a sense] his very own self; and let the wife see that she respects and reverences her husband [that she notices him, regards him, honours him, prefers him, venerates, and esteems him; and that she defers to him, praises him, and loves and admires him exceedingly].*"

She receives her letter of appointment from National Bank Limited, and commenced her employment a week later as the Marketing Manager of the Bank for their products and services. She loves the job, her fantastic salary and benefits, and her work colleagues. Everything! All is indeed going well for Mary Jenkins again. Exciting!

Shaun McGregor and Mary Jenkins had an exciting twelve-month period of courtship *without sex*, after which they got married on Christmas day, exactly one year after her cousin Priscilla Evans was married. It was a royal wedding, and Bishop John Barnes joined both of them at the Shekinah Pentecostal Church, London. They are now happily married with a baby boy they had after the marriage and his name is David. The Shekinah Glory of God manifests in full measure for Mary Jenkins. Glory!

After the wedding, they proceeded to their honeymoon. For full details of this extraordinary honeymoon in paradise, get the sequel book titled: *MR AND MRS MCGREGOR'S HONEYMOON ON THE ISLAND OF SANTORINI, GREECE.*

The afflictions and anguish Mary Jenkins went through turned out to be training to transform her to be a much better person, and excellent vessel of honour suitable for God to use all to His glory. The loss of her job, death of her boyfriend Alan Brown, no husband, fibroids, breast cancer, and her evangelical work all eventually worked together for her good, and effectively built her up in patience and character making her a good soldier of Christ indeed. Perhaps you are going through tough times similar to Mary Jenkins, be encouraged and know that the Most High God is at work behind the scenes perfecting all that concerns you to also show forth His glory.

Holy, Holy, Holy is the Lord

Glorious, Glorious, Glorious is the Lord

Hallelujah to the Most High God

Hosanna to the Most High God

Marvelous is the Lord of lords

Majestic is the King of kings

Heavenly Father, thank you for all your love

I give you all the glory Lord

SPREAD THE GOOD NEWS

Well done! You have successfully finished reading this book. I believe you must have picked up some principles that will help you grow in the Word of God, and spiritually as you apply them in your life. It is the application of the principles you have learnt that will bring about a transformation in your life and also give you your desired results. So, keep on practicing what you have learnt.

Now that you have read this book, and you are blessed, I would like you to tell your family, friends, and colleagues about it and spread the good news of the principles you have learnt. Recommend this book to at least twenty people you know, and you can even get some copies for your loved ones as a gift. As you do this, you become a blessing to others and also enlighten the world from where you are. Thank you and God bless you abundantly.

MICHAEL NWADUBA

BIBLIOGRAPHY

1. The Holy Bible containing the Old and New Testaments. Authorized King James Version. Reference Edition. Thomas Nelson Bibles, A Division of Thomas Nelson, Inc. Copyright 1989 Thomas Nelson Inc. Printed in the United States of America.
2. The Living Bible. Parents Resource Bible. A Life Application Bible. Edysyl Publications. Parents Resource Bible. Copyright 1995 by Tyndale House Publishers.
3. The Amplified Bible. Copyright 1954, 1958, 1962, 1964, 1965, 1987 by The Lockman Foundation.
4. The Thompson Chain-Reference Study Bible. Second Improved Edition. New International Version. Copyright 1973, 1978, 1984 by International Bible Society.

All scriptural references in this book are taken from the
King James Version, and are in italics,
except where indicated.

NOTES

1. Orchestra instruments – https://www.naxos.com/education/enjoy2_instruments.asp - (Accessed 5 October, 2017).
2. Orchestra instruments – http://www.philharmonia.co.uk/explore/instruments – (Accessed 23 October 2017)
3. Gym equipment – http://www.gymventures.com/gym-equipment-names-and-pictures/ - (Accessed 5 October, 2017).
4. Sex positions – https://www.menshealth.com/sex-women/45-sex-positions-guys-should-know – (Accessed October 5, 2017).
5. Palma Cathedral – http://www.northsouthguides.com/mallorca_cathedral.html – (Accessed 5 October, 2017).
6. John Assaraf: How to set and achieve goals' video - http://www.bing.com/search?q=Internet+video- +How+to+set+and+achieve+any+goal+you+have+in+your+life+by+John+Assaraf&src=IE-TopResult&FORM=IETR02&conversationid=&adlt=strict - (Accessed October 5, 2017)

FOR INFORMATION, ENQUIRIES, OR BOOKINGS TO SPEAK:

Please send all correspondence directly to:
Email: mikenwaduba@gmail.com

OTHER BOOKS WRITTEN BY THE AUTHOR

1. A Simple Guide for Bible Study.
2. Questions and Answers on Tithes: Covenant of Prosperity.
3. Mr and Mrs Evans' Honeymoon on the Island of Majorca, Spain.
4. Healing Balm for the Soul.
5. The Holy Spirit and Supernatural Power
6. Mr and Mrs McGregor's Honeymoon on the Island of Santorini, Greece.

To order the above books log into: *www.Amazon.co.uk*

ABOUT THE AUTHOR

 Michael Nwaduba is a Minister of God with a calling to write and evangelise. Prior to God's calling into ministry, he obtained qualifications in Business Administration, and Accountancy. He worked for nearly two decades as a finance officer for various establishments including being a Church Administrator for a Pentecostal Church in London.

He teaches the truth in the Word of God with a passion. He firmly believes in the integrity of the Word of God. You will find his books interesting and easy to understand because of the simple style he adopts as an author. You will also find biblical and practical life examples in his books.

Minister Mike is also a lawyer. He obtained his LLB (Hons) Law degree from London South Bank University, London, United Kingdom. He is a member of RCCG Victory House, London, and the former Personal Assistant (PA) to Pastor Leke Sanusi, Continental Overseer, RCCG Europe, and Special Assistant to The General Overseer (SATGO).